PRAISE FOR TIFFANY REISZ

"Stunning . . . Transcends genres and will leave readers absolutely breathless." — *RT Book Reviews* **on the Original Sinners series**

"Daring, sophisticated, and literary . . . Exactly what good erotica should be." — **Kitty Thomas on** *The Siren*

"Kinky, well-written, hot as hell." — **Little Red Reading Hood on** *The Red: An Erotic Fantasy*

"Impossible to stop reading." — **Heroes & Heartbreakers on** *The Bourbon Thief*

"I worship at the altar of Tiffany Reisz!" — *New York Times* **bestselling author Lorelei James**

The Chateau

Print ISBN: 978-1548681951

MP3 CD Audiobook ISBN: 978-1541459069 (Tantor Audio)

CD Audiobook ISBN: 978-1541409064 (Tantor Audio)

Cover design by Andrew Shaffer. Cover and interior images used under license
from Shutterstock.com.

www.8thcirclepress.com

First Edition

THE CHATEAU
by Tiffany Reisz

8TH CIRCLE PRESS
Lexington, Kentucky

CONTENTS

DEDICATION

To the ones still waiting and the ones we are waiting for . . .

I wasn't young, I wasn't pretty. It was necessary to find other weapons.

— PAULINE RÉAGE

"Tell me a secret you've never told anyone before."

"Is that an order?" Kingsley asked.

A hand on his neck, a thumb digging into his throat, pressure to the point of pain.

It was an order.

Kingsley told him a secret.

I

WINTER

The dream always begins the same way. In the winter. In the woods.

Kingsley stands in snow surrounded by shadows. None of the shadows are his because he's not really there. He leaves no footprints as he walks. He does not see his steaming breath as he breathes. He is a ghost in this white forest, but he is not the only ghost here.

Before him stands a door.

It's an arched wooden door alone in the woods. It belongs to an old chapel, but there is no church here, no chapel, no house. Only a door. Kingsley can walk around the door, but nothing will happen. Nothing will happen at all until he steps through it. The iron latch is cold enough to bite his bare fingers, but he doesn't feel this either. He lifts it and passes through the door, because that is where the boy in white waits for him.

The moon is full and high, and the snow is bright, and he can see the young man so clearly it's almost as if it were daytime, almost as if it weren't a dream at all.

The boy in the clearing is beautiful, his hair so blond it looks almost white. His hair is white and his clothes are white, not snow white but a purer white, a baptismal white.

Kingsley speaks a word—either the boy's name or "sir." When he wakes he can never remember what word he says.

The boy, luminous in his pure white clothing, stands next to a table made of rough stone and on the stone table is a chess board made of ice.

Even though it is a dream, and no one has spoken but him, Kingsley knows he is supposed to sit and stay and play the game. It's the rules. If he doesn't play, he'll wake up, and the last thing he wants is to wake up now, to wake up ever.

He sits opposite the young man with the white-blond hair. The chess board is between them. Everything is between them.

Kingsley moves his pawn.

"You're not really here," Kingsley says to the boy with the snowy hair and the silver eyes. The boy's beauty renders the dream a nightmare because Kingsley knows when morning comes, the boy will be gone and nowhere does such beauty exist among his waking hours. Not anymore.

"How do you know?" the boy asks, moving his king.

"You look eighteen," Kingsley says, moving another pawn. "You're twenty-five now. I'm twenty-four."

The boy moves his king again. "In your memory I'm eighteen."

"That isn't how you play," Kingsley says. "You can't move the king like that."

"It's my game," the boy in white says. "I move my king however I want. Don't you remember? Don't you remember the way I moved my King anywhere and everywhere I wanted him to go?"

Even in the snow and the cold, Kingsley grows warm.

"I remember."

Kingsley moves his bishop.

The boy in white moves his king again.

"I don't know how to win this game," Kingsley says. "How can I win if I don't know the rules?"

The boy in white narrows his silver eyes at him. "You've already won."

"I have?"

"To play is to win, if you're playing with me. Isn't that true?" the boy asks with an arrogant smile in his eyes.

Kingsley knows this is true though it galls him to admit it. He doesn't care who wins the game as long as the game between them goes on forever. He moves another pawn and the boy in white captures it.

To be the pawn captured in that boy's hand . . .

"How do you keep finding me?" Kingsley asks.

"You came to me," the boy says. "I'm always here."

"I lost you," Kingsley says. "Seven years ago. I lost you."

"No," the boy says, smiling for the first time. His face is like Michelangelo's David, passive and powerful and carved from pale marble. His eyes are granite and if Kingsley had a chisel he knows he could chip away at the boy's chest until he uncovered an iron and copper wire heart beating inside a steel ribcage.

"No?"

"You lost you," the boy says. The smile is gone and it has begun to snow again. When it snows, Kingsley knows the dream is almost over. All he wants to do is stay asleep a little longer. All he wants to do is stay asleep forever.

"How do I find you again?" Kingsley asks. "Please, tell me before I wake."

"You don't find me," the boy says. "I find you."

"Find me then."

"When it's time."

"When will it be time?"

The boy in white moves his hands over the board and

Kingsley looks down. The ice king lays on the board broken in two pieces.

"When?" Kingsley asks. He is a child again, asking a thousand questions in the quest for a single answer. The snow is falling harder now, heavy as rain and hot as tears. "Tell me when, please . . ."

The boy leans across the board as if to kiss him, but instead of a kiss, Kingsley is given an answer.

"When you find you."

Between the kiss and the answer, Kingsley would have picked the kiss.

2

PARIS, FRANCE. 1989.

Kingsley woke up covered in cold sweat. His body ached like he had a fever, but he didn't—not of the sort that would ever break, anyway. For a long time he stayed in his solitary bed with his eyes closed, trying to remember as much of the recurring dream as possible. They had started a month ago when he returned from a successful mission in the Swiss Alps. Something about the snow there, something about the blood on the snow when he'd completed his dark task, had opened a door in his mind that Kingsley usually kept locked and guarded. The boy in the dream escaped that hidden room. There would be no locking him back in again now that he was out.

Ah, well, it was Kingsley who probably needed to be locked up. Seven years since he'd last seen the boy in white, and here Kingsley was, dreaming strange fever dreams of the lover he'd left so long ago, waking up sweating and hard. He ought to be ashamed of himself, but that would require shame. If Kingsley ever had any shame, he'd lost it when he lost his heart to that terrible blond monster whose hallowed name he refused to whisper even in the privacy of his own mind.

Outside his window, footsteps echoed off the pavement. A woman walking briskly in high heels. He gave himself permission to miss the boy in white who invaded his dreams, but only until the sound of the woman's sharp heels faded from hearing. That was all. He didn't weep nor did he shake. He simply lay naked in his bed and burned.

The sheets smoldered and the pillow warmed from the inside out like it had a core of hot coals instead of down. The air around his body turned to steam. He stretched his arms over his head and slid his wrists under the brass bar of the headboard and tried to pretend he was tied to it.

I want you.

I need you.

Use me. Hurt me. Destroy me because you're the one who created me. Kill me because you're my only reason for living.

Find me because I'm lost without you.

In his mind Kingsley spoke those words, in his mind and never aloud. He was a man now, not a boy. He didn't beg anymore. He didn't debase himself for love anymore. And he didn't want to.

Liar.

His time of remembering was almost up. As the sound of the woman's footsteps waxed, waned, and then died, the fire in his heart burned itself out, leaving him once more with nothing in his bed but the soot and ashes of his memories.

Find me then . . .

When it's time . . .

When will it be time?

When you find you . . .

What the fuck did that mean?

"You fucking monster," Kingsley said with a sigh. "You even

piss me off in my dreams." And, because he could, he added, "Asshole."

Slowly Kingsley opened his eyes, wincing as the bright white light of morning slammed into his optic nerve and caused the back of his brain to recoil. There existed the slightest possibility he'd had too much wine last night. He rolled up in bed and for a moment stayed there, knees bent to his chest, head down, arms around his ankles to stretch his back. At least the pain in his ribcage was gone, more or less. He'd taken one hell of a beating on that mission in the Alps, enough of a beating that he'd been given a full six weeks off to recover before being sent out again. He wished they'd hurry up and give him something to do. The more downtime he had, the more time he had to sleep. The more he slept, the more he dreamed . . . and the more he dreamed of the ice-hearted boy in the snow-filled forest, the more he wished to never wake again.

Like it or not, Kingsley was awake. He got out of bed, the white sheets damp with his sweat. The cold hardwood flooring kissed the soles of his bare feet. Two wine glasses sat on the floor at the foot of the bed. Kingsley drank the last two swallows in each and set the empty glasses back down for the cleaning lady, a local widow, to tend to it. He wasn't lazy. He simply took enormous pleasure in trying to scandalize her with how much he drank and how often he fucked. So far, she hadn't been impressed.

"I personally thanked a whole platoon of Patton's boys after the Liberation in '45. You'll have to do more than five girls a week to impress me, little boy," she'd said to him once. He'd kissed her cheek and whispered in her ear that he knew other ways to impress her, which had earned him a well-deserved swat with a kitchen towel on the seat of his trousers.

Maybe he should put a third glass by the bed for her. Or a

fourth, each with different-colored lipstick on the rims. That might do the trick.

Smiling at the thought, he walked naked to the small galley kitchen in the garret flat on the third floor of a house that he occupied between missions. He never said he "lived" there because that wasn't the point of the flat. He lived while he worked and when he wasn't working, he ceased to exist. Until someone knocked on that door with a file, a passport, money, and a target, he was a ghost.

He was a hungry ghost that morning, but unfortunately the refrigerator was bare. And his companion from last night—a twenty-year-old Swiss university student named Nina (or was it Zina?)—had left around two in the morning. Usually if one of his girls stayed overnight, he'd make an offer: *You feed me, and I'll eat you.* The line never failed. Since he'd woken up alone this time, he'd have to find his own breakfast. Horrible thought.

Kingsley turned on the cold water in the kitchen sink. He stuck his head under the faucet, washing the last of the cobwebs out of his skull with a quick whore's bath. He dried off with a kitchen towel, chuckling when he noticed the red marks on his skin that Nina's fingernails and teeth had left on him. She'd called him "delicious." She'd meant it, too, attempting to cannibalize him with nibbles and bites and licking kisses all over his stomach, sides, and hips.

She'd been a playful little thing. Even made him laugh a few times with her dirty mouth. He'd thought he'd forgotten how to laugh. He wouldn't mind seeing her again, which fairly well guaranteed he never would. These days he couldn't afford to get emotionally involved with anyone. He was gone too often. Even when he was back in his flat for an extended period of time, it was usually because he needed a few weeks to sleep off his injuries. Nina—no, it was definitely *Zina,* he decided—was sweet and like everyone he slept with, she deserved more than he could give. The more he liked someone, the less he saw of them—for their sake. But try passing that line of reasoning off onto a lovesick university student waiting by her phone. No, he wouldn't see Zina again, even though she'd left her phone number on the counter signed with a red lipstick kiss.

After washing up, he found his cleanest pair of jeans, a black sweater, black scarf, and was halfway to the door when he stopped at a sound.

Footsteps.

Inside the house, coming up the staircase.

Jeanne wasn't due to clean today. And the house was owned by his employers. No one lived in it now, except for him. Unless Zina was returning with breakfast, the footsteps meant one of two things: either someone was coming to kill him or someone was coming to give him a job. Considering he was supposed to have two more weeks off, he doubted his visitor was here simply to say "*bonjour.*"

Kingsley quietly pulled open the cutlery drawer in the kitchen, the one where he kept his Beretta. He waited behind the door, gun in hand. He wasn't scared. Not yet. That would come later if he survived. That was something they'd never warned him about in training, that he would never stop being afraid no matter how many years he did this job. Only made sense, he supposed. An old fox ran as hard from the hounds as the young fox. No one ever got used to being hunted.

The footsteps paused outside the door and then came the knock.

Tap, tap.

Pause.

Tap, tap, tap, tap.

Kingsley sagged against the wall with relief. He wouldn't have to shoot anyone today.

"Lieutenant?" said the voice from outside the door, and

Kingsley growled with barely repressed fury. Maybe he would shoot someone today after all.

He opened the door. At the top of the stairs stood a young man with disheveled brown hair wearing a foolish grin and holding what appeared to be a blue bowling ball bag.

"Good morning, Lieutenant," the young man said, grinning like a cameraman had just told him to say "Cheese."

"Bernie," Kingsley said as he leaned on the doorframe. "I thought we had this talk."

"Which talk? Oh." Bernie grimaced and switched the bowling bag from one hand to the other. "Right. The one where I don't call you by your name or rank?"

"Right."

"Sorry, Lieutenant."

Kingsley dropped his chin to his chest. Poor Bernie. He looked like a twelve-year-old boy who'd never grown up. He'd merely gotten taller, like someone had pulled him like taffy or stretched him on a rack.

"I mean, sorry, ah . . . John," Bernie said.

"Better," Kingsley said. "Thank you."

"You're welcome, Lieutenant."

Kingsley used his gun to rub his forehead, despite knowing there was the slightest risk he'd accidentally shoot himself in the head. He'd take that risk.

"Bernie, we have to have the talk again."

"I've asked you not to call me Bernie," he pointed out. "You still do."

"It's affectionate," Kingsley said. The young man's last name was Bernard. "I only call that because I like you. Did you bring breakfast?"

"Ah, no," Bernie said, glancing around as if hoping to find a breakfast that someone else had inadvertently left behind. "Was I supposed to?"

"It's protocol, Bernie. It's in the manual."

"Protocol, right," Bernie said again. "Well. I'll be back. You'll be here?"

"I'll be here. If I don't answer right away, it's because I'm in bed cleaning my gun."

Bernie glanced at the gun in Kingsley's right hand.

"Looks clean to me."

"It's a euphemism," Kingsley said. "You'll figure it out when you hit puberty."

Kingsley shut the door in Bernie's face, and put his gun away before he shot someone accidentally or on purpose.

At first, he heard nothing.

Then he heard footsteps receding. Then he heard those same footsteps returning. Then he heard that knock again—*tap-tap*. Pause. *Tap-tap-tap-tap.*

"Bernie?" Kingsley said through the door.

"It's a wanking joke, yes?"

He smiled only because Bernie couldn't see him.

"Good job, Bernie. Breakfast?"

"Yes, Lieutenant."

"And Bernie?"

"Yes, Lieutenant?"

"Don't forget the coffee. That's also protocol."

"Yes, Lieutenant."

"And Bernie?"

"Yes, Lieutenant?"

"Stop calling me Lieutenant."

3

B ernie could never remember not to call him by his name or rank, but at least he knew how to fetch a decent breakfast. Kingsley hopped up on the kitchen counter and sat with his legs crossed like a schoolboy, devouring a croissant smothered with fresh strawberry jam. He washed it all down with a large stout cup of coffee, black, just the way he liked it. Meanwhile Bernie sat waiting at the little yellow table for two under the kitchen window. The garret flat was so small and narrow that Kingsley could have extended his leg and kicked Bernie in the head, had he any desire to do such a thing. Since Bernie had fed him and brought him coffee—above and beyond the call of duty —Kingsley left him un-kicked.

For the moment.

"You had company last night," Bernie said, nodding at the empty wine bottle and the two glasses by the bed. A small brass bed, barely big enough for two, but that was fine by Kingsley as he was happy to let his companions sleep on top of him. Or, on occasion, underneath him. And who needed a big bed? The best sex he'd ever had in his life had been in a cot.

"I have company every night," Kingsley said.

"Is that safe?" Bernie asked.

"Are you worried I'll catch something?"

"Yes," Bernie said. "A bullet."

Kingsley reached over and turned the radio volume up a couple notches. He didn't want them being overheard. He was supposed to be playing the part of an American in Paris. Anyone hearing him speaking French like a native with a classic Parisian accent to boot might get suspicious. The Police's "Don't Stand So Close to Me" was playing on the American radio station. Kingsley had always liked this song for some reason. A reason probably best left unexplored.

"I only fuck university students," Kingsley said between bites. "They don't even know where to buy pot, much less guns."

"You might blow your cover."

"Fucking university students *is* my cover," he said, pointing to a small desk pushed against the back wall. On it sat a blue Smith-Corona Galaxie Deluxe XII typewriter with paper rolled inside and stacks of typewritten sheets on either side of it. They were all fake, of course. His cover was "John Kingsley Edge," a twenty-seven-year-old American mystery novelist—as yet unpublished, living out his Hemingway-in-Paris dreams. And the words on those pages? Taken word for word from *The Mirror Crack'd from Side to Side* by Agatha Christie, the one English novel Kingsley had been able to find in the used bookshop two streets over. He doubted the Swiss and the Dutch and the Algerian and the German students he'd fucked the past three weeks were big enough fans of Miss Marple to notice, especially since he'd changed Miss Marple's name in the book to Mr. Stearns.

Bernie's eyes were still on the two empty wine glasses.

"Wish they'd let me go undercover," Bernie said wistfully.

"Do you even speak English?" Kingsley asked, raising an eyebrow at Bernie. Poor Bernie. He sounded like a little boy wishing to be a spy when he grew up. Instead he was nothing more than an errand boy for the real spies. Probably as close as Bernie would ever get to his dream job.

"A little," Bernie said. *Un peu.*

"You need more than a little English for this work," Kingsley said. "I'm fluent, and I can speak without a French accent." What he didn't say was that he hated hiding his accent. It gave him a headache. Still, when he was out on the town meeting girls, he usually didn't have to talk much to get them back to his place.

"How did you learn English so well? Are you actually a secret American? If you're a secret American, does that mean it's French you learned? No, you're too good at it. You'd have to be a native—"

"Bernie, you know the rules."

Kingsley had a working theory about how someone as dense as Bernie had managed to weasel his way into the inner circle of a very small, quiet, and secretive military intelligence agency. Long ago, he'd heard a story about the infamous Hope Diamond. When the owner of the cursed jewel, Harry Winston, sent the diamond to Washington DC, he hadn't bothered with armed guards. No, he'd put it in a regular box and shipped it via the good old-fashioned United States Postal Service. No one expected something that valuable to get shipped through the post office, just as no one expected a man as young and dumb as Bernie to be carrying important intelligence documents either. Hiding in plain sight was the best place to hide.

Either that or Bernie was the nephew of someone very well-connected.

"What's America like? Tell me that, at least," Bernie said.

"Barbaric," Kingsley said. "They eat butter on their croissants."

Bernie screwed up his face in an expression of purest French disgust. "So you hated it there?"

"No, I didn't hate it there," Kingsley said, trying not to smile. "I did at first. It grows on you though. Like a tumor."

"I bet American girls like French men. Right?"

"They like Englishmen better. They assume Frenchmen will cheat on them."

Bernie's eyes widened. "That's rude. Why?"

"Because we do."

"We do?"

Kingsley shrugged and nodded.

"That's not very nice of us," Bernie said, frowning.

"I don't make the rules. But they will sleep with us for a night or two if you know enough English to get them into bed."

"I know enough."

"Say something in English," Kingsley said before finishing off the last of his coffee.

"Euh . . ." Bernie paused so long Kingsley had time to finish off his breakfast. When Bernie started speaking again, it was in English. Very bad English.

"I 'aave . . ."

"Go on, Bernie," Kingsley said, not only in English but in his flawless American accent picked up from his mother who'd been born and raised in Maine. "You have what?"

"A zhab . . . *pour* . . ."

"*For.*"

"For you."

"You have a job for me?" Kingsley repeated, lighting a Gauloise. He only allowed himself to smoke after eating these days. He wanted to quit, but the last thing he needed on a mission was his hands shaking as he went through nicotine withdrawal. He'd planned on cutting back by smoking only after he'd had an orgasm, but some days that was almost half a pack.

Three meals a day. Three cigarettes a day. It was as close as he got to self-restraint.

"I have a zahb for you," Bernie said and smiled, proud of himself.

"I'm supposed to be on leave," Kingsley said. "Medical leave."

"Your physical results came back—you're in perfect health. Try to stay that way."

"I'm still sore," Kingsley said, which was true . . . ish? "There's no blood test for that."

"They said you'd say that. So I'm supposed to tell you that if you're in good enough shape to bring five different girls home five nights in a row, you can work."

Kingsley pursed his lips but couldn't argue the point. It was his own fault he'd gotten caught. Of course the house was being watched. Spies spied on spies. It's what they did.

"Give me the dossier," Kingsley said, wiping his hands off on a towel. Kingsley might be tasked with killing the target contained in the files—usually KGB or someone else the government had deemed too dangerous to continue being allowed to walk God's green earth a week longer—but that didn't mean he had to get crumbs all over their fucking dossier. The first dossier he'd ever been given had contained pictures of his target . . . and his target's wife and three small children. Killing was the only part of his job he took seriously.

Bernie opened his bowling bag and took out a file folder, which he handed over.

"It's a woman," Kingsley said, staring at the photograph clipped just inside the flap. "A beautiful woman."

"You think?" Bernie asked. "She's wearing a widow's veil over her face."

Women didn't wear black veils anymore. Kingsley couldn't remember the last time he'd seen a woman in a widow's veil, even at a funeral. They were no longer in fashion. They caught the eye. They made you look.

"A woman wouldn't wear a veil over her face unless there

was something under there worth veiling," Kingsley said. "Trust me, she's beautiful."

Kingsley could see the woman's eyes through the open weave of the tulle. She was staring directly at the camera, which was rare. His targets never knew they were being targeted. Even most Frenchwomen smiled when they knew a camera was on them. Not this woman, even though it was clear she knew someone was photographing her. She didn't look amused and she didn't look defiant and she didn't look shamefaced or shameless or even curious. She simply looked bored. Any woman who looked bored while being stalked and photographed was likely a very dangerous woman indeed.

"Why am I killing her?" Kingsley asked. He found it was hard to imagine this chic lady with the white fur collar of her black coat turned up had done anything to deserve being assassinated. Then again, he'd learned in his line of work that one could never judge by appearances.

"You aren't," Bernie said.

"I'm not? Then what am I doing with her? Surveillance? Reconnaissance?"

"Rescue."

Kingsley narrowed his eyes at Bernie. This woman was not a woman who needed rescuing. Kingsley would bet his life on it.

"What's going on here?" he asked Bernie.

"The colonel says this is an 'unofficial' assignment."

"All our assignments are 'unofficial.' "

"This is extra un-official," Bernie said. "You can even turn it down if you want. Although the colonel might not be happy if you did that."

"Let's keep the colonel happy. Tell me everything."

"Apparently a man has disappeared," Bernie said. "Six months ago he disappeared for a week. Came back and didn't tell anyone where he went. Now he's gone again. He called the same phone number the day before both disappearances. Her phone number, they think."

Bernie nodded at the file, at "her."

"So?" Kingsley said. "A man has a right to run off with a woman if he wants to. Not telling people where he is makes him thoughtless, maybe even an ass, not a criminal. Or her."

"They don't want to arrest her. Or him. They just want someone to go in and talk him out. He's young."

"If they have her phone number, can't they find her address? Send his mother to go talk to him."

"Untraceable number, apparently. She's got friends in high places. Someone's protecting her privacy. Makes her very hard to find. The only option is for someone to meet her, talk their way in. Like you."

Kingsley closed the file. "This assignment is a shit sandwich," he said. "I'm not getting involved with someone's family soap opera. It's none of our business if somebody's kid wants to screw an older woman."

"I guess it would be none of our business," Bernie said, "except the missing man is Colonel Masson's nineteen-year-old nephew, Leon."

Kingsley stared at Bernie. Stared *and* glared.

"What?" Bernie asked.

Kingsley opened the file again.

"Bernie, in the future, tell me the important part first."

"Sorry," Bernie said. "Should I start over then?"

"Yes, start at the beginning," Kingsley said, uncrossing his legs and dropping down to the floor. "And go slowly. Pretend I'm you."

"Why would I pretend you're me?"

"Ah . . . just tell me," Kingsley said.

"We don't know her name," Bernie began. He clasped his hands in his lap and one foot danced along the floor. "She goes by Madame. That's all."

"Madame?"

Bernie nodded. "We think she's the leader of a cult."

"A cult? Really? In France?" Kingsley couldn't keep the surprise out of his voice. "Are you sure you're not thinking of the Catholic Church?"

"This is a sex cult."

"So it is the Catholic Church."

Bernie blinked, his eyes dim as a five-watt bulb.

"Go on," Kingsley said. "You now have my attention."

"Some men . . . important men, have disappeared over the past ten years. They'll be gone a week or two with no word to their families or friends at all, and then they'll simply reappear, glassy-eyed and confused, standing outside their front doors with no idea how they got there."

"Important men. Such as?"

"The son of an English duke. A minor Spanish prince. A wealthy North African financier. And now—"

"The colonel's nephew."

Bernie shrugged. "He was last seen getting into a wine-colored car. That was one month ago."

"White wine or red?"

"Oh," Bernie said. "I don't know that part."

Kingsley met Bernie's eyes. "You're someone's nephew, aren't you?"

Bernie looked sheepish and guilty. "Yes."

"Whose?" Kingsley demanded.

"My aunt's."

Kingsley counted to five in both French and English and then smiled at Bernie. "So it's a sex cult. Run by a woman who goes only by Madame. And the colonel wants me to go there and check on Leon, and convince him it's time to come home. Where's this woman live?"

"Apparently her château is off the map. The phone number is untraceable."

"She does have friends in high places. Wait, did you say château?"

"Yes, she lives in a château," Bernie said. "Does that mean something to you?"

"Maybe," Kingsley said. "But I can't remember why."

"Will you take the job?" Bernie asked.

"Why me?"

"Why you?"

"Why am I being sent on this job?" Kingsley asked.

"I don't know. I'm only the messenger."

"You're a messenger who eavesdrops. Why me?"

Bernie flushed. He looked guilty as a little boy who'd seen his first naked girl in a movie. "I might have heard the colonel say something about you being a good fit for the job."

"Why?" Kingsley asked, eying Bernie meaningfully.

"He used a phrase, but I don't know it."

"What phrase?"

"It's English," Bernie said. "Something like, uh . . . *oeuf trader*? Egg broker?"

"Rough trade?" Kingsley asked.

Bernie's eyes lit up. "That!" Then he paused. "What's it mean?"

"It means the colonel thinks I'll fuck anyone," Kingsley said. He decided not to tell Bernie the phrase specifically referred to working-class men who had sex with men with money and *for* money. That was a conversation Bernie was not ready to have yet. Or Kingsley.

"But . . . you will fuck anyone."

"I won't," Kingsley said, insulted. "I'll fuck *almost* anyone. There's a difference."

"Who wouldn't you fuck?" Bernie sounded skeptical.

Kingsley flipped another page in the file. "Nazis."

Kingsley found the file woefully lacking in useful information. No addresses. No photographs apart from the one of Madame. There was a phone number written on the file. That was about it for useful information.

"I need to know more about her," Kingsley said. "What else did you overhear?"

"Three different agents have already tried getting to Madame. Only one of them has gotten further than a first phone call. It's like she gives them a test, and they all fail, but they don't know what the test is, so they don't know how to pass it."

"I'm not saying I'm doing this job," Kingsley said. "But if I were going to do it . . . what do I do? What's the first step?"

"You're supposed to go to a payphone. Call the number on the file. When whoever answers, you say 'looking glass.' " Bernie was speaking French to him, but the password—"looking glass"—he'd said in English. That seemed significant, though Kingsley couldn't say why.

"Looking glass?"

"A mirror," Bernie said.

"I know what it means," Kingsley said. "If I can get to her, what's my cover?"

"Tell her you're a friend of the family, and they've asked to look into Leon's disappearance. She's made all the other agents immediately, so the less you lie to her, the better. She'll probably make you, too, but she might still bite if she likes you. They don't think she's dangerous. I mean, she probably won't try to kill you."

"Probably?" Where had Kingsley heard that before?

Bernie nodded, smiling.

"Anything else?" Kingsley asked. "Anything at all? Anything that might help me not get 'probably' killed by her?"

"Oh, one thing. They worship a book."

"Every cult worships a book. It's called The Bible."

"No," Bernie said. "Different book."

Once more he went into his bowling bag and produced the book in question.

"This book," Bernie said.

Kingsley didn't take it from him. He only looked at it. It was *Histoire d'O—Story of O*—by Pauline Réage, the most notorious novel of sadomasochism of the twentieth century. In the book, a young woman's lover takes her to a house in Roissy where she's ravished and imprisoned and trained to be the perfect slave. No, not a house.

A *château* . . .

"Lieutenant? Something wrong?" Bernie asked.

"Nothing's wrong," Kingsley said. Quite possibly something very right. "Tell the colonel I'll do it."

"You're braver than I am," Bernie said.

"I know. Now get out."

"But—"

"Out. I'll be in touch when I can."

Kingsley held the door open for Bernie. The poor boy had to scramble to push all his papers back into his bag. It appeared there was an actual bowling ball in his bowling bag. Kingsley decided that either Bernie was literally the worst spy in the entire world or the best.

"Leaving, leaving," Bernie said. "But don't you want the book? You might need it?"

He held it out to Kingsley again.

"You keep it. Read it. You might learn something," Kingsley said, before shutting the door in Bernie's face.

He didn't need to keep the book, after all.

Kingsley had his own copy.

Was this real life?

Was this really happening?

This woman, Madame, not only ran a sex cult, but a cult that worshipped *Story of O?* Crazy, right? It had to be crazy. Rumors, misinformation, you couldn't trust stories like that. They were all urban legends, blown out of proportion. More likely that Madame was a madam. Instead of kidnapping important men, she probably operated a brothel that catered to rich, deviant men, and those rich, deviant men lied to their not-so-deviant wives about how they ended up in the pocket of this woman. That was Kingsley's theory. And it was very possible that's why his little corner of France's intelligence community wanted to know where she was and exactly what and who she was doing. The colonel's nephew strapped to a bed by a beautiful woman might give up secrets he didn't know he knew.

In the wooden crate at the foot of his bed, the one he used for a makeshift bookcase, he found his copy of *Story of O*. He'd first read the book when he was a boy, sneaking it from his parents' bedroom shelf when they were out. He told himself he'd only kept the book because it had his mother's initials written inside it. *K.B.* The same as his. But that wasn't why.

He'd read it a dozen times since, this strange slim novel about a woman whose name is nothing but an O, a hole, and the terrible things done to her that she hates while they happen and misses when they're over. Sometimes when he read the book he imagined himself as one of the mysterious men who used O for his own perverse and violent pleasures. And sometimes—often even—Kingsley imagined he was O.

Kingsley opened the book to an earmarked page and read. *To say that from the moment her lover had left, O began to await his return would be an understatement. She turned into pure vigil, darkness in waiting expectation of light.*

Kingsley closed the book and put it back in the crate. He watched the street from behind the window curtain. The second Bernie's putting red Citroën pulled away from the curb, Kingsley flew into action. He burst out of the door of his flat, ran down the three flights of stairs, and out onto the street where he nearly bumped into an old woman carrying her groceries. She swore at him, and he muttered a quick "*Je suis désolé*" before running off again down the street to the next block over where he knew he would find a payphone.

As soon as he arrived, Kingsley pushed the door open so hard he almost wrenched it off the hinges. He grabbed the receiver, put in his coin, dialed the number, and panted while he waited, waited while he panted.

One ring.

Two.

Three rings.

Four.

The rings ceased. Kingsley heard silence, white noise, a breath.

"Looking glass," he said in perfect English, sounding as American as possible.

More silence.

A long silence.

A long and terrible silence.

Then finally . . .

"Not again."

Kingsley laughed softly. The woman, for it was a woman who'd answered, sounded deliciously annoyed.

"I'm sorry," Kingsley said, already playing the slave. He remembered this game. Oh, he remembered it well. Remembered more than anything how much he loved to play it.

"Go on. Tell me your name." She spoke in French.

Her voice sounded impassive, detached, elegant, educated, sinister, and civilized. Yet she hadn't asked him for his name; she'd ordered him to tell it to her.

His cover of "John Kingsley Edge, poor American writer playing Hemingway in Paris" was almost on the tip of his tongue when his real given name slipped out.

"Kingsley," he said, dropping his American accent to speak to her in French. "Or King. Or whatever you want to call me."

"Kingsley," the woman said. "You sound scared."

"Out of breath. I ran to the phone. I was in a hurry to talk to you."

"I'm flattered. You're nervous."

"Yes," he said. Not a lie. He didn't know why it wasn't a lie. Women didn't make him nervous. Men didn't make him nervous. It took someone facing him with a gun in their hand to make him nervous. Only one person had ever made him nervous without the gun.

"Good," she said. "Very good." Her voice was cool and soothing, like a psychologist's voice made for probing the deepest recesses of the psyche and soul.

"Tell me how you heard of me, Kingsley," she said.

"A friend," he said. "His name is Leon."

"Leon," she repeated.

"He stayed with you a few months ago for a week. When he came back he told me about you. He's gone now, but I found your phone number in some papers of his."

"Leon is your friend and he told you about me . . ."

"He said you're beautiful under your veil."

There was a long pause after that. Had Kingsley gone too far or had his arrow struck his target?

"Many men have tried to find me," she said. "They never find me."

"I don't want to find you," Kingsley said.

"Tell me who you want to find," she said.

Kingsley closed his eyes tight and returned to his dream.

"I want to find me," he said at last.

"Very good," she said. She sounded pleased with him. Already he was desperate to please her. He remembered this feeling, this need to please. It had lingered in his blood, dormant like a virus and already he felt the first hint of dizziness, the first flush of fever.

"Tell me what you look like," she said.

"Six feet tall," he said. "Eighty-two kilo. I'm twenty-four, and I look twenty-four. Brown hair. Brown eyes. Hair needs a cut. It's wavy, not curly. People tell me I look Greek. I guess I'm darker than your average Frenchman."

"That's not what I wanted to know."

Kingsley smiled. "Women find me very handsome."

"They do?"

"I've had seven beautiful girls seven days in a row," he said.

"Are you bragging?" she asked.

"Just offering corroborating testimony," he said, proud of himself for that line.

"Arrogant boy," she said.

"Sometimes."

"If we meet, I'll humble you," she said.

"I need it."

"You won't like it."

"You don't know me."

"You won't like it," she said again.

"Maybe not," Kingsley said. "But I might love it."

"Ah," she said and it was a delighted sound like he'd heard women make when he was touching them for the first time and found that spot, that special little spot that wanted, needed, demanded touching. "Ah," she said again.

"I want to meet you," he said. "I want you to humble me."

"You want me to humble you." She sounded amused by him, like a teacher speaking to a too-eager pupil. "Very well. Tell me the phone number from where you're calling."

Kingsley read it off the payphone to her twice.

"Good," she said. "I'll call you back."

"When?" he asked, but she'd already hung up.

He stared at the phone as if it would answer his question for him, but it did nothing but buzz until Kingsley replaced it on the cradle.

"Fucking sadists," he said to himself. There was no telling when she'd call back. A minute. An hour. A day. He had no choice but to wait and to wait and to wait. Wait like a servant. Wait like a slave. Exasperating. Infuriating. Insulting.

God, he'd missed this.

As Kingsley expected, Madame didn't call him back right away.

Not for one hour.

Not for two hours.

Not for three hours.

Not for four.

She was testing him. He knew it. She was testing him, and he had to pass this test if he were to be allowed to meet her.

Kingsley waited.

He waited and he waited and he waited. Luckily he'd picked the payphone booth next to an alley where few people ventured. He didn't have to fight anyone for custody of the phone, but that didn't make the wait any easier. He paced the alley, never walking out of earshot of the ring. He sat down in the phone booth and read the phone book until he almost fell asleep. And he would have fallen asleep if it were three degrees warmer outside. An old man walking his dog gave him increasingly suspicious and disgusted looks all four laps he made of the alley. Even the dog seemed to be judging him. Finally Kingsley leaned out of the phone booth and yelled to them both, "It's for work, all right!" The old man muttered something about "bizarre young people these days" and took his dog away—briskly.

By late afternoon, he'd been waiting for the phone to ring for six hours. At least it had warmed up enough that he could almost, perhaps, *maybe* take a quick nap while sitting on the floor of the phone booth with his coat wrapped around his knees. He got settled in and closed his eyes. Just as he was about to drift off, someone knocked on the phone booth door.

Kingsley sprang immediately awake. And when he saw the girl standing outside the door, he leapt to his feet, a smile on his face.

"Pardon me, sir," she said. "Do you live here?"

She spoke French like a native. He knew he was supposed to play dumb, to act like he only spoke English or stilted French, as part of his cover.

But.

The girl was magnificent. Black hair in a loose bun. Onyx eyes. Skin a deep olive like his, maybe even darker. She had a little beauty mark on her chin and her lips were a dusky hue, full and mischievous as if they wanted to slide into a smile but knew better than to encourage him. All her clothes were chic. Chic brown leather knee boots with a little heel. A brown skirt, a belted brown coat, and a red newsboy cap tilted rakishly over her right eye. She didn't look very old—maybe eighteen or nineteen—but she carried herself with a sophistication beyond her tender years.

Since she was so very magnificent, he was compelled to respond with his own fluent French. So what if he blew his cover? He'd blow anything for this girl.

"Do I live here?" he asked. "On this street?"

"In the phone booth?"

She smiled and he decided they should have two children. Both girls. Or maybe one boy and one girl. He wasn't picky.

"No," he said. "I'm waiting on a call."

"Oh," she said. "I'll find another phone then."

"You can use this one," he said. "It's not mine. I don't own it. It's public. You're the public."

"But I'm not public. I'm *very* private," she said.

Maybe three children, he thought. The third would be an accident. Unplanned. Likely the result of him ravishing her one time too many while on holiday in Saint Croix. He wondered if she liked being spanked. He would try to find that out before tomorrow morning.

"Then you shouldn't use my public phone," he said. "We should find you a private phone. I have one back at my place."

"If you have a phone, why are you using a phone booth?" she asked. She was looking at him with unabashed appreciation. She might even find him as attractive as he found her.

"It's for work. I think."

"If you're working I should leave you alone then," she said. "I'll find another phone on my own."

"You're Jewish."

She furrowed her beautiful brow. "Are Jews not allowed to use phones?" she asked.

"I noticed your necklace," he said. A gold Star of David pendant danced in the hollow of her throat. "I like it."

"Are *you* Jewish?" she asked.

"No," he said. "I'm just so happy you aren't Catholic."

She laughed and her laugh bounced off the sidewalk into the sky and jumped into the nearest passing cloud. Kingsley hoped wherever that cloud went it would rain her laughter onto the world.

"Is it so bad to be Catholic?" she asked.

"I went to Catholic school," he said by way of answer.

"Is it like I hear it is?" she asked.

"Worse. We can raise our children Jewish. I'll convert."

"Are you circumcised?" she asked.

"Not yet, but if you'll give me a minute, I have my Swiss Army knife on me."

"You're awful," she said, grinning.

"I'm half-American. That's where my rude behavior comes from."

"What if I like rude behavior?" she asked.

"God bless America," Kingsley said.

"Does he?"

"What?"

"Bless America?"

"I don't know, but Americans say it all the fucking time. There's another American saying: What's your phone number?"

"I don't have a phone," she said. "That's why I was looking for one."

"Then what's your address? I'll write you letters. Long letters. Stirring letters. Letters that will break your heart," he said.

"What if I don't want my heart broken?"

"Then I'll write you another letter to put it back together."

"Sounds dangerous to my cardiovascular health. I don't know if you should write me."

"Can I write your beauty mark then?" he said, nodding at the little black dot on her chin. "I have a lot to say to it."

"Oh, that's not a beauty mark," she said.

"What is it then?"

"It's a tick," she said.

He laughed so hard he mentally impregnated her a fourth time. *C'est la vie.* He'd always wanted a big family.

"Then I'll write letters to your tick."

"His name is Georges," she said.

"Does Georges like boys?" Kingsley asked. "Because I want to kiss him."

She shook her head in that way women did to tell men they were both cute and annoying.

"Would you like to go have coffee with me?" she asked. "There's a café on the next street."

"Yes. Yes, I would. I would like that . . . but not today. I'm, well . . ." He pointed at the phone booth.

"Working?" she said.

"Yes."

"Tomorrow?"

"I'll be gone tomorrow. I should go now," she said, glancing at the end of the street, a pretty pout on her face. "It was nice to meet you, Monsieur. Good luck with your work. Georges and I will miss you. *Au revoir.*"

The girl in the red cap and the brown boots walked away and Kingsley watched her go. At the last second before she disappeared from view, she turned around and waved at him. Then she was gone. She'd been so insanely, indescribably stunning that he could only think that she'd been a test. Madame had hired a teenaged model to charm him and tempt him with coffee at a café and the promise of more.

Madame better fucking call him soon if he gave up the most beautiful girl in the world for this job.

He waited four more hours.

Four.

More.

Hours.

Kingsley was five minutes away from giving up on this assignment, going back to his apartment and taking a long hot bath when the payphone rang.

He'd been sitting on the concrete until his tailbone had gone numb when the shrill sound pierced the cold evening air, and he jumped up so quickly one might have thought someone had shot a gun at him.

Kingsley picked up the receiver. "Hello?"

"Don't talk," came the woman's voice over the line. "I have no time for mindless chit-chat."

Kingsley stayed silent.

"Good," she said. "You can take an order. Here's another. There's a hotel in the thirteenth arrondissement. It's called The Opulent. It isn't."

Kingsley smiled.

"Be there in an hour on the hour. Precisely on the hour. Come unarmed and alone or do not come at all. Room four. It will be unlocked. Go in. Shut the door behind you but don't lock it. Face the window, curtains closed. Wait for me on your knees."

"What's the address?" Kingsley asked but she'd hung up again already.

He put the phone on the receiver and leaned back in the booth. The call happened so fast and was so bizarre, he almost didn't believe it had happened. He repeated what she'd told him. *The Opulent. 13th arrondissement. Room 4. Close the door, kneel by the window, facing the window, curtains closed.* He looked up the address in the phone book. It would be an easy trek on foot. He'd make it in plenty of time if he left now. He ran his hands through his hair, retied his scarf, and was about to leave the booth when the phone rang again.

He answered it but this time he didn't speak.

"You learn quickly," the woman said.

He still didn't speak.

"Your ability to learn quickly has earned you an answer. Ask me a question. Don't waste my time or yours on something stupid like what my name is."

Kingsley opened his mouth and didn't know what to ask at first and then he knew in an instant. "How do I pass the test?"

"Ah," she said as she had before. That pleased little "ah"

again. He was glad he'd given up the girl in the red cap. He'd needed that "ah."

"There is a test, isn't there? When men try to find you," Kingsley said, "you test them. I heard this. How do I pass the test so I can be with you?"

"You pass the test by taking the test," she said.

And, of course, she hung up again before he could say another word.

Kingsley checked his watch. Head down against the wind and feet moving fast, he made it to the 13th in half an hour. Ten minutes and two wrong turns down blind alleys later, Kingsley found The Opulent. A nondescript building, he hardly would have noticed it unless he'd been looking for it. Three stories high, gray stone facade, simple glass front door.

He went inside and nearly collapsed from the relief of being immersed for the first time all day in real warmth. The radiator in the lobby groaned and sang, and he stood by it, warming himself as if it were a roaring fire. In the faded red velvet lobby, he shucked off his overcoat and shed his scarf. A long-legged girl in a short black skirt eyed him with avarice and interest from across the room. There were two other girls there, wearing more lipstick than clothing. The Opulent was clearly the sort of hotel that rented out its rooms by the hour. Kingsley was surprised he'd never heard of it before.

Without a word to the sleeping clerk, he headed up the narrow stairs beside the front desk and walked down the threadbare carpet to room 4. The door wasn't locked. He entered it, as ordered, and shut the door behind him. There was no overhead light. When he flipped the switch by the door, only the lamp on the bedside table came on.

By its weak and jaundiced light, Kingsley could see the room wasn't nearly as squalid as he'd been expecting. It even smelled like someone had cleaned in there sometime in the last two weeks. The wallpaper was dark green, with golden vines entwined with golden apples. The bed was large, a queen-size, and covered in a forest green comforter and gold tasseled pillows. The rug was also a deep green and under it lay an ancient wood floor full of pockmarks from a hundred years of boots and high heels. Across from the bed hung an ostentatious gilt mirror, a cheap rococo replica that had likely acted as the sole witness to a hundred years of depravity in the bed it reflected. The only other item of interest in the room was the telephone.

Kingsley knew he ought to call his superiors and make a report. Yet something stopped him. Something in him didn't want this to be about work. It already felt more like pleasure than business. Besides, he knew nothing yet. To call now would be to waste their time.

Thoughts of work faded from his mind as he tossed his coat and scarf over the back of an old and humble-looking red leather armchair. He faced the window and closed the gold curtains. He knelt on the rug and waited, ready and willing. And if the readiness was perhaps feigned, at least the willingness was not.

Right on the hour, the door opened behind him.

In the novel *Story of O*, the woman, O, is taken to a château, and the minute she's inside the house, four men take turns ravishing her. Kingsley wondered if such a thing was about to happen to him now. Would he be grabbed, stripped, violated, raped? Myriad lurid scenarios ran through his mind. But it seemed the mysterious stranger in the room had other ideas. He heard the door lock. He heard a woman's prim footsteps, first on the hardwood floor and then on the rug. Then he sensed her standing directly behind him. He inhaled deeply and smelled lavender water, the kind his mother used to wear.

"Don't speak," the woman said. It was the voice from the phone. "Only speak when I ask you a direct question. I'll speak in French. You answer in English. If someone is eavesdropping it'll make it a little harder on them. Do you understand?"

Comprenez-vous?

"Yes," Kingsley said, *en anglais*. He wondered how she knew he was fluent in English. Apart from saying "looking glass" to her, he'd spoken French the entire time.

"I'm going to touch you," she said. "If you have an objection to that, then I don't know why you're here."

Again, Kingsley did not speak. He had absolutely no objection to being touched. Not by her, anyway.

He waited, eyes closed, and felt a soft touch on his head, a stroke of fingers through his hair.

"You lied to me," she said.

Kingsley tensed, but didn't speak. He knew better than to say anything to that sort of accusation.

"You told me you were handsome. You aren't," she said. "You're exquisite."

Kingsley almost said something to that. Something like, "Will that be a problem?" But she'd only made a statement. Until she asked a question, he wasn't allowed to speak.

"If I were a painter, you'd be my muse," she said. "You belong in oils on canvas."

Not being allowed to say "thank you" to a compliment of that magnitude was mild torture.

She stroked his hair again. His eyes were open, but he couldn't see her as she stood beyond the farthest edge of his peripheral vision. That explained partly why the curtains had to be closed. Otherwise he could have seen her reflection in the window.

She touched his forehead and now Kingsley felt the silk of gloves against his skin. Her touch was gentle, soothing, and the second he relaxed into it, she put a knife to his throat.

Kingsley froze.

"I don't want to kill you," she said.

That made two of them.

"Very good," she said. "Even with a knife at your throat you hold your tongue. Someone's trained you very well."

Kingsley still did not speak. He knew he could overpower her if he needed to, but would she make a fatal stab first? Better to wait it out, behave, play along.

"Someone sent you to me. Who was it and what did he tell

you?" she asked. "If you tell me even one lie I will slit your throat. And yes, I will know if you lie."

She'd asked him one direct question. Therefore he was allowed to speak.

"I'm employed by an intelligence agency without a name," he said. "French military. Officially unofficial. Leon isn't my friend. He's my commanding officer's nephew. They think you're holding him against his will. They asked me to get him out. If he wants out."

"Leon is your commanding officer's nephew," she repeated, sounding amused. "So that's the game, is it?"

"I don't care about the boy," he said. Kingsley wasn't sure what she meant by "the game." He hoped he lived long enough to find out.

"Then why did you come here?"

"My own reasons."

"You wish to serve, do you?"

Kingsley whispered, "Yes."

She said nothing. The blade remained flush against his neck, cool and sharp.

"You betray your mission easily," she said. "Why is that?"

"Because fuck my mission. Leon is nineteen. And I don't want to lie to you."

"And why is that?"

"For my job I have to lie to everyone. I'd like to tell the truth to someone before I forget how."

"There may be a Leon at my home," she said. "What does he look like?"

"I don't know, other than he's nineteen. The only picture I was given was of you."

"A picture of me. Was it flattering?" Her tone was mocking.

"I haven't see you in person yet," he said. She'd been standing behind him ever since coming into the room. "But if you're as beautiful in person as you are in the photograph, then it's you who should be an artist's muse."

Did the flattery please her or annoy her? Kingsley wasn't sure. After a moment's hesitation, she took the knife away from his jugular.

She stroked his face, his cheeks, his lips. She still wore her gloves, and he ached to feel her flesh on his flesh. He had no doubt that was the reason she wore them.

"I'm quite familiar with the agency you belong to," she said. "They've been dogging my every move for years. I made the mistake of knowing a little too much about one of your brothers-in-arms. They won't let me be. I would very much like your agency to leave me alone. My family and I live a quiet life in a quiet house near a quiet village. People come to me, people in need, and I take them in. Do you think such a person deserves the scrutiny of your agency?"

"No," Kingsley said, although he didn't entirely believe her. He highly doubted she lived a quiet life in a quiet house near a quiet village.

"If I were to take you to my home and allow you to see Leon, would your agency leave me and my family alone?"

"It might help," Kingsley said. "I don't have that authority. I can't make you any guarantees, but I'll tell them to leave you alone if Leon is safe and happy."

"If I let you come to my home, you will have to serve."

Kingsley felt a cold thrill of excitement at the thought of "serving," the thrill like a feather sliding up the center of his back, like that moment when a hand or foot fallen asleep starts to tingle and come back to life.

"You've served before, haven't you?" she asked. "I can tell from how patiently you wait. Only those who've served know how to be humble."

Kingsley tensed. He didn't talk about *him* with anyone, ever.

He didn't particularly want to start now. But he knew he must keep playing if he wanted to win.

"Yes, I've served."

"Did you serve a woman or a man?"

"Neither."

"Mysterious. Animal?"

"Perhaps."

"Vegetable?"

"No," he said, smiling.

"Angel? Demon? God?"

Kingsley considered his options.

"All of the above," he said.

"Ah," she said. Again that "ah," that lovely "ah."

He wanted to make her "ah" and "ah" and "ahh . . ."

She lightly tugged his right earlobe. "Your neck muscles went very tense when I asked about the one you served. Interesting." She spoke French again—*interressant.*

Abruptly she ceased touching him and sat in the armchair, crossing her legs at the ankles like a lady. He was so shocked that he looked at her without waiting for permission.

She didn't seem to mind.

She was wearing a well-tailored ankle-length navy pinstripe skirt and jacket, a navy fascinator with the veil pulled down. This close to her, he could see enough of her face through the veil to know he'd been right. She was beautiful. He still couldn't place her age, however, not that it mattered to him.

"If you come with me, Kingsley," she said, "I might decide to kill you. Do you accept that risk?"

"Yes," he said simply and without hesitation.

"Why?"

"Better to be murdered by beauty than to live without it."

She took a moment to absorb that. Behind the veil her eyes narrowed. "Do you know this phrase—worth his salt?"

"It means a man is worth his pay," he said.

"Workers in ancient Rome were paid with salt. It's where we get the word 'salary.' In my home, salt is still the official currency. Blood. Tears. Sweat. Semen. Choose one. That's how you'll pay me for taking you in."

Kingsley started to answer, and she held up a finger to stop him.

"Think carefully before you choose," she said. "It seems an easy question. It is not by any means."

Kingsley thought it over.

Sweat meant manual labor.

Tears meant psychological torture.

Blood mean physical torture.

Semen . . . well, it was obvious what that meant.

"If I knew you better," he said, "I would choose blood. Maybe even tears. Never sweat. But since I don't . . . I'll have to go with come."

"You might regret your choice."

Kingsley only shrugged.

"Aren't you worried about that?" she asked.

"I regret everything anyway. What's one more for the butcher's bill?"

"Very well," she said. "I accept your payment. Stand up. I'll have to examine you. Would you like to take your clothes off, or would you rather I do it?"

Her tone indicated she didn't care either way.

"I will," he said. She lifted her hand as if to say, *Get on with it.* Kingsley stood up to undress. He didn't make a show of it. He had a feeling she wouldn't approve of theatrics. Without hurrying and without dallying, he stripped completely naked. If his body did anything for her, she didn't say so. He wasn't aroused, but he was in that state where he could be easily if someone wanted that from him. She'd used the word "examine," however, so he had a feeling she was simply checking him for weapons.

"Please," she said, waving a hand toward the bed. "Sit."

He sat as ordered and waited.

She rose from her chair and came to him. He watched, curious, as she first removed her white gloves and then replaced them with latex gloves from her small blue handbag.

This was going to get personal.

"Open your mouth," she said, tilting his head back slightly. He did as he was told, and she slipped a finger into his mouth. He almost gagged, but he'd learned to control that reflex. She made a little clicking sound with her tongue, the sort a mother makes to soothe a fussy child. Was she looking for hidden weapons or counting his teeth? Whatever it was, it was fairly humiliating and dehumanizing, which was likely her intention.

She pushed him backward, and Kingsley lay flat on the bed.

"I won't hurt you," she said as if she could sense his sudden tension. "Not until you ask me to. But I see you've been hurt."

She ran her fingers over a small scar on his side. A gunshot wound. She touched a larger scar left from a knife wound on his bicep, a clinical sort of touch, not sentimental or even sensual. She probed the scar tissue like a doctor insuring herself he was healed enough for whatever she had planned for him.

"It was men who hurt you, yes?" she asked.

Kingsley nodded. "Yes."

"Of course, it was men," she said and laughed. "It's always men."

"Did men hurt you?"

She slapped him—a quick hard nasty little slap that shocked the hell out of him.

"No questions," she said. She didn't look angry at him for speaking out of turn. The slap was a mother's slap, striking her toddler's hand before he could burn himself on the hot stove. But it stung like fire. He had to tell his cock to calm down.

She was a slim woman, with the classic coveted "French silhouette" achieved only by good genes or self-starvation. Slight as she was, nothing about her seemed weak. Her eyes . . . he'd seen them before, through the sights of his long gun when he'd been tasked with assassinating an assassin. This was a dangerous woman.

And this dangerous woman was running her hands all over his naked body, sliding them along his thighs and over and under his knees, down his calves, and even across the bottoms of his feet. She briefly cupped his testicles, stroked his cock once— but only once!—and, when she'd touched every square inch of him, she pushed his thighs apart and carefully worked one finger inside him.

She smiled. He could see it even through the veil.

"You like it," she said.

He didn't answer. He didn't have to. His body was already telling her.

"You'll do well in service," she said, removing her finger. "Polly will love you."

She snapped off the gloves, tossed them in the rubbish bin, and stood up. With a precise little gesture of her hand, she indicated he was to stand up, too. He did, naked, aroused, eager, and nervous. But not scared.

"Look there." She pointed at the gilt-framed mirror on the wall. "What is it?"

"A mirror," he said. "A looking glass."

"Hold up your right hand," she ordered. He did. "In the mirror, what hand are you holding up?"

"My left," he said.

"That's where we're going," she said. "Through the looking glass where everything is backwards. Do you understand?"

"I understand."

"Put your clothes on. Meet me at the car in front of the hotel in five minutes. If you're one second late," she said, "I will leave without you, and you will never see me again."

With that she was gone.

Kingsley dressed quickly, not wanting to miss his chance. Before he ran out of the room to follow her, he stopped and looked at the mirror again. The looking glass. Their destination.

Through the looking glass where everything is backwards. He knew what that meant. He knew immediately. He might have known from the second she walked into the room.

Where she was taking him, the men served the women.

Where she was taking him, the women ruled the men.

Considering every wound on his body, heart, and soul had been inflicted by a man—the deepest by a boy—Kingsley couldn't get to her château fast enough.

8

The car waiting out front for him was a 1950's-era burgundy sedan with large wheel fenders and whitewall tires. A Ford Custom, maybe. A tank, definitely, but an elegant tank. He opened the back door and sat next to Madame. There was a driver up front, a tan man in his late thirties with a jagged scar across his cheek. Kingsley had also noted the license plate. He was supposed to be working, after all.

"I apologize in advance," she said. She held up a black length of fabric.

Kingsley sighed.

"If it's any comfort, I'll allow you to speak freely once you're blindfolded," she said.

He won by playing, he told himself. He won by playing.

Kingsley didn't fight when she wrapped the black scarf around his head. She secured it over his eyes and tied it in the back.

"Does it bother you?" she asked. "Too tight?"

"No," he said. "It's fine."

"Put your head in my lap," she said. He did as told. The driver pulled away from the curb and into traffic. He lay on his side and found if he pulled his knees in just a little he could fit on the leather bench seat. Her thigh was soft under his head, and he felt her body warmth through her stocking and skirt.

"Comfortable?" she asked.

"Very. I've never known a kidnapper as considerate as you."

She laughed softly, a warm sensual chuckle.

"You're in my care now," she said. "And you haven't been kidnapped, if you recall. You called me. You wanted me."

"True," he said. "But I was told you'd kidnapped Leon."

"He left his home by choice. I didn't take him."

"He's nineteen."

"Yes, and his family is raising the hue and cry. We'll see if we can't calm their nerves. What about you? Do I need to call your mother and let her know you're safe?" She tapped the tip of his nose.

"My mother's dead," Kingsley said.

"My condolences," she said. It sounded as if she meant it. "You're very young to have already lost a parent."

"Two," he said. "She and my father died in a train crash outside Paris ten years ago."

"Ten years ago? I remember that crash," she said. She'd started stroking his hair again. Gently, so gently, it seemed like it was being ruffled by a light breeze and not by a woman's hand. "That must have been awful for you."

"They were going on a honeymoon. A second honeymoon," Kingsley said. "At the funeral someone said it was good they'd died together, that they would have wanted that."

Madame swore, hissing a very unladylike string of very unladylike words.

"What?" Kingsley asked, laughing.

"No decent parent wants to leave a child orphaned. What a terrible thing to tell you."

"I survived it," Kingsley said. "I think." *Je pense.*

"Poor sweet boy. You may sleep now if you like. You should. I'd like you to rest. And if you continue to please me, you'll have a long night ahead of you."

"You want me to sleep so I won't know how far you're taking me from Paris."

She exhaled heavily, clucked her tongue again. He exasperated her, but she seemed the sort of woman who enjoyed being exasperated. She wasn't happy unless she was correcting a stupid man who'd said a stupid thing. Luckily for her, there were plenty of stupid men in the world.

"I want you to sleep because you're tired, Kingsley," she said. Her voice was as tender as her touch. "You spent all day out in the cold. You must be tired and sore. You need a good meal and a long hot bath and a woman's touch."

"Sounds nice," he said. He shifted and got very comfortable in the warm car that sped along the autoroute to destinations unknown. He was tired, exhausted even, with a deep sort of fatigue that he couldn't blame solely on spending most of the day outside in the cold waiting for a payphone to ring. He was tired the way the fox is tired after the hunt. He yawned.

"See? You are tired," she said.

"What do they say?" Kingsley said. "No rest for the wicked."

"Not true at all," she said, tapping the tip of his nose again. "That's where I'm taking you—where the wicked rest."

"I need it then," Kingsley said. "What do I call you?"

"Madame. That's all."

"Madame," he said, letting his body go slack. "If I dream will you wake me?"

"Why would I wake you up from dreaming?"

"I have bad dreams," he said.

"What do you dream of that scares you so? And you a grown man?"

Kingsley sighed, shrugged.

"Tell me, Kingsley," Madame said. "It's only a dream. You give it power by treating it like an omen."

"Lately, I've been dreaming of the one I used to . . . *serve,* for lack of a better word."

"Dreams or nightmares?"

"Dreams while they happen. Nightmares when I wake up and realize it was just a dream."

"Ah," she said, and that was all. Kingsley could tell she had thoughts aplenty that were left unsaid on that particular subject, though.

She dipped her head and kissed his temple. "You poor boy," she said again.

"It's fine," he said.

"No, it isn't it. But it's fine it's not fine."

"That makes no sense."

She gently tugged a lock of his hair.

"Not all problems are meant to be solved," she said. "Some are meant to be endured. All too often we learn more from living with the question than we ever would from the answer."

"But I want the—"

"Shh . . ." Madame said, stroking his forehead with her silken fingertips. "Sleep now. And don't be afraid of your dreams. I'm here. And if the one you served shows up in your dream, say, 'Go away, I'm with Madame now. She's protecting me. Shoo-shoo.' *Oui*?"

"*Oui, Madame*," he said, and fell asleep smiling at the thought of telling his monster to "shoo-shoo."

When he woke, he was in another world.

9

The car had stopped, engine off. Kingsley was awake and alert behind his blindfold several seconds before he heard Madame's voice ordering, "Wake up. We're here."

Her voice was sweeter than any alarm clock. The way she patted his shoulder, slightly rocking him, reminded him of how his mother would wake him in the mornings before school.

"Here, let me get that for you," Madame said. He sat up and held still as she untied the scarf. "Much better. I like to see that beautiful face."

"Thank you," he said. His relief was so profound to see again that he'd thanked her, forgetting she was the one who'd blind-folded him in the first place.

She tapped her lips with one finger. Oh, so he could only speak freely to her when blindfolded. Otherwise he wasn't to speak unless asked a question. He would learn the rules of this new world soon enough.

The driver opened the door for them and Madame stepped out. Kingsley followed. The driver held out his arm, which Madame took. They walked ahead and Kingsley followed, lagging behind to take in his surroundings.

He'd been to beautiful homes before, luxurious homes, ancestral homes of counts and the old kings and their courtesans. He'd expected something like that when he'd heard of Madame and her château. Like Madame herself, her home didn't disappoint. Large and looming, it was more than deserving of the name "château." A massive stone box with five windows along the top story and four along the bottom, the shutters a pale blue. The exterior was made of river stone, all different colors of earth and clay, cloaked in climbing green ivy. The drive was long and twisting, leading to a tall iron fence covered in vines that surrounded the property. Outside the fence lay a forest, deep and dark. Yet for all that, Kingsley saw it more as a home than a castle. And what made it a home to him instead of a castle was simply this: There were lights on in every single window. Soft warm light and figures making shadows against the glass. People lived here. Lots of them. Someone had cracked a window for fresh air, and he heard voices, laughter, the pleasant mingle of friendly conversation. The people who lived here seemed happy.

In case they weren't, he counted five possible exits if he had to make a run for it.

"Kingsley?" Madame called for him. "Come in. You don't want to catch cold, do you?"

"No, Madame," he said, keeping his smile on the inside. She was treating him like a child. It didn't arouse him in the least to be infantilized, but he had to admit he did appreciate being fussed over. His superiors used him for his abilities. His lovers used him for his body. Nobody actually gave a shit about him. And surely Madame didn't either, although it seemed to be her kink to pretend she did. If that was her game, he was happy to play along for now.

He increased his stride to catch up with Madame and her driver. She held out her arm and placed her hand on the small of his back to guide him through the front door and into the house. How many hundreds of times had he done the same thing to a woman on his arm? He couldn't recall a single instance when a woman had ever done that for him. Or even a man. Madame was chivalrous. He almost told her that before remembering he wasn't allowed to speak.

"*Merci,*" she said to her driver, who took her hand and kissed the back of it. "If you'll find Polly for me and send her to my salon, please. Your coat, Kingsley?"

She helped him out of his overcoat and passed it to the man who was apparently both valet and driver and likely anything else Madame asked him to be.

She tut-tutted over his coat. "Not very warm," she said, eyeing it with disapprobation. "But young people never dress warm enough in winter. I've finally broken Polly of the habit, but not Colette. Short skirts in January? I'll never understand this generation. Do I sound like a fussy grandmother?"

"A little," he said, though he thought she resembled a fussy grandmother as much as he resembled a fussy grandfather.

"Ah, perhaps. But you'll feel the same when you're my age, my boy."

The driver-valet disappeared into a side room with their coats. Seconds later the man returned with a pair of slippers. He bent to remove Madame's shoes and replace them with gold silk slippers, and disappeared again. It was all so graceful and well-choreographed that Kingsley imagined that was the thousandth time her valet had removed Madame's shoes for her, the thousandth time he'd replaced them with slippers. Kingsley was certainly through the looking glass now. He found it civilized. For a man who was paid to lie and kill and steal, a happy home with well-mannered men—*gentle* men, even—seemed a kind of paradise.

"This way, dear." With a neat crooking of her fingers, she beckoned for Kingsley to follow her.

They walked down a short hallway and Kingsley found the château as warm and inviting inside as out. True, it was elegant, tastefully decorated in warm reds and golds with plush Persian rugs covering the dark floors, but it wasn't intimidating for all the luxury. Always the spy, he counted steps and exits as they walked down a short hallway and into a small sitting room. A fire had been lit and it alone provided illumination to the room. He hadn't seen any over-head lights, yet—only lamps. The room was so deliciously warm Kingsley could have laid down on the floor and fallen asleep again.

"Welcome to our little château," Madame said. She sat on a red-striped divan and gestured to the rug at her feet. Kingsley sat on it cross-legged. "Do you like it here?"

Finally, another question. He could speak.

"It's very nice," he said. "Not like I pictured from reading *Story of O*."

"Appearances can deceive. So you have read the book?"

"Stole it from parents when I was a boy and read it when they were out."

"Wicked boy," she said, tut-tutting again, although he could tell she secretly approved. "My husband gave me a copy of it a week before our wedding. I was an innocent, a virgin. Only eighteen years old. He was thirty. He had *ideas* for us. It seems I may have gotten the wrong idea from it. Well, not the wrong idea. An idea he did not intend . . ." Her voice trailed off and she smiled at the fire.

"You want to know something funny about the book?" she said. "When *Histoire d'O* came out—you're too young to know this—nobody would believe that a woman wrote it. It was too violent. Too terrifying. Too sexual. They thought a man had written under a woman's *nom de plume*."

"Whoever said that hasn't met the women I've met," Kingsley said.

"They certainly never met me."

Kingsley laughed. With a graceful lift of her hands, she raised her veil and met his eyes.

For the first time Kingsley saw her face in full. Her skin was smooth, with only a few laugh lines here and there around her mouth and eyes. She had the face of a woman of thirty-five. But when she removed her hat, he saw that her hair was white. White-white. Not white-blond. Not silver. Not gray. White and pinned back in an old-fashioned sort of knot at the nape of her neck. The color and style made her look older, yes—almost fifty, if he was forced to guess—but it also made her look like a snow queen from an old fairy tale. He could have looked at her all night had she let him.

"I know you're here to see Leon," she said. "And you will. Privileges are earned here, however. Are you willing to earn that privilege?"

"Of course," he said. *Bien sûr.*

"You may rest tonight, or you may serve tonight. I'll allow you to decide that," she said. "Before you answer, remember how you promised to earn your keep here."

He remembered.

"What is your choice?" she asked.

"I'll serve," he said. He had sex every night with strange women. Why should this night be any different?

"Very good." She nodded. "Ah, there's our Polly."

"Here's your Polly," said a woman standing in the doorway to the salon. Polly looked about his age, maybe a little older but only by a year or two. She had auburn hair that fell in fat curls to her shoulders. She wasn't slim like Madame, but boasted magnificent curves. Full hips, full breasts, with a narrow waist that accentuated both. She was wearing a white silk nightgown and matching robe. He liked Polly already, if only because he was shallow and she was lovely—a young Mae West in stature though with a sweeter smile.

"Polly, this is Kingsley," Madame said.

"Another stray you've brought home?" Polly asked, smiling. With a name like Polly there was little chance she was French. And the more she spoke, the more Kingsley could discern French was not her native tongue. She had an accent, American or Canadian, and he wanted to speak with her in English. He hoped she would allow it.

"A relative of one of our gentlemen is concerned for his well-being. Kingsley's come to see that we aren't mistreating the young man or holding him hostage."

Polly grinned at Madame like they were sharing a secret joke at his expense. "I'm surprised you let him in."

"Kingsley's promised to pay in full for being allowed into the house," Madame said.

"He is very pretty," Polly said. "I can't blame you for bending the rules a little for him."

"Rules are made to be bent. Kingsley wishes to serve tonight. Would you like to take him? He'll need to be fed and bathed and given a place to sleep, unless you want him in bed with you. If not, we'll let the girls fight over him."

"They'd tear him limb from limb," Polly said. "Though from the way he's smiling, he might enjoy that. I better take him if we want him in one piece by morning."

Kingsley's eyes widened. Did he have any say in who he slept with here? It didn't sound like it. Of course, if all the women here were as alluring as Madame and Polly, then he hardly had much cause for complaint.

"We'll see how we rub along," Polly said, grinning. "Anything else, Madame?"

"I'm thinking . . . he might be the one for Colette," Madame said.

To that Polly raised her eyebrow. "She'll be happy to hear that. She's getting impatient."

"She is. And I hate to make her wait much longer."

"It may snow tonight," Polly said.

"It might indeed."

Kingsley couldn't begin to guess what the two women were talking about. Who was Colette? What was she waiting for? Was she waiting for him? And what did any of that have to do with the weather forecast?

"He's been a good boy for me," Madame said.

"He'll be a good boy for me, too," Polly said.

"You're a treasure," Madame said to Polly. Madame's smile was luminous and genuine. The affection between the two women was obvious. "Kingsley, go with Polly now. Do everything she tells you to do. Understand?"

"Completely," he said.

"Do you have any questions for me?" Madame asked.

"I can ask?"

She nodded. "I'll allow one question. Polly can answer your others."

One question?

"How many times have you lied to me tonight?" he asked.

Madame's eyebrow arched high. Polly looked at him with new respect.

"Only once," Madame said. Then she grinned. "But it was a big one."

Polly snapped her fingers. Kingsley didn't want to make her do it twice. He rose quickly and followed her from the room, but not before looking back one last time at Madame. She had a strange look on her face, like she was trying not to laugh. Or perhaps trying not to cry.

Once they were alone in the hallway, Polly spoke directly to him for the first time.

"You're interesting," she said in French.

"I could say the same to you," he said in English.

She paused mid-step and looked at him.

"Are you American?" she asked, sounding hopeful.

"Half-American. Half-French. You?"

"Canadian," she said. "Toronto. I was born here but we moved to Canada when I was four. Do you mind speaking English with me?"

He shrugged. "Not at all, if you don't mind a French accent. Suppressing the accent is hard on my brain."

"I love the accent. See? We're rubbing along well together already. What do you think of us so far?" Polly asked as she led him into the kitchen and gestured at the table for him to sit.

"Not what I expected, frankly," he said, sitting.

Polly tilted her head. "Why is that?"

"I was told this was a cult. That Madame was a dangerous cult leader, some kind of pied piper who seduced men away from their wives and families. So far, you all seem fairly . . . *tame*. No offense."

"None taken," she said, standing behind the chair opposite him. "But I don't think we're quite as tame as we seem." She smiled and went to the stove where dinner awaited in large copper pots.

"You're being awfully nice to me if this is a cult. Or maybe that's how it starts—you butter me up and make me drop my guard and then you come in for the kill."

"For the kill? You think we're going to kill you?" Polly asked, taking bowls from the cabinets.

"You said the girls would tear me limb from limb," he reminded her.

"Joking," she said. "We have some girls here who like to play-fight over their favorite boys. It's only for fun. At most you'd wake up tomorrow sore and smiling."

"My kind of fight," he said. "But Madame did put a knife to my throat and threaten to slit it if I lied to her."

"That was only a test," Polly said. "She's not really going to kill you. That's not her style."

"What is her style?"

"If she decides to break you, she won't kill you," Polly said with a grin that made his stomach lurch. "She'll just make you wish you were dead. Hungry?"

10

A t the look on his face, Polly patted his head and told him not to worry about Madame. And once he started eating, he stopped worrying. After twenty minutes at Madame's home, Kingsley had already decided he would drag this assignment out as long as possible. The late dinner Polly provided for him was delicious. Some kind of thick vegetable soup spiced with basil, pepper, and thyme, served with a steep glass of cabernet.

"Good wine," he said after a sip. "Spiked? Poisoned?"

"Madame would never ruin cabernet by spiking it. Champagne, maybe. But never the good wine." Polly's eyes twinkled with amusement as she sat down in the chair across from him.

"The house is very cozy for a cult, too," Kingsley said. "Not that I'm complaining. I was expecting a drafty castle with stone floors and dungeons."

"You're in the new part of the house," Polly said. "Built in 1910. Some famously alcoholic Edwardian architect added this wing to the old house back then. The original house is exactly what you would think of when you think of a château. Very drafty. A nightmare to keep warm in winter. The new wing is where we stay from November through April."

"Can I see the old house?"

"Tomorrow . . . if you survive the night," she said with dramatic relish.

"I think I'll make it till morning," he said. "I've survived scarier sorts than you."

"Oh, I'm not very scary, I know. That's one reason I came here," she said. "I like being in charge of men, but I'm not much of a sadist. My mother was very disappointed in me for that very reason."

"Your mother? She wanted you to be a sadist? My mother wanted me to be a doctor."

"Oh, yes," Polly said. "Like I said, I was born here, in this house. It was very different, though, in my mother's time."

"Your mother lived here?"

"For years. When she fell in love with my father who was a slave here, Madame kicked us out."

"Kicked you all out?"

"It's the rules. No monogamy. No falling in love. Unless it's with the house."

"Hard rule to follow," Kingsley said. "Not being allowed to fall in love, I mean. The heart wants what the heart wants."

When he'd fallen in love as a teenager, that relationship had broken fourteen rules in their school's student handbook. Kingsley had gotten bored on afternoon and counted.

"I say 'kicked us out,' but Madame wasn't cruel about it," Polly said. "Mom knew the risks and left on good terms with Madame. Good enough that Madame took me in when I wanted to come back."

"What did your parents do after you all left here?"

"Mom took us back to Toronto and started her own little château there, just our family. My father was her husband and slave, and she had a few other men who submitted to her. My brother served, too." Kingsley goggled at her. "It's not like that," she said, grinning. "It wasn't sexual. Well, not my brother, obviously. My father, yes. He worshipped my mother. Lived in abject servitude to her and loved it."

"But your brother?"

"He was raised to serve women. He did the cooking and cleaning at home. I had the paper route. You look so shocked," she said, reaching out and tweaking his nose playfully.

"I am," he said.

"All over the world right now," she said, "girls are being raised in homes where they're expected to serve men—first their fathers and then their husbands. The boys get the jobs outside the home and the girls do the cooking and cleaning inside the home. So many countries, so many cultures, it goes without saying that the women serve the men of the household. For some reason—sexism—when it's reversed, when the fathers and the sons are expected to do the cooking and the cleaning, people assume we've all gone insane."

"I hadn't thought about it like that," Kingsley said. His sister had done most of the chores when they were growing up. Polly had a point.

"Most men don't. They simply take it for granted that they're kings in their castles. Then the daughter grows up and moves out and the wife gets fed up and leaves him, and the poor man who's left behind can't even boil an egg."

"I take it the men in this house do the egg boiling?"

"You know how to boil an egg?"

"If you gave me a recipe," Kingsley said. "Although . . . you did serve me dinner."

"Dinner that was cooked by a man. And you're new here. A baby. We take very good care of the new babies in this house. That being said, they aren't allowed to stay babies for long."

He grinned at that and kept eating.

"I came back two years ago. It was time to leave home . . .

leave home and *come* home," Polly continued. "My mother's a force of nature. Here, I can relax. Be myself. I'll never be the Valkyrie my mother is, and Madame is just fine with that. She relies on me. I'm her second-in-command."

"Are you going to command me?"

"If you keep being so handsome," she said, "I'll have to. Or I'll never forgive myself. Are you finished eating?"

"Yes, thank you."

"Did you enjoy it?" Polly asked.

"I haven't had home-cooked food in so long I almost came from the first bite. I live on coffee and cigarettes." He could use a Gauloise right about now, but didn't want to be rude.

Polly grinned. She smiled easily and often, and he liked that about her.

"We'll fatten you up," she said. "Angelo's cooking is half the reason I stay here. And half the reason I can't fit into any of my old jeans anymore. No one is complaining."

"I'm not," Kingsley said, and Polly gave him that look women did when a man complimented them and they weren't quite sure they believed the compliment. But she should. She had a lush, full figure. The gown and robe did far more for her lovely curves than a boring pair of jeans ever would.

"Wash your dishes and dry them, and leave them in the rack," she said, pointing toward the sink. "When that's done, come up the stairs right outside the kitchen. I'll be in the third room on the right. I need to start your bathwater running."

"You're giving me a bath? Really?"

"Baby," she said, her eyes twinkling. "Of course I am. How hot do you like your bathwater?"

"Boil me like a lobster."

"Only if I can eat you after," she said, and with a swish of silk, she left him alone in the kitchen.

Alone. All alone. Or was he?

Kingsley glanced around and made sure no one was watching him, no cameras, no spyholes.

A telephone hung on the kitchen wall. He could use it right now to call his superiors. They could trace the call, find the house. He didn't do it. So far he'd been treated with nothing but kindness. No one was holding him prisoner. If he were going to betray Madame's privacy, it would have to be for very good reason, and so far she hadn't given him one. Still, he did glance at the phone, checking to see if the house number was listed on it. No luck there.

After doing his dishes, as ordered, he found the back stairs and went up. The second story was even cozier than the more formal downstairs. The hallway was covered in long red rugs and the lights were turned down low. The house had gone quiet since he'd arrived. No more voices and laughter. A sleeping house. It was late. Almost midnight. From behind one closed door he heard the unmistakable sound of a woman quietly having an orgasm. Ah, so not everyone was sleeping.

Another door in the hallway hung slightly ajar, and Kingsley couldn't resist peeking inside. At first he wasn't sure what he was seeing. The room was quite dark except for one small nightlight in the shape of a sleeping lamb. By the window he spied something he never expected to see in this place—a bassinet, white with sheer netting draped over it. He crept to the bassinet. A small baby slept inside, lying on his back, tiny hands clenched into tiny fists, and a little square blanket decorated with leaping sheep pulled to the baby's chin.

"Kingsley?" came a whispered voice from the doorway. He turned and saw Polly walking toward him.

"Sorry," he said, his voice as low as he could make it. "The door was open."

"It's fine. This is Jacques," she said as she adjusted the baby's blanket.

"Yours?"

"Ah . . . Yes and no," she said, smiling tenderly down at the baby boy. "Come on. Your bath is ready."

Reluctantly, he let her lead him from the room. He wouldn't have minded watching Jacques sleep a little more. He hadn't been around a baby in years.

"What do you mean yes and no?" he asked as Polly led him down the hall.

"We all help with the rearing of children," she said. "He's not my son, but he's as much my responsibility as his mother's."

"Do the men help raise the children here, too?'

"Of course. Why do you ask?"

Kingsley felt a knot form in his chest. He ignored it.

"When Madame said she had a family here, I thought she meant it the way, you know, cult leaders call their 'flock' their family."

"Not quite," she said. "We are very much a family here. Jacques is the first baby born here in a long time, but there have been other children in the house. Myself included. And several more on the way."

"Who is Jacques's father?" Kingsley asked.

"No idea," she said with a shrug. "Not that it matters."

Her answer was offhand, yet spoke volumes.

"Paying in salt," Kingsley said.

"What was that?" Polly said.

"You breed the men here, don't you?" Kingsley asked.

Polly winked at him as she pulled him gently into the room. "Smart boy," she said. "Now you're catching on."

So . . . it seemed life at the château was not so tame after all.

K ingsley let Polly lead him by the hand into her bedroom. It was sumptuous and sensual with pale blue walls and a grand blue bed, with draperies hanging over the padded silk headboard and a large steamer trunk at its foot. He studied the room in silence. He must've been quiet for too long, because Polly squeezed his hand.

"Don't worry," Polly said with a teasing smile. "I won't use you for breeding stock."

"I wasn't worried," he said.

"Oh," she said. "So you do want to be bred?"

"Not at the moment," he said. "I'm free for breeding tomorrow."

Polly laughed. "Come on, you. Bath time."

The bathroom, too, was elegant, if decadent. A large claw foot tub was already filled with steaming water and rolled white towels were stacked on a rough wood table by the pedestal sink.

"Do I take my clothes off or do you?" he asked. "I don't know the etiquette here yet."

"We don't go for a lot of rules around here. The etiquette for the men is to serve the women with enthusiasm and good humor. The etiquette for the women is to treat the men with mercy. We tend to spare the rod."

"What if the man likes the rod?"

"Do you like the rod, Kingsley?"

"What kind of rod are we talking about?" he asked. "Never mind. Whatever kind of rod it is, I probably like it."

"Interesting," she said. "I'll keep that in mind. As for removing your clothes, I'll do most of the work. Only because it pleases me to undress you tonight. Tomorrow it may please me to watch you undress yourself. That's why we have so few hard and fast rules. As long as you strive to do your best to please the women of the house, you'll do fine here."

"How many women are in this house?" Kingsley asked as Polly pulled his sweater off over his head and went to work unbuttoning his jeans.

"Ten counting Colette, though she's not officially a member of the household yet." Polly pushed his jeans down to his ankles and he stepped out of them.

"And how many men?"

"Eight. Nine, counting you. Madame doesn't allow equal numbers. There can never be the same number of men as women. Too easy to pair off. All the men are used by all the women. If you fall in love and want to be monogamous, like my parents, that's fine, but you don't do it in this house."

"Ten women and nine men . . . where does everyone sleep?" Kingsley asked, trying to sound merely curious while he pumped Polly for information.

"Only the women have rooms of their own," she said. "The men sleep wherever they're told to. On the floor if ordered. In bed with one of us if ordered. On the lawn if ordered. Or the roof or the bathtub or wherever we say."

"With Madame?"

"If ordered. Though I don't know if she's ever ordered one of the boys to sleep with her."

Kingsley stepped into the bathtub. The water was hot, very hot, just the way he liked it. The heat seeped into his wounds and his aching muscles, and he felt more relaxed than he had in months.

"I don't like the idea of sleeping alone on the ground," Kingsley said.

"In that case," Polly said and flicked water into his face, "you'll just have to please us, and you'll get to sleep in a bed every night."

"I suppose I will. If I must, I'll make the sacrifice."

"Don't get ahead of yourself. You have to earn a place here. And you haven't done that yet."

"How does a man earn a place here?" he asked.

"Madame tests you. If you pass, you may stay."

"When will she test me? I mean, if I wanted to stay."

Polly lowered her voice. "Don't look now, but you're already being tested."

Before he could ask another question, she dumped a wine glass filled with soapy water over his head.

The bath was hardly the sexual sensual affair he'd anticipated. With a rough sponge, Polly scrubbed him with a vengeance from head to toe and dunked him under water twice to rinse his hair. He needed the scrubbing after last night's sex and the day's long miserable public payphone vigil. Kingsley decided he liked that Polly didn't make the bath into something sexual. That would give it a meaning he didn't want it to have. He hadn't been taken care of in a long time. He used and was used in return. When was the last time someone had paid him a simple kindness like a home-cooked meal and a hot bath? Too long, he decided. He hadn't even known he missed someone caring if he had dirt under his fingernails or not. By the time she'd finished with him, he was red and raw and squeaky clean.

"Good. Your fingernails are very short," she said, inspecting his hands. "That's a requirement in this house."

"I can't imagine why," Kingsley said. She gestured for him to stand up, and she tossed him a plush white towel.

"You're very handsome when you're wet and being a smartass," she said. "I might have to do bad things to you tonight."

"*Bad* bad things?" he asked as he roughly dried his hair. "Or good bad things?"

"Good bad things."

"Those are my favorite kind of bad things." He wrapped the towel around his waist and leaned back against the bathroom counter. He felt good. Relaxed and clean and warm. In a house this warm, it was easy to forget that winter waited for him outside. Outside and in his dreams.

Polly stepped close to him and unwrapped the towel from his waist and tossed it on the floor.

"Tell me what your favorite bad things are," she said. Then she kissed his bare shoulder. His bare clean shoulder. He could smell himself and he smelled like warm skin and soap. Polly was close enough that he could smell her—simple floral shampoo and maybe a touch of vanilla behind her ears.

"My favorite bad things?" he asked. "Just this morning I was lying in bed imagining my wrists tied to the headboard."

"Were you hard thinking about it?"

"A little."

"Nothing little here," she said, taking his cock in her hand. "Were you alone?"

"I was. The girl I'd brought home had already left."

"So did you masturbate?"

"No," he said. "I thought about it, but I try not to give those fantasies too much power over me. Especially if they're not going to come true."

"Maybe tonight," she said, "they will. If you're good."

Kingsley resolved to be very *very* good. Polly ran her fingers through his still-damp hair, but not in a sexual way. Not really. She was pushing the long strands off his face.

"There," she said. "That's better. You need a haircut."

"You should have seen my hair in high school. Down to my shoulders."

"Why did you cut it?" she asked.

"I joined *la Légion.*"

"They have no respect for pretty-boy hair."

"Should I get used to being treated like this?" he asked when she picked up a fresh dry towel and ran it over his hair again. He laughed as she rubbed it in his face, like the fun babysitter one hoped to get instead of the mean one.

"You all get special treatment on your first night."

"Would you like me to give you some special treatment?" Kingsley asked as Polly dried off his thighs. She seemed to be taking her time with the task.

"Oh, but that's the best part of being a woman in this house," Polly said smiling up at him. "It's not special treatment at all. It's just how it's done here."

Polly took his cock in her hand, lightly, not stroking it, merely holding it. It felt good simply to have her soft fingers wrapped around his hardness.

He moved in to kiss her. She put her hand over his lips and grinned.

"Kisses are earned."

She gave his cock a little tug before letting it go. She switched off the bathroom light and led him into the bedroom. Instead of turning on a lamp, she pushed open the heavy curtains. The moon was bright white and full. Polly looked radiant in her white night-gown, which glowed in the moonlit dark. She turned from the window, faced him, and said, "Have you ever let a woman take you?"

"I . . . what do you mean?" he asked, equal parts curious and nervous. "Woman on top? Of course."

"That's not what I mean. What I mean is . . . have you ever let a woman fuck you?"

Kingsley opened his mouth but nothing came out.

Polly laughed a little. "I take that as a 'no.' Don't worry. You're very young. How old are you? Twenty-two?"

"Twenty-four."

"Very young."

"I'm very experienced, I promise. I've been with a couple of men. And Madame's finger was up there today, which was uncalled for." But not unappreciated.

Polly winced. "Yes, sorry about that. We never know where your sort is hiding bugs and whatever else you all hide up there."

"I promise you, I've never put anything business-related up my ass." That wasn't strictly true, but she didn't need to know that.

"What about pleasure-related?"

"What did you have in mind?"

"Let's see what's in the toy chest." She knelt by the large steamer trunk at the foot of the bed and pushed it open. There was no lock, no key. Kingsley couldn't resist peering inside as Polly rummaged through it.

"Are those cuffs?" he asked when he saw two loops on a chain.

"They are. Caught your eye, did they?" she asked. They weren't quite handcuffs, not the sort he'd used for business and pleasure. They were some kind of thick, dark rope. She tossed them onto the bed, and Kingsley's heart rate increased.

"Turn the covers down while I'm digging," she said, waving her hand to shoo him off. While drawing back the blue-and-white silk quilt and top sheet, Kingsley smiled to himself. As attractive and buxom and curvaceous as Polly was, it wasn't so much the prospect of having sex with her that excited him as it was the idea of her dominating him in whatever way she most desired. Once he'd been a slave to a beautiful sadist, but that was years ago. Seven years ago. Seven years ago according to the calendar. Seven thousand by the calendar of his heart.

"Here we are," she said, pulling a black drawstring bag from the trunk. She carried it over to the bed and laid it on the covers. "Lie down," she said, and Kingsley did, rolling onto his side to face her. She untied the string of the bag and laid out five different dildos of varying widths and sizes.

"Pick one," she said as she sat across from him on the bed.

"What?"

"I'm going to fuck your ass tonight. Pick one."

Kingsley blinked a few times.

"If you don't hurry up and pick one," Polly said, "I will. And you might not like what I choose."

"You're letting me choose?"

"It doesn't make much difference to me. It'll make a big difference to you."

Kingsley blew out hard through his lips while he looked at the range of toys Polly had laid out in front of him. One was five inches. One was six inches and narrow. One was six inches and very thick. One was about eight inches with a bit of a curve and not too wide. And the other was roughly the size of his forearm.

"I . . . I am overwhelmed by the options. It's a veritable cornucopia of dildos."

Polly stroked his cheek with the back of her finger. "It's cute that you're shy."

"I am not shy. I am not," he said, playfully swatting her patronizing hand away. "I'm a whore."

"You say that, but here you are, too nervous to pick out the dildo you want fucked with. Such a shy boy trying so hard to pretend he isn't shy . . . so, so cute."

"I'm deciding, okay," he said, holding up a hand in surrender. "It's a big decision. Or an average-sized decision," he said, picking up the five-inch dildo. He tossed it back into the pile.

"Precious."

"I've never done this with a woman before."

She giggled. "Adorable. I'm in love."

"I'm not adorable. I'm devastating."

"Devastatingly adorable. Such pretty eyes, too." She pinched his nose. "Pretty hair." She pulled on a wavy damp lock that had fallen over his eye.

"Stop that."

"And pretty hips," she said, caressing his side and hip with her hand. "Boys have such beautiful curves. Better than women. Don't tell Madame I said that. She doesn't like you boys getting big heads."

"Big heads or big *heads*?" he asked.

"I should spank you. I think I want to," she said, singing the threat at him.

"I think you don't," he said, singing back.

"Speed it up, you adorable whore," she said, giving his ass one vicious pinch to make her point. "I'm dying to play with your body."

"Were all these dildos made in America?" he asked.

"I don't know. Why?"

Kingsley held one up, tip facing her. "No foreskin."

Polly glared at him. "Pick."

"Hmm . . ." Kingsley said. "Who will it be tonight . . . David or Goliath?"

"Kingsley, if you don't pick soon, it'll be all five of them—at the same time."

"Fine, that one." Kingsley picked the second-largest one. Not for the width so much as the length.

"Oh . . . ambitious, aren't we?" she asked, still grinning.

"I've taken bigger."

"When?" she demanded.

"High school."

"If you've taken bigger," she asked, "then why didn't you pick the biggest one?"

"Because," he said quite seriously and solemnly, "high school was a long time ago."

I t had been a long time since Kingsley had laughed so freely with a girl. Polly rolled onto her back in a giggle fit, swept up in the silliness like a child. God, what a beautiful, bizarre looking-glass world this château was. Hard to believe he was getting paid for this assignment. Not that he cared—money couldn't buy him what he wanted. He cared about nothing tonight except giving his body to Polly to do with as she pleased.

And it seemed she pleased to kiss him. A quick kiss, more affectionate than sensual. If it wasn't necessarily the kiss he wanted, it was the kiss he needed. A unique pleasure it was, being kissed by a woman laughing too hard to give a proper kiss.

"I want your tongue in my mouth," she said, "but I'm afraid I'll accidentally bite it off."

"I might need it later," he said.

"You'll definitely need it later. Maybe sooner," she said with a meaningful waggle of her eyebrows. Still smiling, Polly left him on the bed while she rummaged around in her toy chest again. When she returned to the bed, she wasn't laughing anymore.

Polly kissed his mouth and pushed him onto his back. She kissed his mouth, and she lifted his hands over his head. She kissed his mouth, and she straddled his stomach. She kissed his mouth, and she sat on his hips. She kissed his mouth and kissed his mouth and kissed his mouth until he couldn't remember what life was like before she'd kissed his mouth.

"*Mon dieu*," he said when she stopped to let him breathe. *My God.*

She'd kissed him so that his lips were already tingling and swollen and aching to be kissed again.

"I am your *dieu* tonight," she said. "I'm your goddess and this bed is our temple, and you're the offering. Offer yourself to me."

"I'm yours," he said. "Use me in any way that pleases you and I will worship you for life. Or at least until morning."

She pinched his cheek, then slapped it lightly. "Naughty boy. I'm a very happy goddess tonight," she said. "Who wouldn't be with such a fine offering?"

Polly slid her hands over his naked chest and stomach. His skin tingled at her teasing. She picked up her rope cuffs and wrapped them around Kingsley's right wrist. Then she looped them through one of the posts of the headboard and bound his left wrist.

"Pull," she ordered.

He pulled against the ropes and they tightened on his wrists. And the second he felt the tightness kissing the point of pain, he gasped. A little gasp. A little "huh." Nothing of note really but Polly had noticed it, read it, and knew exactly what it meant.

"Masochist," she breathed, her eyes fluttering in happiness. She scored his chest with her sharp, sculpted fingernails. "I love being with masochists. Twice the pleasure for me."

"How so?" Kingsley asked, lightly panting as she dug into his inner biceps with those wicked fingernails of hers.

"When I touch you gently, you like it," she said, caressing his arms with her whole hands. "And when I hurt you, you like that, too." She dug in her nails and scratched his arms with force. She didn't break the skin, but she almost did . . . and *dieu*, he loved it. He loved it enough his shoulders arched off the bed.

"You adorable little boy," she said, her voice a purr now.

"I'm six feet tall," he said. "Twenty-four years old. I am not little nor a boy."

"The more you try to convince me you aren't a little boy, the more like a little boy you sound," she said. "Next you'll be stamping your foot and pouting at me."

"Never," he said and kicked the bed with his heel.

"Adorable," she said and bent to kiss him again. She dug her fingernails deep into his sides as she pressed her tongue into his mouth. Her nails were filed sharp as knives. His cock hardened and his pulse quickened as she pressed them into his flesh.

Polly pulled back from the kiss and put two fingers over his lips.

"Listen to me," she said. Her tone was serious, her expression authoritarian.

He was listening.

"You're my new toy," she continued, "but I'm a big girl and big girls don't break their toys. I want you to do everything I tell you to do so you don't get hurt. I won't be happy if you disobey me and end up in pain in all the wrong places."

She stroked his cheek with the back of her finger as she said this, a tender touch, affectionate. This girl did take good care of her toys.

"Listen to me," she said again. "Pull your knees to your chest. I want you open for me, and that takes time and a little help."

He lifted his knees to his chest as ordered while Polly coated her fingers in a thick lubricant.

"Breathe out when I push my fingers into you," she said. "I'm going to put a plug in you to open you for me. I have a feeling you'll like it."

He drew in a deep breath and let it out as she eased the plug in. It felt, well . . . *weird* was the best word he could come up with for the sensation. Weird at first. When she let him lower his legs down to the bed again, the plug shifted into place, pressing against that sensitive spot inside him that rarely got the attention it craved.

"Good?" she asked.

"Yes," he said, breathless.

"And this?" She wrapped her hand around his cock again and stroked it with long, firm, and wet caresses. "Feels good, doesn't it?"

"Yes . . ." he breathed and arched again.

"Your eyes just rolled back so far in your head, I bet you could read your own thoughts," she teased.

"I have no thoughts," he said. "Other than, *Don't stop, please.*"

"I won't stop if you won't stop," she said. "Keep moving your hips like that when I stroke you. It makes all the muscles in your stomach dance and your cock drip."

He hadn't even realized he was doing anything with his hips until she'd mentioned it. He was rolling them slowly along with her strokes, trying to eke out as much pleasure from each tug of her hand as possible. It felt a thousand times better than when he stroked himself. His wrists were tied over his head to the headboard, just as he'd fantasized about that very morning. That morning? It felt like a year ago that he'd woken up from his dark winter dreams. What sort of dreams would he have while a prisoner in this peculiar female paradise?

"Tell me what you're feeling, Kingsley. I love to hear it," she said. "How's the plug feel inside you?"

"It's . . . ah, hitting a good place," he said.

"And your cock?"

"It's very happy right now."

"I can tell," she said. "It's quite big, isn't it? I hope it won't break your heart that I won't let you inside me."

"That does break my heart."

"You'll come tonight, I promise."

"My happiness is restored."

"Madame says I'm too soft on you little boys. She once made a boy wait a whole week to come."

"She is a sadist, isn't she?"

"I told you so. It's worse than I can even explain. You'll just have to see for yourself."

"I'd love to see for myself," he said.

"In this house, beatings are privileges and privileges are—"

"Earned."

"Very good. Keep this up and you might earn one."

Kingsley kept it up. He wanted to come very badly, but he had learned enough self-control not to spill in a woman's hand even if that woman's hand was silky soft and yet deceptively strong. Her hand felt so good that when she abruptly stopped touching him, he groaned.

"You really are a slut," she said, and from her tone it was clear she meant that as a compliment. She pinched his hipbone hard enough to leave a bruise. "Don't you dare forget you're here for my pleasure, not the other way around."

"I'll never forget it again," he said.

"It's funny," she said, raising her nightgown to her thighs so she could straddle him again. "I'm with Frenchmen all day and the language does nothing for me. But you speaking English with a French accent . . . well, it works for me. Can you tell?"

She sat down onto his hips and he felt her wet heat on his lower stomach.

"I can tell," he breathed.

Polly shifted back so that the tip of his cock slid through the wet slit of her pussy. It was torture to not push his hips up and enter her. She reached under her nightgown and adjusted him so that the head of his cock rested against her clitoris. Then she draped the flowing folds of her gown around them, over her thighs and his. The silk was light as a feather and like a feather, it tickled and teased his skin. All his senses were alive, on high alert and vibrating with pleasure. He could see her flashing, laughing eyes. He could smell her arousal, rich and fragrant. He could feel the silk of her gown and the satin of her body. He could hear his own desperate breathing and maybe hers, too? And when she lowered the straps of her gown to her elbows and bent over his mouth, he could taste the warmth of her skin as she allowed him the privilege of sucking her lavish, lovely nipples.

"There we go," she whispered, running a hand through his hair. "Just like that. Move your hips the way I like. Rub my clit until I come."

He nodded, her nipple still deep in his mouth. She had the sort of magnificent firm full breasts that he could happily suck on all night, the kind of breasts that turned rational grown men into hormone-ravaged teenaged boys again. It was pure erotic bliss to lay there flat on his back, his arms tied over his head to the bed while moving his hips in tight circles as his dripping cock massaged her swollen clitoris. He could feel that tight knot of flesh throbbing against him. Or maybe it was him throbbing against her. No matter, they both moved and throbbed together.

She made beautiful sounds as she neared orgasm. The softest sighs. The quietest gasps. She pushed her clitoris against his aching erection again and again. Her wetness bathed him and the heat that emanated from her body was deliciously scalding. She pushed harder, moved her hips in tiny spirals and it took everything he had to not come when she came, because when she came it was incandescent. Polly let out a hoarse cry as she pumped against him rapidly. Finally she stopped, frozen, and let out another tense moan. A few delicious seconds passed where she did nothing but rest her weight on him as Kingsley continued to kiss and lick her beautiful nipples.

She finally sat up with a flip of her auburn hair. She pulled her gown up to cover her breasts. A national tragedy, in his opinion.

"Well," she said. "That was fun, wasn't it?"

"*Trés,*" he said, falling into French. "I hope I pleased you."

She kissed his mouth, and with her sharp teeth bit his bottom lip to make him flinch.

"Does that answer your question?"

"I'm not sure," he said, grinning.

"Turn onto your stomach," she ordered.

Now that did answer his question.

13

The ropes around his wrists were long enough Polly didn't have to untie him. Kingsley simply rolled onto his stomach and moved back into place, the ropes twisting into a knot. The pressure on his wrists was comfortable, but tight enough to feel like a pair of strong hands. Strong hands on his wrists, Kingsley lying prone, someone about to take him . . .

Just like high school.

"I see you smiling," Polly said as she moved off the bed to do whatever it was she needed to do.

"Just remembering," he said. "It's funny. I don't usually smile when I remember . . ."

"What?"

"Anything,"

Polly kissed the back of his shoulder. "I'll give you a memory to make you smile."

Kingsley let out a breath of pleasure as Polly laid her hand flat on the small of his back and caressed him there.

"This is my favorite part," she said.

"Back rubs?"

"No, silly boy. Backs are my favorite part. Boy backs. My

favorite body part," she said. "Right here." With her fingertips she lightly scored the center of his back where his tailbone met his spine. "Maybe that's why I love doing this so much. The view of you is divine . . ."

With a compliment like that, how could Kingsley object to anything she wanted to do with his body? Polly whispered instructions in his ear. He did as told, and he did it with pleasure. He pulled his knees up under him and spread them. Polly worked the plug out of him carefully.

She positioned herself behind him and started to slowly . . . slowly . . . slowly enter him. Too slowly.

Polly told him to lay flat, to stretch out his legs—however was most comfortable for him. He was under the strictest of orders to tell her the second he felt a moment's pain. But there was no pain, no discomfort. Fullness, yes. Not pain. Not like he'd known once.

"You like this, don't you?" Polly said as she kissed and licked the back of his neck. "Being taken? Penetrated? Used?"

"Very much."

"Say it then," she said.

"Say what?"

"Say you like penetration. You said you aren't shy, so say it. Or are you shy?"

He opened his mouth, laughed softly. "You make me feel shy. It's an accomplishment."

"Kingsley . . ." Polly said as she nibbled on his earlobe. "Say it or I'll stop fucking you . . ." Her voice was teasing, but the order was an order. It had to be obeyed.

"I like being penetrated," he said. "There. Happy?"

"So very happy. If I keep doing this," she said and thrust into him, "will you come?"

"Yes."

"You're sure?"

"I would bet my life on it."

"You've come from penetration alone before?"

"I have."

"High school?"

"Wouldn't you like to know?"

Polly, of course, pinched him for not answering. Pinched him and fucked him a little harder. Her thrusts into him were firm and steady, purposeful but not too hard, deep but not too deep. Every retreat wrenched a moan from his lips and every return thrust sent him panting. The inflexible object inside him stroked neglected nerves with every pass, massaging deep muscles with every welcome invasion. Tethered to the bed and rooted in place, pinned down and penetrated, Kingsley could have stayed there forever. But that was his arousal doing the talking. Or was it? Against the sheets, his cock throbbed. As Polly pushed into him, he pushed back. As she withdrew, he pushed down.

"Do you like it?" she whispered in his ear.

Do you like it?

Kingsley lowered his head with a groan and when he raised it again, he was far away in another time, another world. A shack—rough wood floors and walls. He was facedown, his wrists tied to the bars of a metal cot. A monster with blond hair and a brutal cock was on top of him, inside him. Earlier he'd been beaten with a black leather belt. By "accident" the blond monster had let go of the tip so that the sharp metal buckle hit him with the force of a whip and left a deep burning red welt on his ribcage that he already knew would turn into a black and blue bruise by the next day.

"Do you like it?" the monster asked as he fucked Kingsley for the second time that night. And because it was the second time, he was open and slick and there was no stopping the cock that pounded him.

"Yes, sir," Kingsley answered. Like it? His parents were dead. He was poor as a church mouse. His grandparents had sent him to an all-boys school against his will.

And as long as that cock kept ramming him, he couldn't have cared less. The cock made everything worth it.

God, he was such a whore.

"You're not allowed to like it this much," his monster decreed.

"Stop making it feel really fucking good then. Christ, do I have to explain everything?" Kingsley demanded. "You're supposed to be the smart one."

He only talked back like that when he was out of his mind from being fucked half to death.

Punishment came in the form of the blond monster's perfect pianist's fingers finding that throbbing welt on Kingsley's back and pushing on it. Kingsley's head came up. He cried out in pain, in pain *and* in bliss. So much of both he couldn't tell one from the other.

"Stupid slut," his monster whispered into his ears. "You can't even suffer right."

"I love you, you fucking monster," Kingsley said. "I should be in my Calc study group right now." Instead he had two dozen welts all over his back and a cock up his ass—which was exactly where it belonged, if you asked him.

"Shut the fuck up," the monster ordered. Victory . . . a dirty word. Kingsley had gotten to him. He would definitely not be shutting the fuck up now.

"I love you," Kingsley said again. "I fucking love you. I love your face and your body and your cock and that black hole in your chest where your heart's supposed to be. I want to die with you inside me I love you that fucking much."

"Really?" his monster said. "Every time I'm inside you, I want to kill you."

It was nine degrees outside the cabin, ninety degrees inside. Kingsley was drenched with sweat, open and wet as a whore on her last customer for the day, so hard he could have fucked a hole through the mattress. His legs and his beautiful monster's were tangled up together in the scattered sheets. One hand pushed on the welt. The other hand grasped Kingsley's long hair and pulled it.

Kingsley cried out as a muscle spasm rocketed up his spine.

"Why do I bother raping you?" the monster said and yanked Kingsley's hair again. "You enjoy it every time. What is even the point?"

"You want me to pretend to hate it? You want me to fight you off?" Kingsley asked. "I'll fight you."

Kingsley tried to fight him, tried to twist and push him off. The result was . . . unsurprising. His monster did what monsters do. His monster bit him, bit the soft flesh between his neck and shoulder, the scruff, and Kingsley went limp like a kitten in its mother's teeth. But one good thing did happen from Kingsley's brief insurrection. He'd made his monster moan. Kingsley wasn't the only one enjoying this . . .

Kingsley laughed as he went limp on the cot again. His monster bit and licked the back of his neck as their bodies moved together. When Kingsley felt warm breath on his ear, the monster whispered, "Do you like it?"

"Kingsley?" Polly said again, her tone sharp enough to cut through the memory. "Do you like it?"

He grinned into the sheets. "Yes, ma'am."

Polly shifted herself upward and the phallus in him went deeper than it had gone before. Kingsley arched his back and let out a ragged groan as he took it. Polly held him by the shoulders as she fucked him. Now more rapidly, and rougher, too. It was what he wanted, what he needed and if she'd made him beg for it, he would have.

The pleasure grew so intense that at one point, he disassociated. His head swam, and he floated off the bed. He hung in the air, suspended by pure sensation. The harder she fucked him the higher he floated and when he crashed back to earth, he crashed hard. His back bowed, his fingers fisted the sheets, his thighs tightened to steel. He buried his face into the bedding and cried out as Polly pressed the phallus into him as far as it would go. Inside him muscles clenched and spasmed, clenched and released as he ground his cock into the bed and came in spurts onto the soft white sheets.

Done. Over. Kingsley went slack even as he lay sprawled, legs spread and still impaled on the bed.

"Tell me when," Polly said softly in his ear. "I'm not a man. I don't have to pull out immediately. I could stay in you all night."

"Don't leave. Not yet," he said. "Please."

"I'll wait until you tell me," she said and kissed his back again.

She stayed inside him as he basked for the span of a few breaths in the last little flutters of pleasure coursing through his body and blood. It was only when he felt pins and needles in his fingers did he nod the signal that he was ready for her to pull out of him.

Polly removed the ropes from his wrists. He murmured a grateful "*merci*" and she only kissed his cheek. He rolled onto his back, stretched like a well-fed house cat.

He heard her in the bathroom and then heard her in the bedroom again. His eyes were closed in spent exhaustion, but he wasn't quite ready to slip into sleep yet.

"My God," she said. "How much did you come?"

Kingsley opened his eyes. The wet spot on the bed was enormous.

"All of it," he said.

"I wish I'd weighed you before and after I fucked you," Polly said. "I bet you lost two kilos."

"I do feel lighter. At least my balls do."

"Don't worry. If they start floating, I'll tie them down."

Kingsley had no doubt she would.

She returned from the bathroom again with a clean white towel and draped it like a shroud over the massive come stain. "This," she said, "is why we make the men do the laundry."

"I thought it was because you enjoyed making men serve you."

"That, too," she said as she slid back into bed and pulled his arms around her. She was so soft and so warm, he could have fallen asleep against her immediately. "Isn't it funny? There are men in this world who would say you and I didn't have sex tonight because you never put your cock inside of me. Wasn't what we just did so much more intense than standard-issue sex? The liter of semen would be Exhibit A."

He laughed softly, too tired to laugh loudly. He was as spent as he'd been in a long time.

"Do you ever have standard-issue sex?" he asked.

"Oh, when the mood strikes me. I probably won't with you. You're a little big for me. No offense."

"I'm deeply offended that you think my cock is too big. Offend me some more, please."

She grinned. "Truth is, I usually can't come from intercourse anyway, so there's no reason to have it. The head of the cock is much better than the shaft for clit stimulation, as you may have noticed."

Kingsley had noticed.

"Will I have standard-issue sex while I'm here?" Kingsley asked. "Or is that also a privilege to be earned?"

"It is," she said. "But I have a feeling you'll be earning it fairly soon."

"Why is that?"

"Because," she said, "Madame likes you."

"Tell me about her," Kingsley said. "She fascinates me."

"You want gossip?" Polly asked.

"I want gossip," he whispered.

"Well," Polly said, throwing her leg over his stomach. "This wasn't always a house run by women. Men used to run it just like in the book."

"No," Kingsley said as he stroked her soft thigh.

"Yes," Polly said, grinning. "There was a coup. Madame won."

"From who?" Kingsley asked.

"Her husband," she said in a hushed tone.

Kingsley's eyes widened. "You're joking."

"My mother told me about it," Polly said. "Madame's husband was twelve years older than her. She was eighteen. He was thirty."

"She told me that. She said she was a virgin when she married him. He gave her *Histoire d'O* as a wedding gift?"

"What a gift, right? Gift? Warning? Very kinky man. He had this wild idea that virgins were blank slates and if he got a young and innocent bride, he could turn her into the perfect submissive and slave."

"He must have never met a teenage girl before if he thought virginity equals submissive," Kingsley said. "All the virgins I fucked in high school threw themselves at me. One literally did. Threw herself on top of me from the bleachers. She almost broke my elbow."

Polly whistled. "Ouch."

"I still fucked her," Kingsley said, shrugging. He didn't fuck girls with his elbow anyway. "So was she a slave in this house? Madame?"

"She was—collared and everything."

"Collared?"

"It's something some of us do when we mark ownership. Leather collar."

"Collars are for dogs," Kingsley said.

"And very pampered little slaves," Polly said with relish. "Back when my mother was here, this house had male and female dominants, male and female slaves. But Madame's husband ran the show. Until something happened. Mom never told me, only that one day her husband was king of the castle and the next day, there Madame was, like Jesus tossing the moneychangers out of the temple. No more king of the castle. He's in exile. She's in charge. It used to be a Roman orgy around here. Now it's all quiet and peaceful and orderly. The men serve. The women are served. Madame likes things genteel and refined. She's very civilized. For a sadist, I mean."

"What about her husband?"

"Oh, he's definitely still in love with her."

"He's alive?"

"She's forty-eight, which means he's only sixty. I've seen his letters to her. They come once a week, sometimes twice. That's a man in love."

"What's he do?"

"She won't tell us any details. Says it's for the best if we don't know. But when she talks about him, you can tell she still loves him."

"If they're still in love, why aren't they together?"

"Iron striking iron," Polly said, punching her two fists together like goats butting heads in battle. "Two dominants. Neither one will submit to each other. They're at an impasse."

"So tragic," Kingsley said. "So French."

"True. If they were Canadian, they would have apologized and made up years ago. Instead they find new ways of torturing each other."

"That's bizarre."

"Even more bizarre, they never got divorced. And she's still faithful to him."

"What?" Kingsley said. "She doesn't fuck the men here?"

"The men serve her but not in that way."

"That's either true love or madness," Kingsley said.

"Same thing sometimes," Polly said. "They've been playing this endless game for fifteen years."

"Should you be telling me all this?" Kingsley asked.

"I could be making it all up," she said, her eyes bright and laughing.

"Are you?" he asked.

"That I won't tell you."

"I thought you liked me," Kingsley said, pouting.

"I do like you. You always torture the ones you like," she said.

"I like you, too," Kingsley said. Then: "No, that's not what I mean."

"You don't like me?"

"It's my bad English," he said, as he slid her nightgown up her thighs. Polly rolled onto her back and opened her legs. "I meant, I *lick* you."

14

The dream is different this time. He is standing in the same winter woods where his dreams always take him. He sees the door standing in the clearing and he passes through it, because he knows he must if he wants to see the boy and play the game of ice chess he never wins.

He opens the door and steps through.

The boy is not there.

Though it is a dream and Kingsley knows it is a dream, he is still bereft. If he could weep in a dream, he would weep until he woke himself. There is no stone table. There is no chessboard made of ice. It's darker in the dream than he remembers from last time. This is not a forest for playing games. This is a dangerous place.

Behind him, Kingsley hears a twig snap.

He turns. Among the shadows, he sees eyes. Bright glowing gray eyes. And teeth. Large long white teeth.

A white wolf steps into the clearing.

The wolf is not white like snow, but baptismal white. It is massive, larger than any wolf he's ever seen in photographs or zoos. When it raises its head, Kingsley and the wolf are eye to eye. He has never known terror like this in his dreams, nor his waking hours. There is nothing for him to do but retreat. He steps back and back again. Back once more and he is through the open door. He knows if he can slam the door shut and lock it, the wolf will be trapped on the other side. He slams the door shut but he is too late. The wolf has already pushed opened the door.

Kingsley runs.

He runs though he knows there is no hope for escape. The white beast is hard on his heels and Kingsley can feel the heat of the animal's breaths on his back. Kingsley hears the wolf's huge paws striking the snow and it sounds like the galloping of a horse's hooves shod with iron behind him. He weaves in and out of trees, hoping to shake the creature off his scent, but there is hunger in the wolf's eyes and there is no other prey in this forest but Kingsley.

He races up a hill, but the wolf is too fast for him, too much. If he is going to die, it might as well be this way, killed by this impossibly beautiful beast. He runs into a snowy glade and lets his pace slow. In an instant the wolf has leapt up and slammed him to the ground. Although he wants to surrender, Kingsley can't let himself give up that easily. He tries to claw free of the creature, but he feels himself being dragged back, toward the jaws, toward his death. He cries out for help.

"Hush," comes a voice from behind him.

Before Kingsley knows what is happening, he's been thrown onto his back in the snow.

On top of him is the boy.

There is snow in the boy's dark eyelashes and snow in his white hair. There is snow on his cheeks and snow on his hands. There is fire in his eyes.

"You," Kingsley says. "There was a wolf."

"Only I'm here."

"Are you going to kill me?" Kingsley asks the boy.

"Not yet," the boy says and smiles. It is a wolfish smile.

Kingsley is panting now in the snow, and though he should be cold, he burns. "What are you going to do to me?"

"This."

The boy kisses him. The kiss is such a kiss that it could melt the snow. And it does. When Kingsley opens his eyes, he is lying in a late spring forest, where winter is nothing but a memory. The ground beneath is soft and wet and warm. Kingsley wraps his arms around the boy, and then his legs, too. The boy forces him down and onto his back again and in a few seconds of tearing and pulling, Kingsley is naked in the forest. When the boy pushes Kingsley back onto his stomach, he smells the fresh living earth underneath his nose. His body sinks into the fertile earth as the boy enters him from behind, his teeth digging hard into the back of Kingsley's neck, his arm around Kingsley's stomach, holding him in place, immobile.

This is a much better game than ice chess in the snow.

Kingsley realizes he's said this aloud when the boy laughs in his ear.

"You won't think so after," the boy says.

But Kingsley doesn't retort. Why should he? This is what he's wanted for seven long years. The boy is buried inside him, his movements deep and brutal. The pleasure is so sharp it's almost agony. With every rough thrust, Kingsley tells the boy a secret.

I love you.

I still love you.

I hate you.

I still hate you.

I want you.

I'll always want you.

I only left you so you'd come and find me.

Come and find me.

Find me and come.

"Shut the fuck up," the boy says and Kingsley laughs. The boy clamps a hand over Kingsley's mouth, silencing him.

Kingsley's hands dig deep in the wet rare earth. The boy is insatiable. His teeth nip every inch of Kingsley's back and shoulders. The boy's other hand is clamped hard over Kingsley's wrist. On the ground, in the dirt, they couple like wild animals—without mercy, without shame. The thrusts are vicious. The grunting bestial. If Kingsley dies from this, he will die happy.

When the boy fills him with a heated rush of semen, Kingsley comes hard enough he sees only white again and the forest is filled with his cries.

It is over now and Kingsley is empty.

"Again," Kingsley begs.

The boy laughs in his ear. "Now I'll kill you," he says.

Kingsley almost laughs. This is something the boy would say.

"How?" Kingsley asks.

"Like this."

And then the boy is gone.

15

When Kingsley woke from his dream, it was still full night. Polly lay next to him in the bed on her side and soundly sleeping. He wanted to wake her, to hear a human voice give him words of comfort. He would have given his right arm for a woman's gentle hand on his forehead and a woman's gentle voice whispering, "It's all right . . . It was just a dream."

Only a dream, he told himself. Nothing more. Even as Kingsley rolled up into a sitting position, his fear of the wolf and the dream were already fading. The pain was gone. The ecstasy, too. It was all gone.

Except the loneliness, the terrible loneliness. That remained.

Two unpleasant urges pulled him from the warmth of Polly's bed. He went to the bathroom to relieve the first, more pressing one. He washed his face in the sink, drank fistfuls of cold water, and found his jeans where he'd dropped them. He didn't know the rules about smoking in the château, so, after dressing, he snuck past the bed and went out onto the balcony, closing the door as quietly as possible behind him.

Before he and Polly had gone to bed together, the moon had been high and white. Now it was hidden behind thick clouds.

The night air was brisk, and he lit up quickly, not wanting to stay out in the cold any longer than he had to. He should have put on his shoes, he realized. Shirtless and shoeless, he started shivering by the third drag. But he didn't rush. He liked the cold, even if he didn't like to think about why. He stood on the balcony, hips against the iron railing and inhaled deep of the January night air. It tingled his nose like mint and tasted sweet as a frozen strawberry on his tongue. This was one of those rare winter nights when it seemed winter would last forever.

Snow was coming.

Madame had mentioned that it might snow. And Polly, too, seemed eager for it. Why they wanted it to snow, he couldn't say, but he knew why he wanted the snow, and he wished he didn't. Snow was his enemy. It made it so much harder if he had to escape on foot.

Kingsley stubbed his cigarette out in the dead potted plant on the balcony. He turned to go back inside when he heard a sound.

A soft, plaintive cry.

A baby's cry.

Jacques.

The balcony stretched for the entire length of the second floor. Kingsley ran down to the nursery and found the balcony door unlocked. He slipped inside and shut the door behind him quickly so Jacques wouldn't feel the cold draft. He went to the cradle. The baby boy was screaming so hard he was shaking, his two little fists balled up so tiny and tight, Kingsley couldn't help but laugh.

He wasn't sure what to do. He hadn't even held a small child since he was, what, fourteen? Some cousin of his father's had stopped by with her little girl. Surely someone in the house would be coming to see to Jacques to change his diaper or feed him. Meanwhile, the poor boy was bleating his head off.

"Shh . . ." Kingsley said, and laid his hand over the top of Jacques's small head. "You'll wake the whole house."

The touch seemed to startle Jacques into silence. The baby's eyes went wide and rolled about as if trying to see who this strange person was who'd dared touch the royal baby head.

"There you go," Kingsley said. "That's better. We're Frenchmen, you and me. We don't fuss like that. We leave that to American boys, right?"

Jacques didn't answer, but at least he didn't take up screaming again.

"How old are you?" Kingsley asked as he stroked Jacques's little head. His skin was soft and his hair fluffy and fine as down. "I'm twenty-four. Twenty-four years, I mean. What are you? Twenty-four days?"

"He's six weeks old."

Kingsley looked up and saw Madame coming into the nursery. She held a glass baby bottle in her hand.

"I'm sorry," Kingsley said at once. "I heard him cry when I was on the balcony and I just—"

"You've done nothing wrong," she said, waving her hand, dismissing his apologies. "Would you like to feed him?"

"Me?" Kingsley said.

"Go on. I know you want to. No man who hates children would run into a screaming baby's nursery. They tend to run in the opposite direction very fast."

"No, I like children," Kingsley said. "I don't really know what to do with a small baby though."

"Only one way to learn. Pick him up carefully, cradle his head. Don't let it fall back . . ."

Kingsley took a steadying breath and then as gently as he could he scooped Jacques out of the crib with both of his hands under the boy. "This is not what I expected to be doing tonight," he said, bringing the baby to his shoulder. He instinctively bounced him a couple times while patting his back.

"What had you planned on doing tonight?" Madame asked. "Before you came to the château, I mean?"

She helped Kingsley put Jacques on his back into the correct feeding position. Though he wouldn't say it out loud, he thought Madame looked quite cute in her pajamas. They were gray silk, embroidered with white-and-black flowers and a mandarin collar. She had such a quiet power about her, even in her night-clothes, that Kingsley had trouble picturing her as any man's submissive. Apparently neither could she.

"I've been on medical leave," Kingsley said as he settled Jacques's head against his bicep. "So I do nothing. Not nothing. Every night I go out, drink too much, find a girl, and bring her back to my place."

"Sounds dull." Madame handed him the bottle. It felt warm in his hand, but not too warm. "You don't seem like a dull person to me."

He shrugged. "It's my cover."

"Here," she said and took the bottle from him again. "Bring it to his lips but don't push it in. When he feels it's a nipple, he'll start suckling."

"Typical male," he said.

Jacques did exactly what Madame predicted. Once the bottle was at his mouth, he latched onto it. Kingsley grinned. Amazing.

"When you grow up," Kingsley said to Jacques, "eating and sucking nipples are two entirely different pleasures."

Madame smiled, and the hard lines of her mouth softened. "Jacques is our first boy in twenty-five years," she said. "We tend to breed mostly girls."

"Where is he now?" Kingsley asked. "Your last boy?"

"Paris," she said. "Working. But like our girls, he's still drawn back to us. He visits me often, brings me all the gossip. The children of this house are all very loyal even if their parents are not. If you're not careful, you'll end up falling in love with this place."

"I'm not careful," Kingsley said. "I might come back just to visit him." He looked down at little Jacques who was happily eating away, his tiny fists dancing around his head in pleasure.

"A good boy," Madame said, approvingly.

"He is," Kingsley said.

"I meant you," she said.

Kingsley smiled as he adjusted Jacques's position on his bicep.

"Does his mother not feed him?" Kingsley asked.

"That isn't the concern of any of the men of this household."

"Sorry. You're right, it isn't."

"Curiosity is human. If you must know, his mother had a very hard delivery. She lost blood. For a week after, she could barely take care of herself, much less him. No nursing. Doctor's orders. Nursing a child takes a lot out of a woman, and she needed all her strength for herself. Now she's under my orders to sleep a full night, every night. She has us to care for her little boy from dusk until dawn."

"It's good she had you all then," Kingsley said.

"People are meant to be together," Madame said, pressing a quick and tender kiss on top of Jacques's head. "I would go mad if I had to live alone."

"It's not so bad," Kingsley said.

"If you like being alone, why do you bring a girl home with you every single night? Hmm?"

Kingsley nodded. "Maybe you're right. Maybe."

"I am," she said. "But I won't belabor the point. Did Jacques's crying wake you up? I would have thought Polly had worn you out by now."

"She tried," he said, and smiled. The smiled faded. "I had another dream."

"Ah," she said.

Madame only gave him a pointed look as she placed a white cloth over his shoulder.

"You'll have to burp him," she said. "Or I can."

"I'll do it. I think," Kingsley said. "Do I . . ."

"Here." Madame helped Kingsley position little Jacques against his shoulder and then Madame patted the baby firmly on the back, twice. Jacques made a little noise, like a hiccup but wetter.

"Is that it?" Kingsley asked.

Madame wiped off Jacque's tiny mouth. "All done. And he's a very happy boy now. But leave him there. He seems comfortable. So do you."

Kingsley felt comfortable and was glad he didn't have to put the boy down yet. Madame sat in the large rocking chair by the white cradle, and Kingsley paced the floor as Jacques wriggled and rooted around in his arms until he settled down again. When he could safely turn his back on Madame, Kingsley quickly lowered his nose to the baby's head and inhaled the scent of talc and lavender. The scent of innocence.

"See?" she said. "It's not so hard. You'll make a good father someday."

"Polly said you don't know who Jacques's father is?"

"It could be any of the men in the house. In time he may show a resemblance, but it really doesn't matter." Her tone was light, her expression indifferent. She truly couldn't care less who'd sired the boy.

Kingsley shook his head. "That would be torture, not knowing if he was mine or not."

"If you lived in this house," she said, "he would be yours. He's all of ours."

"Still," Kingsley said. "I would need to know."

"That's not our way," she said, and she said as if that ended the discussion. But then she smiled again, her face softened. "He likes you. Usually he's fussy with men."

"Hard to believe we were all this little once. He seems so . . . defenseless."

"That's what he has us for," she said. "We protect the defenseless here."

"Do you? You don't know me from Adam, and you let me in your house and into the baby's room?"

Madame sat back in the rocking chair, crossed her legs at the ankles, and rocked slowly. "Kingsley Théophile Boissonneault. Age twenty-four. Birthday November second. After your parents died when you were fifteen, you had to move to Maine in America to live with your maternal grandparents. After the death of your sister while she was visiting you at the St. Ignatius Catholic School for Boys, you accompanied her body to France to be buried. You joined *la Légion* at seventeen. You work for an unnamed agency under the umbrella of the French Armed Forces that does 'special assignments,' which is a euphemism, I think, that means you kill people. You went through officer training two years ago. After a successful mission in the Swiss Alps two months ago, you were promoted to first lieutenant. You were also injured during the mission—two broken ribs that seem to have healed very nicely—but otherwise you have been given a clean bill of health, physically and psychologically."

Kingsley only stared at her a good long while.

Madame kept rocking. "Do you think I would let just anyone into my home? Near my family? Near me?" She pointed her hand at Jacques in a graceful gesture. "Near him?"

"How do you—"

"I have friends in interesting places," she said.

"Dangerous places," Kingsley said. "The colonel is a very dangerous man. If you have someone near him, feeding you information, get him out now. For his sake. For yours."

"Your concern is very touching," Madame said. "We'll all be fine, I promise."

"You knew who I was before I even called."

"I'm glad you didn't lie to me too much. I would have known. I like lying, but I don't like being lied to."

Kingsley could think of nothing to say. She'd stunned him into silence, which, like making him feel shy, was quite an accomplishment.

"Is that everything there is to know about you?" Madame asked.

"Yes," he breathed.

"Are you certain of that?"

"I think. What else is there to know?"

She returned to rocking again. Kingsley returned to pacing the floor with Jacques. Then she said something that might have caused him to drop the baby if he hadn't been so well-trained.

"Kingsley, who is Marcus Stearns?"

16

By the time she'd asked that question, he'd managed to put his mask back on. His cavalier mask. His mask of indifference.

"Marcus Stearns was my sister's husband," Kingsley said. "A teacher at the school I went to in Maine. A student and then a teacher."

"But he was more than that, yes?"

Kingsley didn't answer. He simply patted Jacques on the back again, and caressed the baby's soft warm cheek.

"Ah, so he was," she said. "In your personnel file, he's listed as your next of kin. The person to contact in event of your death. An important position in your life."

Kingsley said nothing.

"Put Jacques in his crib," Madame said.

He stared hard at her. He didn't want to let go, and she knew it.

She smiled a wicked smile. "If you want to hold him, you will answer my questions. If you don't want to, you must put him down."

"You'll use a baby as a weapon?" Kingsley asked. "You *are* a sadist."

"You want to hold Jacques. I want answers. Either put him down or answer my questions."

Kingsley took a deep breath. Little Jacques's hand latched onto Kingsley's collarbone, the fingernails digging into his skin like five tender needles.

"Why is Marcus Stearns listed as the next of kin in your files?" Madame asked.

"He was married to my sister."

"Your sister who is dead. He's not family to you anymore."

"I have no one else," he said. "It was either him or a couple of my father's cousins I haven't seen in years."

"He was the one you served, wasn't he?" Madame asked. "The angel. The demon. The monster. I imagined it was a priest at your school when you told me. I thought he was someone much older, someone with power over you. But no. He was just a boy."

"He was not 'just' anything," Kingsley said.

"Ah, so I'm right," she said. "Your master married your sister. And you call me a sadist?"

Kingsley said nothing again. He didn't trust his own voice.

"Funny. I say 'sister' and nothing happens to your eyes," Madame said. "I mention him, and I see lightning, thunder." She waved a hand over her face to mimic a storm.

"Maybe I want to throw lightning at him," Kingsley said.

"That's passion," she said. "You must still love him."

"I hate him. I'd kill him if I saw him again."

"I could say the same for my husband," she said.

Again, Kingsley said nothing.

"Put Jacques down in his cradle if you won't talk," she said. "Those are the rules."

Kingsley wasn't ready to relinquish the little boy yet. He'd forgotten how solid babies were. Even when tiny, they had heft to them. They weighed somehow more than their actual weight. Was it life that gave them that weight? Was it the weight of the soul he felt? The whole of the tree fit inside a single seed. Did the whole of a man's life live inside this tiny form Kingsley could cradle against his shoulder?

"What do you want to know about him?" Kingsley asked.

"Everything," Madame said.

"Everything. All right. I'll tell you everything. He's beautiful," Kingsley said. "You've never seen anyone more beautiful than him. Before him, I never loved a boy. Never even thought of it. I loved girls. I'd had my first when I was twelve, thirteen? Fifty by the time I was sixteen. Then I saw him."

Kingsley closed his eyes as if he could hide from the memory. The memory found him anyway.

He continued, "His hair is like spun gold. His eyes are the color of a January sky before it snows. He even smells . . . he smells just like winter. He's smart. Too smart. There's an American phrase for when they want to say someone is stupid. They say, 'He's not the sharpest knife in the drawer.' "

Madame smiled.

"And Marcus?" Madame asked.

"He *is* the sharpest knife in the drawer. I cut myself on him."

Even in the dark he saw the glint of pleasure in her eyes.

"Tell me more," she said softly. "That's an order."

He didn't need the order. He couldn't have stopped talking now if she'd cut out his tongue. The vein had been opened. The blood had to flow.

"He's tall. Very strong. Lean, though. He's like a wolf," Kingsley said, remembering his dream. "A white wolf. Dangerous because he's hungry. Dangerous even when he's not."

"How so?"

"Because you see something that beautiful, like a white wolf, and you want to pet it." He shook his head. "Don't. You'll lose a hand."

"Or your heart?" She was teasing him now.

"At least I had a heart to lose. He's got ice in his veins. Stone for a heart." Kingsley took a breath. "And even worse, he plays piano. Beautifully. Everything about him was cruel. Even his virtues."

"Go on." Madame's eyes had taken on a lupine hunger of her own. "I love to hear you talk of him. It's like watching you flay yourself."

"We were talking once, sitting next to each other on a bed. I kissed him . . . out of nowhere, I just kissed him before I went mad from wanting to kiss him. He kissed me back, but only for a second. Then he pushed me down onto the bed. Held me down so hard he nearly broke my wrist. It popped. I remember it popping under his hand."

"Did you like it?"

"It made me hard."

"His kiss?"

Kingsley whispered, "The pain." *La douleur.*

"La douleur exquise?" she asked.

He smiled. "*Exactement.*"

"Did he love you?" she asked.

"I loved him. He owned me. If there was love, it was because he loved the owning, not the thing he owned."

"You were lovers?"

Kingsley placed his hand over Jacques's ears.

"Not in front of the children," he said to Madame.

She smiled again. "You *were* lovers. Tell me what it was like with him."

"The first time was in the woods, this forest that surrounded our school. I wanted him . . . God, I never knew you could want someone like I wanted him. I didn't know it was possible. I pursued him. It didn't work. Then one day, I don't know, instead of following him everywhere like I'd been doing, I ran."

"You ran?"

"Into the woods," he said. "Something about the way he looked at me, I knew I should run. He caught me. Our first time was in that forest, in the dirt. I was in so much pain after, I had to crawl back to school. One boy at school . . ." Kingsley paused to laugh. "He asked me if I'd gotten attacked by an animal."

"Hardly an ideal first time with someone."

"It was exactly what I wanted," he said. "Does that sound sick? It does to me, but it's true."

"Sick? No. You were so young, both of you. Too young. Like I was when I got married. You don't know yourself yet. Someone tells you what you are and you, well, you believe them."

"He knew what I was. He knew, and he was right."

"It seems he did."

"I told you he was smart."

"Regrets?"

Kingsley shrugged. "He was too good at it. How's that for a regret?"

"What do you mean, too good?"

"After him . . . it was years before I was with another man. I thought it would be too much like being with him."

"Was it?" she asked.

Kingsley shook his head. "No. No one is like being with him."

Madame made a soft murmuring sound, a sound of pleasure.

"Tell me more about him. More, more, more," she said, turning her hand to indicate he must keep talking. "Your pain is a fine wine on my tongue." She laughed at her own eagerness.

"You're a sadist," he said, smiling.

"Real sadism is an art form. I'm an art lover, and you, right

111

now, you're the Louvre. Tell me more about how he hurt you and let me see your face while you do."

Kingsley turned to her, let her see his face, let her see his pain. He didn't want to, but he needed to. The masochist in him needed to give that to her.

"He broke me. In so many ways, he broke me. He broke me until I was happy I was so broken. The more pieces of me there were, the more pieces of me there were for him to break into even smaller pieces. By the time he was done with me, I was nothing but shards. If I'd spent another day with him, I would have been the dust on the bottom of his shoe."

"A perfect pair then. A true sadist with a true masochist. Perfect and rare."

"Perfect," Kingsley repeated. "Maybe for a little while."

"Why did he marry your sister if it was you he wanted?"

"Money. His trust fund. He got millions when he got married."

"He was trying to take care of you," she said.

"We were poor," Kingsley said. "Me and my sister after our parents died. Too poor to even see each other, separated by an ocean in more ways than one. If we had money, we could all be together. The three of us. She wasn't supposed to fall in love with him. When she found out it was me he was . . . When she saw us kissing, she didn't take it well."

"She killed herself?"

"He does that to people," Kingsley said. "You feel like you can't live without him."

"Is that why you joined *la Légion*? You can't live without him, so you signed up to die?"

"Or I just wanted to take orders from powerful men," he said. A joke, but not really. "Why are we talking about this?"

"I like seeing men naked. Nothing strips a man more naked

than the things that cause him pain and the things that make him afraid."

"He was both of those."

"Marcus?" she asked.

Kingsley smiled.

"Why are you smiling?"

"Because I know something about him you don't know," he said.

"What is that?" she asked.

"His real name."

Madame smiled, but this time it was a cold smile. She clearly didn't like that Kingsley knew something she didn't know. Knowledge was *her* weapon. *Her* power.

"What is it? Rumpelstiltskin?" she said.

Again, Kingsley smiled but didn't answer. He wouldn't if she'd put a gun to his head.

"Keep your secret," she said. "If it makes you smile like that to keep it."

"Worthless secret," he said, the smile fading. "I haven't seen him in seven years. I only call him by his name when I dream of him and sometimes not even then, if I wake up before ..."

"Before what?"

"Before he kisses me."

He looked at her once, then looked away. "Let's talk of something more pleasant," he said. "Wars. Famine. The Black Plague."

"Let's talk of fears then. What are you afraid of?"

"I'm afraid of someone knowing my fears," Kingsley said.

"Our fears are the bastard children of our longings. You hold one of my children. Let me hold one of yours."

"I'm afraid of dying," Kingsley said.

"A very human fear. The nothingness waiting for us on the other side of our last breath."

"It's not that so much. Before I was born, I didn't exist. Not existing doesn't scare me. I did it for eons. I'm afraid of dying *before . . .*"

"Ah," she said. "Dying before what?"

"Dying before I have children," Kingsley said.

"And?"

"Dying before I can see him again."

"You said he taught at your old school in Maine. You could probably find him in two phone calls."

"I can't," Kingsley said.

"*Pourquoi pas?*" Why not?

"I don't want to find him. I want him to find me."

Madame tilted her head to the side and tut-tutted like he was a naughty boy who'd said a very dirty word. "Men," she said. "You'd rather die fighting than surrender to happiness. You are your own worst enemy."

"You know what they say," Kingsley said. "Keep your friends close and your enemies closer. Being my own worst enemy is as close as it gets."

"What is it, really? What keeps you from finding him?"

"Jealousy," Kingsley said. "Not a trait I'm proud of."

"Jealous of what?"

"That he's moved on. He could have a dozen lovers worshipping at his feet as we speak. He could be married; he could have children. Our first time together . . . There are still pieces of me there in that forest. I need to believe, you know—"

"You need to believe there are still pieces of him there, too?"

Kingsley only shrugged.

"Poor child," she said, shaking her head.

"You're wrong about one thing," he said. "I can't find him

with two phone calls. Last summer, I had a weak moment. I called our old school to talk to him."

"And?"

"He's not there. And he'd left instructions not to give out any information at all about him to anyone. I'm not vain enough to think it's me he's hiding from. But still . . ."

"If he would have answered the phone," Madame said, "what would you have said to him?"

Jacques yawned against his shoulder, and without thinking Kingsley kissed the top of his small head. "I would have said . . ." Kingsley swallowed, his eyes burned.

"What, Kingsley? What would you have said if your Marcus had answered the phone?"

"I was in the hospital when I called. I think I would have . . . I would have said, 'Please, come get me. I want to go home.' "

He met Madame's eyes. She was looking at him almost in shock, almost as if he'd slapped her across the face instead of simply answering her question. "Like a little boy," she said, "sick at school, calling his *maman*."

She held out her hand as if to touch him, to comfort him, but then seemed to think better of it. She lowered her hand to her side and turned her back to him as she stood at the balcony doors.

Jacques had fallen asleep on his shoulder. As much as he wanted to keep holding him, Kingsley carried the boy to the cradle and gently lay the infant down again on his back. He gazed down at him a long time. Madame came and stood at his side.

"Tell me what you're thinking," she said.

"I put Jacques down. Game over."

"The game is never over. Tell me what you're thinking."

"Do you remember," he began, "being a small child and falling asleep in the backseat of the car or in the sitting room on your father's big chair? And a few hours later you would wake up in your own bed? You remember that?"

"Oh yes," she said, a slight smile flitting across her lips. "I was a picky eater. My mother would make me sit at the table until I finished my dinner. I was a child during the war. We were lucky when we had food at all. But I wouldn't eat. I'd sit there, stubborn, defiant, until I finally fell asleep at the table."

"She'd carry you to bed," Kingsley said. "While you were asleep, your mother or your father would carry you, yes?"

"Of course."

"Do you remember that moment when you woke up and didn't know where you were? That moment you were confused and afraid and lost? Then you realize you're in your own bed, and you're there because someone who loves you has carried you there and tucked you in . . ."

"A perfect feeling," Madame said. "The beauty and inno-cence of childhood in one split second, the moment you wake up lost and confused and then know you're safe and you're home. Is that what you were thinking of?"

Kingsley nodded. "I was thinking that's something I want to feel one more time in my life." He smiled. "But it's a stupid dream. That doesn't happen when you're grown."

Kingsley adjusted the blanket over Jacques. He didn't want it too close to the boy's face.

"What bed is it?" she asked.

"Hmm?" Kingsley looked at her.

"When you imagine yourself waking up in that bed, what bed is it? Who's bed?"

Kingsley knew he was expected to answer. And he would. After he took a breath or two, then he could answer. "One night I talked back to him. I did that a lot."

"What did you say?"

"He was making me suck him off," Kingsley said.

"Making you?" Madame said.

Kingsley grinned. "And he didn't like the way I was doing it. I told him if he didn't like my style he could do it to himself."

"I'm remembering my marriage."

"He punished me by making me sleep on the cold hard floor of the old cottage where we'd go to be together. I know I fell asleep on the floor. I remember wishing for a pillow. But when I woke up a couple hours later I was in the cot we shared." He paused, trying to remember something he'd spent seven years trying to forget.

"My God, how did you survive that boy?"

"I'm not sure I did," Kingsley said. "You know, it probably didn't even happen like that. I probably woke up for a few seconds and crawled into bed with him and forgot I did it. I'm sure . . . I'm sure that's what happened. He wouldn't have picked me up . . ." He met Madame's eyes. "Would he?"

He didn't know why he asked her except perhaps he thought only another sadist would know the answer.

"You want me to say 'no,' " she said, "so you can tell yourself he didn't love you. I'll say 'no,' for your sake. No, of course he didn't lift you while you were sleeping to put you to bed beside him. No sadist would ever do anything so tender. We're heartless and cruel and incapable of love."

"I thought so," Kingsley said.

Madame leaned close, touched his face gently, the same way he'd touched Jacques. "I told you I liked to lie, too, sometimes," she whispered.

He closed his eyes and turned his face into her hand.

"You should go back to Polly," Madame said, lowering her hand. Kingsley was certain he noticed some reluctance on her part when she did. She inclined her head toward the cradle. "In about ten minutes, that one will be screaming for a nappy change."

"I will leave him in your capable hands," Kingsley said.

He started for the balcony door.

"Take the hallway," she reminded him. "It's warmer."

He would have objected—grown men didn't need coddling —except he liked her concern. He went to the hall doorway.

"Goodnight," he said.

"Sleep well," she said. It sounded like an order. "I hope you don't dream of him again."

"*Merci. Moi aussi,*" he said, but already knew he wouldn't dream anymore that night.

He started to open the door when Madame spoke again.

"Thank you for telling me your fears. You're beautiful when you're naked."

"I've heard that before."

"I'd like to see you that naked again," she said.

"I might not like it."

"Ah," she said with a smile, rocking in her chair again. "Perhaps you should not have told me your fears then."

18

Once in the hallway, Kingsley glanced over his shoulder to see Madame's eyes close. He shut the door.

Now was his chance.

So far, he'd been on the guided tour. He'd been itching to do a little reconnaissance on his own. A window had just opened up, with Madame preoccupied and Polly asleep. If somebody caught him snooping around, he could simply say he'd gotten lost on his way back to Polly's room. He was new there, right?

Quietly as he could, he slipped down the hall on his bare feet. He wasn't looking for Leon—not specifically, not yet. What Kingsley really wanted was to find the catch. There had to be one. If something seemed too good to be true, it probably was. And this place definitely seemed too good to be true.

Beautiful, intelligent, kinky women.

An elegant luxurious château.

Quiet. Serenity. Refinement. Fucking amazing food.

A sadist. An exquisite, vicious, delicious sadist . . .

Oh, there had to be a catch.

He passed a gold carriage clock on a hallway table and

checked the time—a little after two in the morning. Surely everyone was asleep.

Or were they?

At the end of the quiet corridor, Kingsley found a set of double doors, heavy oak and richly carved. He pushed one open a crack and smelled old, cold air. He shivered but slipped through the doors and into what had to be the older wing of the house.

He found himself in a foyer on black-and-white chessboard tile. A fanlight window provided the only light to the small anterior room, but he saw another set of doors before him.

There was no way he could plead ignorance if he got caught in the old château.

Here's hoping he didn't get caught.

Surely Madame really wouldn't kill him. Still . . . he wished he'd thought to wear his shoes.

Kingsley pushed through the doors.

Once inside he stopped, blinked, let his eyes adjust. It wasn't nearly as dark as he'd expected in this ancient wing of the home, nor nearly as cold.

Nor as quiet.

He heard voices. He started forward.

The long corridor was dark and gloomy with a musty scent of rooms in need of airing out. Red carpeting on dark wood floors. Dark wood-paneled walls. Closed doors with heavy wrought-iron latches. It made him think of a convent for some reason, not that he'd ever been in one. Or an old hotel. He liked it. If he owned a place like this, he'd do exactly what Madame had done—turn it into a private little kingdom for her and all her lovers and kinky friends. A safe place. A hiding place where he didn't have to hide.

Kingsley moved toward the voices.

As he crept down the hall, he checked every room. The

doors were unlocked. The rooms were empty, except for antique furniture—beds, dressers, tables, and cold fireplaces—covered in linen sheets. No bodies. No skeletons. No whips or chains. No cuffs and no canes. Certainly no prisoners. He also found no radiators, which backed up Polly who'd said the old wing was too cold in winter to use. Pity. This part of the house must have been built and furnished in the late eighteenth or early nineteenth century. His father had been an importer, and though Kingsley didn't know much about the antiques trade, he did know a real Louis XVI chair when he saw it.

Near the end of the hallway, he saw a closed door with flickering yellow light sneaking out from under the sill. He pressed his ear gently to the door. He heard murmurs followed by laughter—a woman's throaty laughter and a younger man's nervous chuckle. Looking down he saw the door had a large keyhole. He knelt and pressed his eye to the keyhole and peered inside.

He saw almost the entire room through the keyhole. A fireplace took up nearly one entire wall—a large stone mantel, leaping red-and-golden fire behind the grate, and a portrait of an old French queen hanging on a scarlet cord from the picture rail. What appeared to be a man and woman's discarded clothing were tossed over the back of a red-and-gold brocade chaise lounge. On a grand bed with embroidered covers and a looming canopy lay a naked man, a young man no more than twenty. Leon? On top of him, straddling his hips, was a lovely woman, thirty-five at the most. She was wearing a loose white gown with a loose bodice that slipped over one bare and delicious shoulder. She had dark skin and dark hair drawn up at the nape of her neck in a knot. The young man reached for the tie of her gown and she slapped his hands away.

"Naughty boy," she said in what Kingsley recognized as an Algerian accent.

"You have my cock. I want your breasts," he said without contrition, without apology.

She rocked on his hips and the young man groaned, then laughed at his groaning. "Behave or I won't let you come," she said.

What a wicked tease, Kingsley thought. She was moving on the boy's cock even as she denied him his own pleasure. He liked this lady.

"I'm trying to behave, Amel. You make it too hard."

"Behaving?" the woman said.

"No, my cock. You make my cock too hard."

"Oh, Leon. You stupid little boy."

So he had found Leon. Leon didn't seem to be the least insulted by Amel's mockery. He grinned broadly. He ran his hands through his pale brown hair, and locked his fingers behind his head.

"See? Behaving now," he said.

"It's good you're new here," she said, poking his chest. "Or you'd be in so much trouble."

"I love to be in trouble almost as much as I love to be in you." He punctuated this statement by lifting his hips off the bed, an erotic undulation that had Kingsley breathing harder.

"I suppose I can be a little nice to you," the woman said, taking Leon's face in her hands and pinching his cheeks. "If you can guess the number I'm thinking of, I'll let you play with my breasts."

"Good game," he said.

"I'm thinking of a number," she said, her head falling back and her eyes closed, "between one and one billion . . ."

Kingsley scowled at Amel from behind the door. Unfair. Truly unfair.

"Hmm . . ." Leon said. "Let me think. Is it . . . four hundred, eighty-four million, three hundred fifty-four thousand, nine-hundred and ninety-one?"

"Ah, you guessed it," she said. "Good boy!"

Kingsley had to bite his tongue not to laugh out loud and give himself away. Should he be watching this couple having sex? Not under normal circumstances. But he was here for work. He had a job to do, and he really ought to learn all he could about Leon's "captivity" here.

The woman—Amel—untied the drawstring on the bodice of her nightgown and allowed Leon the liberty of slipping it off her shoulders and baring her breasts. She had full breasts with large dark nipples, and Leon sat up on his elbows and latched onto one immediately.

Amel grinned as he sucked her. "Not too much," she said. "I'm tender."

Leon must have obeyed because the woman gasped and smiled. Whatever the young man was doing to her nipples, she liked it. She rocked her hips on his cock again, and Kingsley grew hard. He ignored his erection. This was work and he wasn't about to wank off in the hallway while on reconnaissance. Amel's little gasps turned into little moans and it sounded like she was close to coming. She moved harder on Leon as he licked and sucked her nipples. Her moans and gasps suddenly turned into a quick cry. Leon looked startled.

"Did you come?" he asked, eyes wide.

"No," she said, laughing. "Somebody just kicked me."

She slid off Leon and lay on her back, propped on the thick luxurious-looking pillows. Kingsley saw then what her volumi-nous white gown had hidden while she was on top of Leon.

Amel was pregnant. Very pregnant.

On her back, the fabric of the gown settled over her swollen stomach. Leon lay beside her, his erection resting on her thigh.

"Can I feel?" he asked.

She took his hand in hers and placed it on her lower belly. "It was there," she said. "A foot, I swear it."

Leon must have felt the foot too because his head twitched and he looked at her in delighted surprise.

"He kicked me!" Leon said. "Rude."

"He knew what you were doing to his mother and didn't like it. Or she knew."

"A girl wouldn't be so rude," Leon said. "How far along are you?'

"Six months," she said. "Too pregnant to be playing with little boys like you."

"I don't think so," he said as he kissed her neck, his hand still on her stomach. Kingsley stared at Leon's hand on her belly and felt a pang of longing.

Longing, not desire. He envied the boy.

"You don't?" she asked Leon.

"I don't," he said.

"You know I don't care what you think," she said, but not unkindly. "I didn't wake you up and bring you here for your brain." She tapped his forehead.

"What did you want me for?" he asked. "Tell me and I'll do it."

"Make me come," she said. "Use your fingers. Make me come hard enough so my fucking back will stop aching for five fucking minutes, and I'll let you come inside me."

"I don't know if I can," Leon said, kissing her on the neck again. She closed her eyes in pleasure. "But I'll try . . ."

He slid his hand under her gown, raised it to her hips as she settled into the pillows and opened her legs. Kingsley watched just long enough to see Leon's fingers slip inside her wet slit before he decided he'd seen enough. His conscience had got the better of him. Kingsley stood up—reluctantly— and walked away from the scene. But not before he heard Amel breathing heavily and then crying out in pleasure. Good for Leon.

Kingsley considered going straight back to Polly, but as long as he was here . . .

At the end of the corridor he found the old servants' stairway and took it downstairs. His bare feet ached on the cold concrete steps, and he had to keep his hand pressed to the wall to find his way in the darkness. No ambient light allowed for the servants. He would have killed for his old military torch.

Kingsley made it down to the lower-floor landing. He found nothing much of interest downstairs except more closed-off rooms. A drawing room. A dining room. A music room with a grand piano under a ghostly white sheet. A music room? He'd love to have a music room with a piano like that and someone to play it day and night. He couldn't play piano, but he vowed if he ever had the money, the first thing he'd do with it would be to buy a house of his own and put a piano inside it.

Really, now, he absolutely had to go back. Except something kept him from leaving quite yet. He entered a parlor and knew that had *Story of O* been real, this is where it would have happened. O would have been escorted into the front door of the old wing on her lover's arm. And she would have been brought here, to this room with the low carved ceilings and tapestries along the walls. Here is where the four men who ruled O's château would have seized her and fucked her and sodomized her. Kingsley wandered the perimeter of the room, peeking under sheets. He found nothing but more furniture.

He checked under a sheet on the wall, expecting to find a painting underneath. Instead, he uncovered a large mirror—gilt filigree, and ornate. Not a reproduction. The real thing. He yanked the sheet off to see the whole thing. The mirror itself was cracked. No, not cracked . . . shattered, like someone had hit the center of it with a mallet.

Or a fist.

Kingsley pulled the sheet off and lifted the mirror away from the wall an inch and he heard a click. The wall panel next to the mirror opened.

Ah. The mirror, of course. The looking glass.

Now he was getting somewhere.

19

B efore entering through the panel, Kingsley had to find a light. He'd noticed a matchbox on the fireplace mantel in the music room, which he returned for. And in the parlor, he found half a candle, wearing wax and dust on its holder, abandoned on a shelf. He lit the candle and slipped through the panel door and into whatever mad world awaited him behind it.

Kingsley was grateful for the candle, for it surely saved him from tumbling down the steep stone staircase that began immediately on the other side of the door. He descended carefully, moving his hand along the walls to steady himself. The surface beneath his fingers was cool and gritty, rough like bare stone. He counted thirteen steps in all. When he was certain he'd reached the bottom, he felt along the wall for a light switch. While he didn't find one, he felt *something*. He brought the stub of yellow candle toward what his hand had discovered.

He saw an old man's face.

Kingsley recoiled, his breath catching in his throat.

Then he laughed. It wasn't a face at all, but a black leather face mask. What were they called? Gimp masks. That was it. Not his taste, but he'd seen men wearing them in some of the more hardcore clubs he'd frequented, sometimes for work, sometimes for pleasure. Kingsley lifted the mask off the hook on the wall. It was finely-stitched and well-made, though the leather had dried out and cracked from long neglect. He returned it to the hook.

Kingsley swept his candle ahead of him before moving even an inch forward. He couldn't see the full expanse of the room, but he saw enough to know that he was in some forgotten place filled with decades-old instruments of torture. The dungeon—for surely that was the only word to call this hidden part of the château—smelled like a cave. Dusty and dank with rot and decay. Kingsley had been in kinky clubs that tried to recreate the medieval dungeons of old. They had the stone walls, the candles, the iron latches. What they lacked was the smell. The scent of the forgotten. The odor of despair.

He stopped to examine a set of wooden and iron stocks, similar to what the Puritans once used to publicly shame offenders. Next to it he saw something like a kneeling bench in a church, no doubt used for spanking and paddling. What else? A rusting suspension rig. And scattered on the floor the remnants of broken canes, leather straps, and a scalpel he almost stepped on with his bare foot. Kingsley picked it up. He saw it had dried blood on it. He flung it from him and wiped his hands on his jeans.

Ten paces from the stocks he found an X-shaped cross, the wooden beams scored with the marks of decades of desperate fingernails. Kingsley touched the scratch marks and remembered leaving marks just like these one long dark night. Not on wooden rails, however, but on the stomach of a beautiful pale-haired monster, petty payback for the cock being shoved down his throat.

In the same cavernous room, Kingsley also found iron brackets nailed deep into the walls, a tall metal cage locked but with no key in sight, and a sort of medical bed with platforms for the legs and cuffs for the ankles. He pictured his red-capped beauty lying naked on the table, strapped here and helpless while he stroked her open pussy, fucked it while she pretended to hate every second of it. He needed one of those tables for his flat back in Paris.

Five paces from the table, Kingsley found a hallway. His candle wasn't guttering yet, but it would soon. He didn't have time to linger.

"Where are you, you monster?" Kingsley breathed, shuddering with need as he wandered down the hall. "You should be here. This is where your kind belongs. And mine." For they were the same, he and his monster. And truly, who was the more depraved—the boy sadist or the grown man who would have knelt to him on this fetid floor? Even now Kingsley was hard, his breaths shallow, his cock aching. Seven years ago, he'd whispered to his master, "There is nothing you could do to me I wouldn't want . . ." And in this cold dark dungeon corridor, Kingsley knew those words were still true. More true than ever. Indeed, the only truth he knew. If his monster were only here now . . .

"I want you," Kingsley whispered. "I still want you with every cell in my body."

As if in answer to his longing, the candle's scalding wax spilled onto Kingsley's fingers, sending pain shooting through his arm, into his chest, down to his groin.

"*Merci,*" Kingsley said to his monster, who he wanted to imagine had sent the burning wax as a gift. Nonsense, of course. Stage one insanity. Still, Kingsley couldn't help but think his monster would have liked it here in this dungeon. And where else in a house like this could you keep a wolf?

Kingsley brushed the wax off his fingers as he went deeper into the corridor. His candle revealed a door in the wall and Kingsley tried to open it. It wasn't locked, but the hinges were rusted. He put his shoulder against the damp wood and pushed. The door split along the hinges. That wasn't quite what he'd intended. Ah, well, too late now. He entered the room.

At first, he found nothing that surprised him. In the center of the small room was a narrow brass twin bed, leather straps hanging loose from the bars of the headboard and the footboard. The mattress was bare and foul, with a rust-colored stain in the center. Kingsley didn't know what was more frightening— that the large stain could be blood? Or something else?

He moved quickly to leave but stopped when he saw the writing on the wall. With a loose bit of stone, someone had scrawled words on every wall. The same words over and over again.

Je déteste mon mari.

I hate my husband.

Kingsley laughed softly. Madame must have been kept in this room once upon a time, and she'd rebelled against her master/husband by decorating the dungeon with these lovely little messages. Cute. He might have done the same if his master had left him unsupervised long enough to cause that kind of trouble.

The words were everywhere, Kingsley saw. On the walls—all four of them. On the floors from corner to corner. On the back of the broken door. Kingsley raised his candle over his head, curious to see if Madame had really written those four words all over the ceiling as well. She had written something there, but not about her husband. Something more chilling.

I don't like this. I want to go home.

"Christ," Kingsley said, reading those words.

"What, Kingsley?" Madame had asked him just that night. *"What would you have said if your Marcus had answered the phone?"*

"I was in the hospital when I called. I would have said, 'Please come get me. I want to go home.'"

"Like a little boy, sick at school, calling his mother," Madame had said.

Or a new bride, terrified of her new husband and the games he forced her to play . . .

I don't like this. I want to go home.

A thousand times Kingsley had cursed the boy who'd owned him. A thousand times he'd screamed and railed and ranted. But never had he said, "I don't like this." Not once. Not ever.

Not even now.

"What did he do to you?" Kingsley said to the ceiling, to the ghost of the girl Madame had once been, the girl who'd been kept a prisoner in this vile room by her husband.

Kingsley's arousal fled. Nausea took its place. Nausea and sadness. He retraced his steps to the panel door, doubling his original pace. He exhaled with relief when he was once again in the parlor, the dungeon locked and hidden behind the looking glass where it belonged. Kingsley hoped it would rot forever.

Kingsley sped quietly up the servants' steps and past the room were Amel and Leon played. No wonder they'd come to the closed wing of the house to have sex. Amel was a screamer. After seeing the stained bare mattress and those words scrawled in the dungeon, the sound of a woman having a loud and lusty orgasm was sweeter than a sonata to his ears. He'd known there had to be a catch to this place, a dark side, a terrible secret. Down in that foul dungeon he'd found it. But instead of making him fear Madame, he felt the deepest admiration for her. She hadn't perished in that dismal cell. She hadn't let her husband break her. She'd survived, escaped, and taken control. No more monsters in the house, and all thanks to her.

There had been a catch, yes, but Madame had caught it. Caught it like a bullet. And now there was nothing in the château but warm and friendly fires, laughing lovers, delicious decadent games, and a beautiful newborn baby with another on the way.

Kingsley found his room again. Polly was still asleep in the bed. He stripped naked as quickly as he could and crawled under the covers, grateful for the warmth of the bed and Polly's body. She stirred awake and drew him close.

"Where did you go?" she asked, pressing her soft body against his. She didn't sound accusatory, only curious.

"I went to smoke," he said. "And I heard the baby crying so I went into his room. Madame was there, and we talked awhile. Sorry."

"It's alright," she said and settled down to sleep again. "What do you think of Madame?"

"I think I want to kill her husband."

Polly laughed. "Stand in line."

20

Kingsley awoke late the next morning. The first thing he did was glance at the glass doors to the balcony. The snow was still coming down. From the looks of the pile on the windowsill, it had accumulated ankle-deep overnight.

It had been a long time since he'd woken up this late and to a sight this lovely. He turned to wake Polly so she could see it, but her side of the bed was empty. Too bad. He would have liked to have served her again. All morning. All day.

But it was not to be. Kingsley rose from the bed and stretched and yawned. He felt no ill effects from last night's erotic encounter. In fact, his body felt better than it had since before the mission that had put him in the infirmary and sidelined him for the better part of two months. He took full breaths. Nothing in his chest creaked or cracked. His muscles idled like a well-tuned engine, ready to take off at top speed any moment. His head was clear and his vision sharp. The snow always did this to him, made him feel more alive.

In the bathroom, he found clothes waiting for him. Black trousers and a white t-shirt made of the softest cotton. Someone had also left him a razor, a toothbrush, and everything else he needed to make himself presentable.

He took a quick brisk shower, shaved, and dressed. The pants were loose on his waist. They must have belonged to a man a little thicker around the middle than Kingsley. Maybe if he stayed here long enough he'd put on some weight. Wouldn't hurt to bulk up a little more. Maybe he'd be able to take punches better when he had more padding on his ribcage.

Thought of food made his stomach grumble. He went to leave the room in search of the kitchen, but when he came to the bedroom door, he found it locked from the outside.

He tried it again, just in case the door was stuck, but no. Locked. This sent alarms off in his head—he hadn't signed up to be a prisoner. Or had he?

Kingsley tried the balcony door. It was unlocked. He still had his shoes, if he wanted to put them on and make a run for it. As much as the snow invigorated him, however, he didn't particularly want to go out in it unless he had to. If this door was unlocked, then he wasn't technically being kept prisoner, right? He decided to wait it out before going out in the cold and in search of open doors and answers.

He didn't have to wait long. Someone must have heard him up and moving about because ten minutes later, after Kingsley had cleaned up the bathroom and made the bed—he was here to serve after all—he heard the doorknob rattling.

Instinct, training, and a dash of paranoia sent him to the corner of the room behind the door. He'd pulled the blade from the razor and he held it now secreted between his fingers and palm. It might just be Polly. It might be someone come to kill him.

It didn't seem to be either.

A man walked into the room carrying a silver serving tray in his hands. He was young, not much more than a teenager with pale brown hair and a face Kingsley had seen before.

"Leon?" Kingsley asked, and the man turned his head immediately toward the sound of Kingsley's voice.

He looked startled at first to find Kingsley where he hadn't expected him. But then he gave a little laugh and smiled.

"We've met?" Leon asked.

"No. Just guessed," Kingsley said. Now that he was seeing him close-up, Kingsley noticed that Leon definitely took after his uncle the colonel. Same high forehead, same line of the jaw, same crook in the nose.

"I brought your breakfast. Hungry?"

Kingsley narrowed his eyes at the young man. "I thought the men served the women here," he said, letting his guard down enough to step out from his corner and inspect what was on the tray.

"I am serving the women. Madame told me to bring you breakfast. I serve her by serving you."

"But why bring me breakfast here? I could have come downstairs. Why was the door was locked from the outside?"

"Midwinter," Leon said with a grin.

"What is Midwinter? The solstice was last month."

"There are local legends that the Germanic tribe that used to live in this region celebrated a festival in winter that involved fertility rites and sacrifices, all that good old pagan fun. Madame is an old-fashioned lady. She's brought it back."

"Old-fashioned is supposed to mean she wears her skirts long and goes to Mass on Sunday. It's not supposed to mean you've brought back human sacrifice."

"There's no human sacrifice," Leon said.

"You sure about that?"

"I think they would have told me," he said. "Or not. I'm still new here."

"Still doesn't answer my question. What's going on?"

"A party. That's all. And you'll be one of the guests of honor at Midwinter. It's important you stay hidden from the other guest of honor."

"Who's the other?"

"Colette. She's the youngest lady here."

Kingsley nodded. Madame had said that name last night. What had she said exactly? *I'm thinking he's the one for Colette.*

"And I can't meet her until the festival?" Kingsley asked.

"Right," Leon said.

"This is all very strange," Kingsley said. "And a little stupid."

"What's wrong with being a little strange?" Leon asked as he put the tray on the bedside table and sat on the made bed. Kingsley glowered. Colonel's nephew or not, he was messing up Kingsley's crisp hospital corners. "We live out here in the middle of nowhere. We have to make our own fun. Nothing stupid about that."

Kingsley pondered this. He was more than a little skeptical.

"If you don't eat your breakfast, I will," Leon said.

Kingsley pulled up a chair to the bed and inspected his breakfast. Croissant, eggs, coffee. He picked up a fork and started in. "Why did you run away? You're nineteen. Nineteen-year-old men don't run away from home. You tell someone where you're going when you go. Your mother's worried." Kingsley would have killed to have a mother at home worrying about him.

"I didn't run away. And it's not easy to talk about, you know? Especially my father. He's . . . He doesn't approve of this place. Or me being part of it."

Kingsley nodded. He could imagine an older man disapproving of the idea of his son being used as a plaything by older women. Although if Kingsley had an adult son and found out he'd become the plaything of a beautiful older woman, he'd probably shake the boy's hand and say, *I'm proud of you, son.*

"It's not my fault my family doesn't understand me."

Kingsley rolled his eyes. "I hope taxpayers aren't paying for your teen angst."

Leon smiled. "Not my fault either if they are," he said. "I'm happy. I don't want to leave. You can tell my family to back off."

"They think you're in a cult. You really are here entirely by choice?" Kingsley asked. "No coercion? No blackmail? No violence?"

Leon stood up and took off his shirt. Kingsley did not complain.

"They don't even beat me," Leon said, showing off his unmarked body. He put his shirt back on again.

"No one pumping you for information?"

"I don't know anything," Leon said. "What can I tell them if I don't know anything to tell?"

"I'm supposed to go back and tell your family that you're happy, you're healthy, and you don't ever want to come home?" Kingsley asked. "I'm sure that'll go over very well."

Leon raised his hands. "I could have moved to Australia. I could have moved to America. I could have moved to Brazil. They would have been sad, but they wouldn't have tried to stop me."

"Brazil isn't a sex cult," Kingsley said. "Except during *Carnival.* I'll tell them I saw you and that you're well and here by choice, but I don't know if that'll convince them you aren't being brainwashed."

"Thank you for trying. If I have to leave, I'll leave," Leon said, lowering his head. "If that's what I have to do to protect this place. But I hope it doesn't come to that. I love it here."

"You're a submissive?"

Leon lifted a hand as if to say, *Does it matter?*

"I serve," Leon said. "I black Polly's boots. I make Madame's bed. I serve at the dinner table. I serve in Polly's bed, or Louise's or Amel's or whoever wants me that night. I get patted on the head like a prize hound. I sleep like the dead every night and wake up smiling."

"It sounds menial if you ask me," Kingsley said. "Your family's old, important, yes?"

"So?" Leon shrugged. "I'd rather sweep floors in a warm happy home than count gold coins in a cold vault. I feel useful here. Valued. They don't care if my family is important. Are you important?"

"No," Kingsley said. "I'm nobody. My father ran a small import company, and when he died, he was up to his eyeballs in debt." Kingsley had learned a new word two days after his parents died—*insolvable.* In English, "insolvent." In any language, it was a word a teenager didn't need to know.

"See? And you're already adored here," Leon said.

"Am I?"

Leon stood up, ready to leave. "Must be," he said. "When I came here the first time, I wasn't allowed in a bed for a week. Somebody likes you."

"Nice to be liked," Kingsley said. Most of his lovers were total strangers for good reason.

"Or . . ." Leon said with a long exhalation.

"Or what?" Kingsley demanded.

Leon shrugged. "Or . . . they could be fucking with you."

21

---

 omeone was fucking with him, but at least it was a painless
 sort of fucking. Whatever Madame's motives were for
keeping him locked up in the bedroom all day, they didn't seem
all that sinister. He wasn't being tortured, wasn't being starved.
Around two, Polly brought him a late lunch. She even stayed
after to keep him company. When he explained he was bored to
tears, she brought him a paperback to read. Though he enjoyed
reading, that wasn't quite what he had in mind to pass the time.

"You have to save your strength for tonight," Polly said,
staying out of arm's length. She was wearing a clingy blue dress
that made it hard for him to make eye contact. She didn't seem
to mind.

"Save my strength? For what?" Kingsley said.

"For Midwinter tonight."

"Yes, but what precisely am I doing at this Midwinter party
of yours?" He reached for her, but she swatted his hands away.
No playtime today, alas.

"Didn't Leon tell you?"

"He told me I would be the guest of honor."

"Oh," she said. "That's not true."

140

"So I'm not the guest of honor?"

"No," she said.

"Then what am I?"

"You," she said, coming to stand between his knees. "You are the *gift* to the guest of honor." She poked the tip of his nose with the tip of her finger.

"The gift?"

She nodded, grinning. Rather maniacally grinning.

"You're being cryptic to torture me," he said.

"You like being tortured," she said, running her fingers through his hair.

"If there's human sacrifice at this party, I'm never letting you fuck my ass again."

Polly sighed and shook her head. "Don't be so vanilla."

"I won't be insulted like this," he said. "You take that back."

Polly's head fell back, and she laughed.

"You wonderful boy," she said and bent to kiss his cheek. She smelled like Madame, like lavender soap. He wanted to bury his face between her beautiful full breasts and breathe her scent for hours. But instead she pinched his nose.

"You won't give me any idea what's happening tonight?" he asked as she stepped away to leave him.

"You'll like it," she said. "Promise."

"I'm trusting you. Now go. I have to read . . ." He picked up one of the books she'd brought him. "*The Adventures of Tom Sawyer.*"

"It's a classic about a very naughty little boy, just like you."

"Any sex in it?"

"You're cute," she said. "I wish I was Colette. Lucky girl."

"Will I ever get to meet this mysterious lady?"

"Tonight," she said.

"I meet her tonight and then we . . ." Kingsley waited, hoping for Polly to fill in the blank.

She didn't.

"Enjoy your book," Polly said.

"It's not very long. What do I do when I finish it?" Kingsley asked.

"You could shave," she said.

"I already did this morning."

Polly stood at the open door and smiled at him.

"You don't mean shave my face, do you?" he asked.

"See? You are catching on."

"I could escape, you know," he said. "It would be easy."

Polly shrugged. "Then escape."

"You weren't supposed to call my bluff," he told her.

She smiled and shook her head. She'd turned into his babysitter again, amused by his antics while trying to maintain a modicum of authority over them.

"I'll leave the door unlocked," she said. "I'm asking you not to leave the room, politely asking. Not an order."

Kingsley sighed heavily. "Why did you have to ask politely? Now I can't escape."

"You're so easy," she said. "If you get to stay, I'm going to chain you to my headboard for a week."

"What about the footboard?'

"The week after," she said with a wink. Then she left him alone and, as promised, didn't lock the door after her.

Alone again, Kingsley collapsed back onto the bed and stared at the ceiling. "This house is bizarre," he said to himself.

He paused.

"I like bizarre."

Kingsley did sit-ups and push-ups until he'd made himself sweaty enough to earn a bath. He bathed while reading, read while bathing and, because Polly told him to, he shaved. It left him feeling quite breezy and exposed afterward, not that he minded. He finished his bath and took his time with the cleanup, since he had nothing else to do but try to eavesdrop. All day he'd heard voices in the hallway—laughter, whispers, even little Jacques crying a couple of times. It did sound like the household was hard at work preparing for a party, but nothing anyone said gave him any clue about what was really happening tonight.

He was, frankly, annoyed to be left out.

By sunset, Kingsley was nearly out of his mind with boredom. When the knob of the bedroom door finally rattled and turned, he was ready to bolt from the room like a horse from a starting gate.

It was Polly again. She was carrying a garment bag over her arm.

"Ready?" she asked.

"For what?"

"We have to get you dressed. You must look your best."

"Now, will you—*please*—tell me what you're getting me ready for?"

"For Colette, silly. I told you that earlier."

"Yes, but what am I doing with Colette? Or for Colette? Or to Colette? Or onto Colette?"

"Oh," Polly said as she lay the garment bag on the bed. "I guess I did forget to tell you that part."

"You did. So will you tell me now what is happening tonight with me and this Colette person?"

Polly unzipped the garment bag and inside he saw a suit. A beautiful suit. Not just a suit but a formal suit—cravat, tails, vest. In fact in looked just like a . . .

No.

No.

No.

Polly grinned. "You'll make a very handsome groom."

22

"Where are my shoes?" Kingsley asked. He'd had enough.

"In the bathroom. Why do you need your shoes?" Polly asked.

"Because once they're on, I'm going to jump off the balcony, run across the courtyard, scale the wall and run to the nearest village," he said. "Or into the nearest body of water to drown myself."

"You don't have to scale the wall. The gate's unlocked during the day," Polly said. "But you really should stay. You'll miss the party."

"I'm not getting married. Hard limit."

"It's all for show, Kingsley," Polly said in a conciliatory tone. "It's not real. Just, you know, pantomime. Symbolic."

He dropped his head back and groaned. "Why does no one ever tell me the important part first?" Kingsley asked the ceiling, the sky, God, as his pulse slowly returned to normal.

"Because you're so handsome when you squirm," she said, patting his cheek. "Now behave yourself. I'm here to dress you."

"I'd rather you undress me."

"Don't worry. I'll do that first."

Polly gathered his t-shirt in her hands and pulled it up and off of him. He couldn't believe he was agreeing to this insanity.

"Pantomime, how French," he said. "Please don't make me wear a clown nose."

"Never," she said. "Unless Madame orders it."

"That's it. Goodbye."

Kingsley took one step, but Polly caught him by the arm and he let her drag her into the bathroom.

Thirty minutes later the result was . . .

"There are two types of handsome men in the world," Polly said. "Those who *think* they're God's gift to women."

"And?"

She kissed his cheek and turned him to the mirror. "Those who actually *are* God's gift to women."

Kingsley surveyed himself. The suit was a classic evening tailcoat tuxedo. Black trousers, black coat, white vest, white collar and cuffs, and a white bow tie. He looked like a young count on his way to the opera.

Or a young count on his way to his wedding.

Not bad. Not what he'd ever get married in. Not that he would ever get married. But if he did get married, he'd wear his dress uniform. If he could find it . . .

He tried to run a hand through his hair, but Polly stopped him.

"It's perfect. Don't touch it."

"Fine," he said. "Can we go now? I've been cooped up in here all day. I'm bored. I'm horny. And I need a drink. And I'm horny."

"You already—"

"I'm *very* horny."

The kiss went on just long enough he thought it might lead somewhere. Then she stopped. "Kingsley."

"Yes?"

"Shut up."

He said nothing, though it wasn't easy.

"Good boy," she said. "I have to get ready. Someone will come for you soon."

She started to leave him and then she turned back at the door and smiled at him. "You'll have fun tonight," she said. "I promise."

"I want to believe you."

She smiled. "Do you really want to leave? If you do, you can go. I'll have a driver take you back to Paris right now."

He believed her. If he asked to leave, she would make sure he was in a car in ten minutes. He'd already talked to the colonel's nephew. The boy didn't seem to be in distress at all—far from it, in fact. Why not leave? Because he didn't want to, that's why. He told himself he was "information-gathering." Sure. That sounded like a good enough excuse.

"I'll stay," he said. "If only to meet this mysterious Colette."

"Oh, you'll do more than meet her," Polly said. "You know what happens after a wedding, right?"

"A reception?"

Polly winked. "The wedding night."

After Polly left, Kingsley paced the room like a caged lion. He only stopped when he realized that was the sort of thing a real groom would be doing. Pantomime? Really? A play ceremony? Insane. But he'd done stranger things for this job before. There were certainly worse ways of earning a living than getting dressed up and fucking girls at parties.

As Polly had promised him, it wasn't long before someone came to fetch him. It was Leon, also in a tuxedo.

"Are you my groomsman?" Kingsley asked, looking him up and down.

"You don't look happy. If you knew Colette, you'd look happy."

"I don't know Colette, but I'm already sick of her. I'm annoyed Madame is putting me through this stupidity."

"I told you they fuck with you here," Leon said. "Didn't I? They fuck with all of us all the time."

"Then why do you want to stay?"

Leon looked at him like he was crazy. "Everyone fucks with everyone all the time. Might as well get fucked with by beautiful women who let you fuck them after. Really, what's there to complain about?"

Kingsley shook his finger at the boy. "You make a point."

Leon waved Kingsley into the hallway, which had been transformed during the day from a decorous passageway into a gauntlet of ornate paper lanterns on every table surrounded by hot house flowers. Orchids and irises and winter roses over-flowed from gilt vases. The stair railing was also decorated with flowers and lights and emanating from the walls of the house was the low hum of music playing somewhere. Kingsley couldn't help but stare agog at the transformation the château had undergone. Holly hung from the ceiling and tall white candles glowed in the mirrors.

"How decadent," Kingsley said, trying to fight off the spell the house was putting him under. His heart was racing with anticipation, excitement, and nervousness. When he passed under a hanging garland of roses, he'd almost forgotten he wasn't actually getting married.

"Maybe so," Leon said. "But Madame likes to indulge her favorites."

"Am I a favorite already?"

"I meant Colette."

Before Kingsley could respond something to the effect of *Fuck Colette*, Leon ushered him through a set of heavy wooden double doors. They entered a glittering ballroom, the sort Kingsley had only seen in films from the thirties.

Once he entered the room, exuberant applause erupted from the assembly. Polly had said there were nine men in the house and ten women, but Kingsley counted at least forty people in the ballroom, all in various costumes. Louis XV ball gowns on some of the women. Nineteenth century breeches and boots on several of the men. But some were wearing contemporary formalwear. Some were wearing almost nothing at all. One woman, resplendent in her white powdered wig, had on a pale peach dress so sheer and tight that he could see the freckle on her delectable bare posterior as she passed him by.

"Who are all these people?" Kingsley asked Leon as they were both greeted with kisses on their cheeks by the delighted—and likely inebriated—crowd.

"Friends of Madame." Leon grabbed two glasses of red wine off a passing server's tray and handed one to Kingsley, who downed half of it in three swallows.

"That's Henri and Jean-Michel," Leon said, pointing to two men—one white and one black, both wearing formal tuxedos but without the tails.

"Henri is Madame's driver?" Kingsley asked.

"Right. And he does everything else for her. He's been here with her for fifteen years. Jean-Michel's mother is Senegalese. He's been here ever since he graduated from the Sorbonne. Five years here, I think. Polly's favorite. But don't tell. They're not supposed to have favorites."

"Hmm . . ." was all Kingsley said. Kingsley wanted to be Polly's favorite.

"That's Nadine and Jacques," Leon said, pointing to a pretty pale lady in a blue velvet Empire-waist gown.

"I know Jacques. We're old friends now," Kingsley said, smiling at the little baby boy in the blue velvet suit. Jacques had a white ruff around his neck like a seventeenth-century prince.

Jacques was getting cuddles and goodnight kisses from a few people in the crowd. Must be his bedtime.

Leon pointed out others and named them. Louise, another of the ladies of the château, a woman of about forty with fiercely intelligent eyes looked haughty and marvelous in a Givenchy gown of black. Even that fierce-looking lady couldn't stop herself from smiling every now and then. And Amal, Leon's lover from last night brushed past them both without saying a word . . . though she did give Leon a little wink.

"Isn't it great here?" Leon asked, beaming. "I don't care what my father says. I'm never leaving."

Kingsley eyed Leon. The young man was a puzzle. He thought about that American phrase he'd learned long ago, the one about drinking the Kool-Aid. Leon had clearly drunk the Kool-Aid. He hadn't even asked Kingsley how his family was, or if his mother had sent a message. Brand new cult members were like happy brides on their honeymoons. Everything was perfect. Everything was a dream come true. Nothing was wrong. Everything was right. True love prevailed and would last forever.

The room they stood in was octagonal, with gray marble floors and floor-to-ceiling windows all around. Outside everything was white with snow—trees and shrubs and statues. Lanterns hung from the rafters, and it seemed the entire party glowed with their light. The string sextet he'd heard echoing through the house sat on a dais playing lively waltzes. Not all the men were handsome and not all the women were beautiful, but every last one of them glowed like they were lit from within by wine and song. It was *joie de vivre* if he'd ever seen it and even Kingsley's lingering suspicions began to wither under the light.

The crowd parted, and Kingsley spied lovely Polly coming to him. Her low-cut red dress was adorned with so many sequins that he could hardly tell the outline of her as she shimmered like a mirage in the desert.

"*Magnifique*," he said to her as she reached for his hands and kissed both his cheeks.

"You like my dress?"

"I meant your breasts."

Polly laughed, and he joined her in her laughter.

"*Merci.*" Polly grinned, her face flushed with happiness. "You're having fun, aren't you?"

"If I was I wouldn't admit to it," he said. But he smiled when he said it.

"It's about to be more fun."

She nodded toward the center of the small ballroom and there stood Madame looking both blithe and lithe in her black double-breasted tuxedo dress, her white hair expertly coiffed in a low knot that gave her a sleek androgynous silhouette. She was a slight woman, but there was no denying she held the gathered in her thrall. The wine flowed and the music played and the partygoers danced and laughed and kissed, but the moment Madame raised one thin arm into the air and snapped her fingers . . .

Silence.

"*Bonsoir, mes amis*," she said, as she turned a slow circle to greet all and sundry. "Welcome to Midwinter."

Everyone applauded and cheered.

"For fifteen years we have held this celebration," she continued, "on the first full night of the first true snow of the new year. What we honor tonight is life. And what better night to honor life than a night when it is cold and snow covers the land? Life is out there, under the snow, sleeping, yes, and waiting to wake. And life is in here. Warmth in the midst of coldness. Light in the midst of darkness. Beauty in the midst of bitterness. And to rebuke the barrenness of this season, we, as we have for three decades, offer up fresh and fertile young blood."

"I said no human sacrifice," Kingsley whispered to Polly. "Hard limit."

"Hush, it's symbolic," she whispered. Kingsley rolled his eyes.

"And so we bring together our Midwinter King," Madame said, holding out a hand to Kingsley. Polly nudged him and he walked over to her. "And our Midwinter Queen in marriage."

Leon and Henri opened the double doors. A girl stepped into the hall. She was wearing a Renaissance-style dress of black and gold. Her dark hair fell down her back in rolling waves and her dark eyes danced in the lantern light. She wasn't more than eighteen or nineteen and she was undoubtedly the loveliest girl he'd seen in his life.

And he would have recognized her in a heartbeat even without the red cap and beauty mark.

No one had bowed to him, but as Colette, the girl he'd met at the phone booth, walked over to him, every man bowed and every woman curtsied. Kingsley probably should have bowed as well, but he was too overcome by the sight of her to move lest he break the spell. Her eyes were on him alone, as if the people she passed were nothing but shadows and only he was present in flesh and blood.

"You," he said as she came to stand in front of him. She held out her two small hands to him and he took them instinctively. They shook in his grasp. For all her apparent composure, she was nervous.

"Me," she said in a whisper. Then she gave him a smile, the exact smile every groom wanted his bride to give him the moment before the marriage. The smile that said, *You, only you, always you.*

He wanted to ask her a thousand questions. Why him? Had there been a test? Had he passed it? Who was she really? How had she found him at the phone booth? And, most important of all, could he kiss her right here right now and never ever stop?

Before he could open his mouth, Madame began to speak again.

"The Midwinter Queen has chosen her King, and now we join them together with ribbons of white to symbolize our Queen's purity, ribbons of red to symbolize the blood of rebirth, and bands of gold to symbolize the endless cycle of life."

Madame brought his right hand together with Colette's and she wrapped a length of white silk around their joined wrists, a length of red silk over the white, and then placed gold band on their left ring fingers. Kingsley wanted to find it ridiculous. He wanted to laugh at the silly paganism of it all. And he might have, if Colette's eyes hadn't been shining with unshed tears. If there was a man in the world who could remain unmoved by the sight of a beautiful girl trying not to cry with happiness, Kingsley didn't want to know him. This—whatever this was— meant something to her, and if it meant so much to her, he would at least pretend to take it seriously. The longer he looked into her eyes, at her quivering bottom lip, so soft and kissable, the less pretending he had to do.

"And now," Madame said, her words cutting through Kingsley's reverie on Colette's lips, "let there be kissing and let there be laughter and let there be new life."

"You're supposed to kiss me now," Colette whispered.

She didn't have to whisper twice.

Their right hands were still joined by the white and red ribbons, and Kingsley lifted her hand to his lips and gently kissed her knuckles, her palm, and all her fingertips. As his lips brushed the back of her hand she made a little sound, a little intake of breath that told him she desired him almost as much as he desired her.

He hadn't expected the girl who'd asked him if he was circumcised at their first meeting to be timid, but she kissed like she'd never been kissed before. Her lips trembled and her breath hitched in her throat as he explored her mouth. She tasted sweet as strawberries and he chased that taste with his tongue. Her head tilted back and she moaned softly in the back of her throat. Around them people clapped and cheered and oh-la-la-ed but they might as well have been a thousand miles away for all Kingsley heeded them. He had one purpose in that moment and that was to make Colette moan like that again. And again. And again . . .

Colette broke the kiss, but only, it seemed, because she had to or she would faint. Her cheeks were pink and eyes damp and wide. She was young, terribly young, and it must have been overwhelming for her to be kissed like that in front of so many.

"Children," Madame said to them. "Let us be about Midwinter's business."

As the music struck up again, Madame untied the cords from their wrists (though she left the plain gold bands on their ring fingers). As soon as they were no longer joined by ribbons, the women of the house—Polly and Nadine and Louise—took Colette by the arms and swept her from the room.

"Shall we?" Madame asked Kingsley, and offered her his arm. They followed at a slower pace behind the ladies, who were running far ahead of them down a long torch-lit corridor. As they left the ballroom, one final cheer went up just as the lights went down.

Things were going to happen in that room.

"Did you enjoy that?" Madame asked once they were alone in the hallway. The ladies were long gone.

"I have no idea what just happened in there," he said. "But I got to kiss a gorgeous girl, so I can't complain."

"You'll do more than kiss her."

"I'm really going to sleep with her?"

"Do you mind?" Madame asked.

Kingsley laughed and the laugh hit the rafters. "No. Not at all. If the lady is willing."

"Oh, she's more than willing. She did choose you. There were, of course, many other options."

"Why me?" he asked.

"All the obvious reasons. You're close to her age. You're very handsome. You made her laugh. You laughed at her. You offered to father her children and convert to her faith."

"Flirting," Kingsley said. "That's all. She's never been flirted with before?"

"Not by the likes of you," Madame said.

"I've had some practice."

"And you have this face," she said, patting his cheek. "Pretty words and handsome faces have been making the hearts and loins of girls come to life since the beginning of time. Plus . . . she said you offered to let her use the phone even though you were waiting on a call from me, and you'd been waiting for six hours."

"It would have been rude not to," he said.

"Even ladies like us can have our heads turned by chivalry. Especially ladies like us."

"I'm glad I pleased her. I look forward to pleasing her all night."

"Polly said you were a very good lover. Colette needs that."

"Has she had bad experiences before?"

"No."

"That's good."

"She's had no experience before."

Kingsley stopped midstep and stared at Madame.

"She's a virgin?" he asked.

Madame smiled. "Not for long."

Kingsley looked for words. He looked for them and didn't find them.

"Don't worry," Madame said, patting his arm. "I'll be there the whole time."

"That's not comforting," Kingsley said.

"You've never had sex while someone watched before?"

"I have, yes," he said, "but this is a little different."

"How so?"

"For starters, I'm not stoned out of my mind."

"I'll give you champagne."

Kingsley had certainly had sex in front of other people before. At seedy clubs for fun. Once on a mission for business. This was different.

"She's never had sex before," Kingsley said. "Don't you think it'll be better for her if we're alone? She might like her privacy. I know I would."

"She wants me there," Madame said. "She wants you there. This is her night. She gets what she wants."

"If I'd known she'd never done this before . . ." Kingsley groaned. "There is an epidemic sweeping France where people are rendered incapable of telling me the important part first." He raised his clenched fingertips in imitation of his Italian grandfather when irritated.

"Unless you're a brute, which you aren't, you won't hurt her. She's already open. We don't let men near hymens. What's that English saying—*like bulls in China shops*? We don't let cattle near the good dishes."

"What do you mean you don't let men near hymens? Am I supposed to take her in the ass?"

"You can if she wants you to. What I mean is that she's used a vibrator," Madame said. "And a dildo. Often."

"Christ, how many dildos do you have in this house?" he asked, smiling despite himself at the thought of Colette opening herself with a vibrator.

"Enough that were you to suddenly disappear, you would not be missed."

Kingsley heard the warning, and kept his mouth shut.

"Colette is very special to me," Madame said. They turned a corner and walked up a curving staircase. "She was born in this house, like Polly. When her mother fell in love with a local barrister, they moved to the village. But Colette came by every day after school as she got older. Came for tea, came for my company, came to learn. She was drawn here the way some seabirds are drawn to the place of their birth. She's my goddaughter. We've been looking a long time for the right man to be her first. I know you won't disappoint us."

"Another English saying," Kingsley said. "I'll give it the old college try."

"Good boy."

"You should know, however, that I never went to college."

That got a rare laugh out of Madame. "Officer training will do," she said. "I know you can take orders."

Kingsley exhaled—loudly.

Madame paused outside a door and took his hand in hers. "You know how poorly women are treated all over the world, yes?"

"Yes," Kingsley said.

"Under this roof, we try to undo a little of that damage the world has done to women. Every girl on earth deserves to have her first time treated with respect. Every girl on earth deserves to feel pleasure."

Kingsley got the message.

"I'll take good care of her," he said.

"I believe you will. But if you don't . . ."

"Yes?"

"I'll see to it no one ever finds your body."

The door opened.

P olly opened the door a crack. She wore a wide smile and her eyes were bright with happiness.

"She's almost ready," Polly said.

A voice from inside the room said something unintelligible.

"Ah, she's ready," Polly said.

Then she shut the door in their faces.

"Bridesmaids," Madame said, shaking her head in constrained amusement. "In the old days the whole wedding party would have watched the consummation. That's how the tradition of catching a garter started. You're lucky to have only me in the room. Unless you're an exhibitionist. Are you?"

"I'm anything I need to be to avoid being murdered by you," Kingsley said.

Madame patted his cheek yet again. "That's the spirit, my boy."

Polly opened the door again. She came out with Louise and Nadine. All three of them kissed Madame on the lips and then Kingsley on each cheek.

Nadine told him "Many blessings" and Louise whispered a

quick "*Merci beaucoup*" and Polly gave him a wink and said, "Go get her, tiger."

"My first time wasn't nearly this elaborate," he said to Madame.

"You should have had a better first time then."

Considering his first time had been on a kitchen floor, and had lasted under ninety seconds, Kingsley couldn't argue with that.

Madame led him through the door. Kingsley glanced around, taking in his surroundings. The walls were covered in gold wallpaper decorated with black flowers. The bed, heaped high with silk pillows and luxurious coverings, was as large as any he'd ever seen. The curtains were drawn to let in the view of the winter night and the dark forest just outside the window. And Colette sat on the edge of the window seat wearing a gown of pale gold, with her long black hair swept over one shoulder. She had her feet tucked under her and her face turned to the cloud-kissed moon.

She looked so painfully young at that moment, Kingsley nearly spun on his heel and walked straight out of the room. But then she turned and smiled at him and she looked so wildly wickedly desirable, he decided to stay.

"I should be ashamed of myself," he whispered to Madame.

"We all should be," she said, patting his back. With a lift of her chin, she indicated he should go forward, and he did as ordered because it was impossible to stay rooted in place with that girl within walking distance. He went to her and sat down across from her in the window seat.

"You," he pointed at her. "You tricked me."

She blushed and briefly buried her face against her knees before peeking up at him again. "I didn't mean to," she said as she rested her chin on her crossed arms over her knees.

"So you didn't need to use my phone?" he asked.

Her blush deepened.

"I thought so," he said, narrowing his eyes at her in playful annoyance.

"I only wanted to meet you," she said. "Madame said she liked your voice. We drove in to take a peek at you. I liked what I peeked. And I think you liked peeking at me, too."

"What gave you that idea?" he demanded.

"You offered to circumcise yourself with a Swiss Army knife for me. But I bet you say that to all the girls."

Kingsley slid his hand along the window seat toward her. He crooked his finger and Colette slowly lowered her hand to his and let him touch her.

"You're nervous," he said, feeling her fingers shake.

"A little."

"What about Georges?" he asked. "Is he nervous?"

She thrust out her chin to display her beauty mark which she'd tried to convince him was a tick. "He's fine," Colette said. "He's very experienced."

"My kind of man," Kingsley said. "I should kiss him in congratulations."

"He'd like that."

Kingsley leaned in and pressed a gentle kiss onto her chin. When that went well, he moved his lips to her lips. He could tell she was nervous from the dryness of her mouth when he kissed her, but soon she warmed to him. She lowered her legs so she could push closer to him, and when he put his arm around her lower back she murmured a little sound of pleasure.

"You like that?" he asked, pausing between kisses.

"I was wondering what your arms would feel like on me," she said. "It's better than I thought."

"What else were you wondering?" he said. Out of the corner

of his eye he saw Madame turning down the covers on the bed and smoothing the sheets.

"A few things," she said.

"Such as?"

"Why are you so handsome?"

He narrowed his eyes at her. "Trick question, right? If I answer that, I'm admitting I'm handsome."

"Not a trick question."

"Oh, then the answer is I'm handsome because you think I'm handsome and yours is the only opinion that matters. What else were you wondering?"

"Have you ever been with a virgin?"

"A few."

"How many?"

"Let's just say I made a lot of big brothers very *very* angry at me during high school. I'm lucky to be alive."

She laughed.

"I'm not kidding. One of the big brothers tried to stab me. I seduced so many girls my grandparents shipped me off to an all-boys school to save my life."

"How terrible," she said, grinning.

"Not really. I found a boy to sleep with there."

Colette's laugh was so light and airy it floated to the sky, parted the clouds and the room filled with moonlight.

"What else were you wondering?" he asked when her laughter faded.

"I was wondering," she said, her voice soft and tender, "what you would feel like inside me."

Kingsley slowly nodded. "A good thing to wonder," he said. "I wondered that, too. Should we find out?"

She grinned again and nodded. "Let's."

Kingsley stood up first and before she could stand he gently lifted her off the window bench and carried her to the bed.

He lay her back against a pile of gold and red pillows.

"I'll go anytime you tell me, Colette," Madame said as she took a seat in a red velvet wing chair near the bed.

"Can she stay?" Colette asked Kingsley.

"Of course. Anything you want." He stroked her face, her burning red cheek. She was alive to his touch, excited and beaming and breathless. A very good combination. He wanted her to enjoy this, wanted her to be ready and not only ready but desperate for him.

"I'm going to give you a magic number," he said to her. "That number is five."

He held up his hand, all five fingers.

"Five? That's the magic number?" she asked. "Why?"

"Because let's say you're at one right now," he said and held up only one finger. "I'm not going to make love to you until you're at a five. We'll start at number one and when you tell me 'five,' then I'll be inside you. Not on one. Not on two. Not on three. Not on four. Only on five. Understand?"

"I understand," she said. "But."

"But what?"

"I think I'm already on three."

Kingsley turned to Madame who was sitting with her legs crossed in the chair, placid as a woman watching the evening news.

"I'm never leaving here," Kingsley said. "And you can't make me."

"Be good and we might let you stay," Madame said. She waved her hand, indicating he needed to give Colette his full attention. He was more than happy to obey that order.

"Don't move," he told Colette as he stood up again.

"Ever?" she asked.

"For the next ten seconds."

She leaned back into the pillows and watched him as he shed his tuxedo jacket, pulled off the bow tie, and opened the collar.

"Much better," she said when he sat next to her on the bed again. "I'm not sure how to undo a bowtie, but I do know how to do this."

Colette lifted her delicate hands to his shirt and undid a single button. Then the button beneath it. She slipped her hands under the fabric and touched his upper chest, his collarbone and neck. He reveled in the curiosity of her fingers. Her touch sent shivers dancing over his skin. She slipped one hand into his hair and stroked it and he turned his head and his lips met the satiny skin of her wrist. He covered her hand with his own and licked and nibbled at her wrist until he heard her gasp.

"What was that?" he said, smiling at her.

"I said 'five.' "

"I think you're skipping ahead a few numbers."

"Tell that to my body," she said.

Kingsley slid both arms around her back, lifted her and laid her down flat onto the bed. He buried his head between her tender young breasts and loudly said, *"You're skipping ahead a few numbers."*

Her laughter reverberated through her and under him. And while her laugh was lovely and vibrant, what he wanted to hear from her was more gasping, more moaning. He untied the gold ribbon at the bodice of her gown and pulled the fabric loose, baring her breasts to him.

Abruptly she stopped laughing.

Her nipples were a warm dusky red like her lips and just as kissable. His cock, already hard, stiffened further at the sight of them. He licked the left one as he stroked the right softly with the pad of his thumb. Licked and stroked, stroked and sucked.

Colette panted as he kissed and fondled her nipples, even digging her hand into his hair again to hold his head against her chest. No need for that. He had no intention of stopping anytime soon. He drew a nipple into his mouth, teasing it very gently with his teeth before kneading the now stiff tip over and over again with his tongue. With his hand he massaged her other breast, holding it and molding it to his palm. Her nipples were very hard and the flesh of her chest flushed scarlet. The urge to take his cock out of his trousers, mount her and pound her was growing stronger. He ignored the fantasy. They would get there soon enough, especially if she kept breathing like that, moaning like that . . .

His hand didn't leave her breast but his lips traveled up to her long neck to nibble on her earlobe.

"Are you wet?" he asked her, a question for her ears only.

"I think so. But maybe you should check to be sure," she said.

With his mouth still on her neck, he reached down and gathered the fabric of her gown in his hands, slowly dragging it over her knees and up her thighs and to her lower stomach. He touched that first, and felt it quiver under the flat of his hand. His thumb traced a circle around her navel and even dipped inside to make her tense and smile again. He moved his hand along her leg and lifted it over his hip to open her up for him. He caught her mouth in another kiss and when she breathed against his lips he lowered his hand and cupped her. She was hot against his palm, her desire incandescent. He slid one finger along the seam of her vulva and found it damp. He slid it along the seam again, a little deeper this time and found her wetness waiting for him. Her labia were slick and she offered no resistance at all when he slid his finger into her body.

Their mouths were still joined when he penetrated her so he could taste her gasping with his tongue. She was burning hot inside and wet enough he probably could have entered her that second without hurting her.

He broke the kiss and smiled into her shining eyes.

"Now what's the number?" he asked.

Between breaths Colette spoke a number.

"Six."

25

"I'm going to spank you for that," Kingsley said.

Colette whimpered. It was about as believable a performance as when she tried to convince him her beauty mark was a tick.

"Or," he said. "I'm changing the numbers to ten. And you're not going to say 'ten' until you're so ready for my cock you think you'll die without it. Are you there yet?"

"Well, I won't die without it yet," she said. "But I'm not very happy living without it either."

"Five," Kingsley said.

"What's five?"

"How many children we're having someday."

"You've already decided?" she asked.

"You object?"

"Five is a lot," she said.

"There's ten women in this house and nine men to take care of our brats. We'll breed them, then we'll let everyone else raise them while we make some more. What do you think?"

"Hmm . . . it's not the worst idea I've heard. We'll try one and see if we like that."

"A wise compromise. I knew I married you in my head for a reason."

That set her giggling again and Kingsley decided he'd had just about enough of that. He slipped his hand out of her and spanked her quick and hard on the side of her naked thigh. It was nothing but a harmless swat, the sort that makes a big sound without so much as leaving a handprint, but it did the job. Colette's eyes went wide, and she immediately stopped laughing.

"Did you just—"

"Yes," he said. "Now what's the number?"

Colette panted, her lips parted and glistening.

"Seven."

"Good. Let's see if I can get you to eight."

Kingsley pressed her legs apart again, even wider, and laid down between her thighs. With his fingers he parted her wet folds and with his tongue he gently licked her open slit. Colette rewarded him with a groaning sort of sigh. She opened her thighs even wider for him and he licked her again, deeper this time, then deeper still. He licked the opening of her body, teasing the hole with the tip of his tongue before focusing all his attention onto her clitoris. She tasted divine and the heat of her inner body was addicting. And if she didn't stop taking those quick needy breaths while he licked her, he might be here between her legs all night.

Kingsley knew this dance required restraint. He wanted her desperately aroused, desperate for him, but he didn't want her to orgasm quite yet either. He knew from vast experience, women were often too tender after climax to take a cock inside them. He didn't want to hurt her—not only because Madame was watching, but because it was her first time.

Reluctantly, he tore himself away from this most pleasant of tasks. He knelt between Colette's thighs and kissed her breasts again.

"Why did you stop?" she said with a sweet pout.

Kingsley grinned against her skin. "I could spend all night with my face buried in your pussy," he said. "But if I make you come, we'll be back at one again in seconds." He kissed his way up her neck and let her taste herself on his lips. "I like you here, stuck at eight."

"Nine," she said into his mouth.

"Little liar," he said.

"Eight and a half," she said.

"Better."

Kingsley rolled back on his knees again and unbuttoned another button on his shirt.

"Eight and three quarters," Colette said.

"You flatter me," he said and undid another button.

"What's your number?" she asked.

Kingsley stripped out of his shirt and tossed it aside. Colette devoured his body with her eyes. He bent over her, caressed her cheek, cupped her breast, lightly bit her bottom lip.

"I've been at ten since I saw you walk into that ballroom," he said.

Colette raised her hand to his face and touched his lips. Her eyes were hooded and dilated with desire. "Kingsley," she said.

"Yes?"

"Ten."

This time he didn't accuse her of lying. He only pulled away from her long enough to remove the rest of his clothes. As he stripped, he watched Colette watching him. She seemed very pleased by what she saw.

He lay next to her on the bed and slipped his hand between her legs again. "I meet your approval?"

"Yes, you—"

At the *yes*, he pushed two fingers inside of her. She flinched with pleasure at the penetration. While Madame had told him Colette had already opened herself with a toy, he wasn't going to take anything for granted. She was wet and she was open, but he was also big. He went as deep as he could into her with his fingers and then spread them apart inside her. Colette whimpered—not quite the sound of pain, but more of slight discomfort. As he kept moving his hand and spreading his fingers, the sounds she made turned back to pleasure and from pleasure to desire and from desire to need.

"Good?" he asked into her ear.

"Very," she breathed.

"Let's practice," he said. "When I push in, you tilt your hips up."

She nodded and he pushed his two fingers into her. Colette did as he'd told her to, lifting her hips to meet his hand. They did it again and this time Colette moaned as he went into her deeper. The third time her head fell back on the pillow. She was more than ready.

And so was he.

He moved on top of her and out of the corner of his eye he saw Madame in her chair shifting forward, fluttering like a mother hen. He almost smiled. If Madame wanted to watch, he'd make sure it was a good show.

Kingsley ignored Madame. He had eyes only for Colette. She was exquisite lying there on her back, her straight dark hair fanned over the red silk pillow—the crimson and the black. Her bare breasts rose and fell with her rapid breaths. Her nightgown was pushed up to her waist and with her legs wide and ready for him. Nothing of her was hidden. With two fingers, he spread the folds again and gazed with pleasure at her wet and waiting hole. He couldn't wait one more second to be inside it.

He positioned the tip at the entrance and slowly lowered

himself down onto her, allowing the shifting of his weight to push his cock into her without force or thrusting. He watched Colette closely as he entered her. Her fingers caught in the sheets and she pulled hard. Her eyes closed tight, and her hips shifted as if trying to make room inside herself for him.

He tested a tentative thrust, and, while she didn't protest or whimper in pain, she didn't seem to like it much either.

Kingsley started to pull out, but Colette said no to that.

"It hurts," Kingsley said. "Yes?"

"Darling?" Madame said. "Does it hurt?"

Colette glanced at Madame and then back at Kingsley. "It's just . . . it's so deep," she said. Kingsley could see she was torn between wanting to push past the discomfort and wanting to push him out of her.

"Too deep?" Kingsley asked.

Colette looked embarrassed. "A little."

"Try her on top," Madame said to Kingsley.

"Are you in charge here?" Kingsley asked her.

"Yes," Madame said curtly. "Always, if you've forgotten. *And* I'm a woman. Put her on top."

"Do you want to be on top?" he asked Colette. Madame might have been in charge of the château, but only Colette was in charge of Colette.

"Can we try something different?" she asked. "I don't think I want that."

Kingsley turned to Madame. He found her smiling instead of scowling like he'd expected. Apparently, he'd passed another of her little tests.

"We'll play," he said. "When you like something, tell me." Kingsley pulled out, as ordered, and kissed Colette until she didn't look quite so chagrined anymore. Poor thing. "You want to play?"

"Let's play," she said, nodding.

He put her legs on his shoulders and entered her again.

"You're in my chest cavity," she said. "That is definitely bad for my cardiovascular health."

Kingsley laughed and pulled out. He put her on her hands and knees and entered her from behind.

"No, no, now I just have to piss," she said. Kingsley pulled out. "Wait, no I don't."

Kingsley pushed her onto her side and knelt behind her, entered her again slowly.

"Ohh . . ." she said.

"Good ohh? Bad ohh?" he asked. He pulled out again and waited for her verdict.

"Ohh ohh," she said. "I think it could work."

Madame came to the bed and picked up a small pillow.

"Lift your knee, darling," Madame said. She fit it under Colette's thigh.

"I've never had an assistant before," Kingsley said as Madame maneuvered Colette into a comfortable position on her side, but with her thighs still open enough he could get into her vagina from behind.

"I told you," Madame said. "I'm in charge. *You're* the assistant."

She said that with a little smirk on her lips and even Colette giggled underneath him.

"No laughing from you," Kingsley said as he slid in behind her, covering her body with his. He kissed the back of her naked shoulder and caressed her thigh and hip and small soft bottom with the flat of his hand.

"Are you ready to try again?"

Colette smiled and nodded.

"Ahem," Madame said.

Kingsley had to fight to not roll his eyes.

"Yes?" he asked Madame. She held a small glass bottle of

what was obviously a very pricey lubricant.

"She's already wet," he said to Madame.

"Do you have a vagina?" Madame asked him.

Kingsley sighed and held out his hand. Madame poured a liberal amount of the viscous fluid onto his fingertips, which he massaged over and into Colette's vulva and vagina. Madame even wiped his fingers off for him when he'd finished. Perhaps there was something to be said for having an assistant.

Kingsley waited for her to return to her chair, but Madame stayed standing close by the bed.

"You're going to stand there?" Kingsley said.

"For now. Carry on."

"You live in a strange house," he said as he mounted Colette again.

"Really?" Colette said. "I like it."

"Don't tell Madame," Kingsley said. "But I do, too."

He started to push his cock into Colette again and this time he went as slow as possible. When he'd gone in a couple of inches, he began to move with short, slow shallow thrusts. He went into her body an inch at a time and then a thrust at time. Unable to resist, he glanced up once to see Madame watching him with avid interest. He hadn't expected it to arouse him to be watched by this lady but it did, very much. He and Madame locked gazes as he worked his way deep into Colette's body. Colette's eyes were closed as he penetrated her fully, so she didn't see Madame reach out and stroke Kingsley's body from his lower back, over his hip, and down his thigh, like a jockey inspecting prize horseflesh. Madame gave him one last little wink before she returned to her chair to watch at a more respectful distance.

"Good show," Madame said as she sat back in her chair.

Well, if he was going to have an audience, at least it was an appreciative one.

26

Kingsley turned his attention back to Colette. As erotic as it was to be watched while fucking, he did have a job to do and that job was to make Colette come. As he moved in her wetness, she made murmuring sounds of pleasure as he pressed into her deeper. She took him easily now, and after only a minute or two of thrusting, he was fully penetrating her. He shifted his weight onto his hands and braced himself over her, letting his lower back and hips do all the work as he thrust his cock into the panting moaning girl. His thighs were hard as steel bars by that point. His years of experience were the only thing keeping him from spilling inside her before he'd even gotten her close to orgasm. He lowered himself onto his side and held her back to his chest, spooning her while he fucked her.

With his other hand he found her swollen clitoris. Colette cried out when he touched it. It was a beautiful cry. That little knot of tender flesh was hard and hot, and it throbbed against his fingertips as he kneaded it. He rubbed it in time with his thrusts. He could feel Colette's vagina tightening around his cock as he pressed her toward climax. She was squirming against him, trying to take more of him inside her, feeling more

TIFFANY REISZ

of his touch on her. Every few thrusts she said his name or "please" or "yes." Finally she said "more."

"Harder?" he asked into her ear. "Deeper?"

"Yes," she said.

"Which one?"

"Both. All. Everything. Just more."

If he hadn't been so hard and ready to come, he might have laughed at her eagerness. He kneaded her clitoris as thoroughly, yet as gently as he could, until she was gone, far gone, over the edge and there was no going back.

He pulled out of her and pushed her onto her back again. With a rough thrust he was back inside her. She arched underneath with shameless pleasure. That's what she wanted. That's what she needed. She needed to be taken and impaled and he was happy to do it. She threw her legs open wide in invitation and Kingsley pounded into her with powerful thrusts, ramming his full shaft into her before pulling out to the tip and ramming it in again. She was at that stage of arousal where he couldn't begin to fuck her hard enough to suit her . . . but he would try. God, he would try.

The room grew fragrant with the scent of her wetness and their sweat. A heady moment for Kingsley with this beautiful young girl spread out under him, his cock splitting her body open, and one of the more fascinating women he'd ever met watching their every movement from only a few feet away. Colette's nipples were hard and he sucked them into his mouth, nipped and tugged on them until the girl was nearly out of her mind with need. She writhed under him, her hips hungrily bucking into his thrusts, eager to take as much or more than he could give. He covered her breast with his hands, holding and kneading them while he rode her. When it seemed Colette had reached the very edge of her arousal, when she hovered there, poised on the brink of the cliff so that even the slightest breeze could send her tumbling over, that's when Kingsley licked his two fingertips and pressed them against her burning clitoris again and rubbed.

Colette arched back again, arched hard, arched so that her shoulders came off the bed. She didn't make a sound when she came, but she didn't need to. Kingsley could feel it happening. Her inner muscles clasped at his cock, clenching it and squeezing it tight. And as she came he pounded into her again and again, rapid-fire thrusts deep into the core of her as he raced toward his own orgasm.

He'd fantasized briefly about pulling out and coming onto her lovely breasts, but the necessary self-control for that act was long gone. His own orgasm was unstoppable. As Colette's body spasmed wildly around him, he released into her with a grunt he couldn't suppress. With thrust after mindless merciless thrust, he pumped his semen deep inside her until he was spent and empty. He poured himself out and into her until he had nothing left to give and she had no will left to take.

And then it was done.

Underneath him, Colette had gone so still he thought she might have passed out. She only moved again when he slowly pulled out of her. Fluid, his and hers, poured from her and onto the already dampened sheets underneath her hips. He had just enough wherewithal to examine her body, his, and the wetness on the bed to make sure none of it was blood. It wasn't. Then he collapsed next to her onto his side.

Colette slowly opened her sleepy eyes, turned her head and looked at him.

"Six," she whispered. Her voice was hoarse and hollow. She had no more energy than he did.

"What's six?" he asked. "How many children we're going to have?"

"No," she said, smiling. "Six is how many times I want you to do that to me tonight."

He'd just ravished her into near-unconsciousness and she was already asking for more. When they wanted him to leave this house, they would have to drag him out kicking and screaming.

"Six?" he said. "That could take a while. Best get started . . ."

He kissed her lips. They were dry from panting, but a girl who'd just had a man in her for the first time needed kissing and lots of it. It might have turned to more than kissing quickly if Madame hadn't interrupted with another one of her "Ahems."

"Drink," Madame said, offering Kingsley and Colette each a champagne flute.

Kingsley helped Colette straighten her nightgown and sit up. She winced, but she didn't complain of any pain. Even he might be feeling a twinge of soreness tomorrow after how hard he'd rode her. He looked forward to feeling his muscles talking to him, reminding him of this night and every little thing he did to this delicious girl.

"Thank you," Colette said as she took her first sip of the chilled champagne. Her nose wriggled from the bubbles. It was adorable enough that Kingsley thought six might be the low estimate.

Parched as he was, he emptied his champagne flute in two swallows and didn't even taste it going down. He lay back on the bed and pulled Colette to his chest. She came willingly, smilingly, and brought many kisses for him with her.

"I hope you approve of my performance," he said to Madame.

"If Colette approves, I approve," Madame said. She placed both empty glasses onto a side table and returned to her chair.

"When can we do that again?" Colette asked.

"I just came out my ears," Kingsley said. "I'm going to need a long time to recover. Ten minutes, bare minimum."

Madame pointed at Colette. "You rest. And you," she said, pointing at Kingsley, "come with me."

"Me?" Kingsley pointed at himself.

Madame didn't answer. She merely gave him the look that brooked no opposition.

"Stay," he said to Colette, giving her a quick kiss on her pouting lips. "I'll be back. Promise."

Kingsley climbed out of bed and pulled on his clothes quickly and haphazardly. Trousers, shirt barely buttoned. He skipped the shoes and walked barefoot with Madame out of the bedroom and into the hallway.

"Where are we going?" he asked Madame.

"I want Colette to rest a while," she said. "It's not good for her to get too attached too quickly. Recipe for disaster, as they say."

"What about me?" Kingsley asked. "What if I'm too attached?"

Madame waved her hand, a gesture to show she was flinging his question aside. "You just made love to a pretty young virgin. Your head's in the clouds. In two days you'll have forgotten all about her and don't pretend otherwise."

Kingsley's steps slowed. "In two days, I hope I'm still in bed with her," he said, blinking. A sudden headache hit him between the eyes and he fought the urge to lie down again.

They were outside another room and Madame opened the door to a simple white bedroom, a guest room, and though there was nothing sinister about it, he didn't want to go in. Madame pushed lightly on his lower back and he felt too weak to resist.

"I'm afraid that won't be possible," Madame said. "You look tired. You should sleep."

Sleep was exactly what he wanted. Kingsley wanted nothing

177

more than to lie down and sleep and sleep and sleep. But it wasn't much after midnight. Why was he this exhausted?

"You . . ." he breathed and raised a heavy hand to his head. "What did you give me?"

"Nothing that won't wear off by tomorrow afternoon. Until then . . ." Madame said. "Lie down. Don't make it difficult for yourself. There's no reason to."

He could have made it difficult. The urge to throttle the woman and flee was almost as overwhelming as the urge to lie down and sleep. Almost.

"What did I do . . ." was the last thing he said as he collapsed onto the bed.

Madame put a pillow under his head as he fell to his side. "It's not personal, dear," she said, patting his cheek. A tender touch, almost motherly. "I like you very much."

"Then why—" he tried to ask again.

Madame touched his eyelids, lowering them closed.

"Shh . . ." she said, a mother to a son. "It's just our way."

Kingsley's head swam, and his brain danced. He forced his eyes open, and he saw a door in the middle of a forest, and a beautiful boy with hair like June and eyes like January stepping through the door and visiting him where he lay on the bed. The boy touched his face, gently.

"Oh, there you are," Kingsley said. "You found me."

"I'll always find you," the boy said and smiled.

"I don't like this anymore," Kingsley said to the boy. "I want to go home."

The boy picked Kingsley up off the bed as if he weighed no more than a feather, threw him over his shoulder, and carried him home.

27

"And that's it?" the colonel asked. "You drank some champagne and fifteen minutes later, you were asleep?"

"Benzo," Kingsley said. "And maybe something else. They're not sure what yet. Knocked me on my ass for twelve hours straight."

Kingsley had told this story already, but Colonel Masson apparently wanted to hear it again. The colonel was in his late fifties or early sixties, but even with his iron gray hair and mustache, he still carried himself with the power and bearing of a man half his age. A military man to the bone—disciplined, perceptive, tight-lipped and tough as nails. Kingsley didn't like the man, but he respected him . . . which is why this whole incident with his nephew was so puzzling and annoying. Surely the man had better things to do than police the sex lives of his relatives.

"What else do you remember of that night?" the colonel asked. "Tell me anything you can recall."

Kingsley sighed as he dug through his already-fading memories.

"Not much," he said. "There was the party, the ceremony.

Madame took me to a room. Things happened that do not need to be discussed in detail, and after, lights out."

Kingsley was sitting on a boring brown chair in a boring brown office in a boring brown office building that was doing everything it could to shout out its incredible boringness to the world so no one would take a second look and discover it was the Paris HQ for the military intelligence agency Kingsley had been assigned to for the past two years.

"I woke up in a room at The Opulent," Kingsley continued. "Same hotel room I met Madame in the day before. I called Bernie to come get me and that was it. Do we need to go over this a third time?"

"Yes," said Captain Huet, who, despite his superior rank and even more superior attitude, was only three years older than Kingsley. "I have questions."

Kingsley sat back in this chair, stretched out his long legs and crossed them at the ankles.

"The answer is yes," Kingsley said. "The sex was very good."

The colonel, who'd been pacing the office, lightly slapped Kingsley on the back of the head. Kingsley sat up straight again. He'd been called out for insubordination more than once in his career.

"Apologies," Kingsley said. "The sex was very good, *Captain.*"

"Another question," Huet said. "I passed the phone call test. I made it to a hotel room and met this 'Madame,' same as you. Why did she pick you and not me?"

"I'm prettier?" Kingsley suggested.

Huet, with his bright blue eyes and Gallic good looks, didn't take that well. He loomed over Kingsley's chair, glaring down at him.

"She asked me if I was willing to let her kill me," Huet said. "But you, you get to go and play Hide the Saber for two nights."

"Did you tell her 'yes'?" Kingsley asked.

"What?"

"Did you tell her that she could kill you?" Kingsley asked.

Huet furrowed his brow. "Of course not."

Kingsley pointed at him and shook his finger. "That's the difference. When she asked me, I said 'yes.' "

Huet threw up his hand in disgust and turned his back on Kingsley.

"Why would you agree to something like that?" the colonel asked, his tone more thoughtful than Huet's.

"Earlier that day, when I was on the phone with her, I asked her how I could pass the test," Kingsley said. "She said you win by playing. If I didn't play along, I wouldn't win. I played along. And, as you can see, she didn't kill me."

Someone else had once asked Kingsley that question—*Will you let me kill you?* He'd said "yes" then, too, and didn't regret it.

"Did she *try* to kill you?" The colonel sounded wistful at the thought of someone killing Kingsley.

"Yes," Kingsley said. "Slightly."

"How does someone slightly try to kill you?"

"She put a knife to my throat but didn't press down," Kingsley said. "I wasn't too worried about her going through with it though. I was in a hotel room. If she got blood on the rug, she might lose her security deposit."

"What were you doing on the rug?" the colonel asked.

"Madame was interrogating me," Kingsley said. "Politely."

"And you told her your name and why you were there?" the colonel asked Kingsley.

"You didn't send me in with much of a cover. Good thing, too. She already knew who I was. She has a mole."

The colonel only snorted.

"Impossible," Huet said. "Do you have any idea how suspicious that sounds?"

"Suspicious or not, it's true. She has someone on the inside. I

181

never told her my last name. She knew it anyway. Knew my birthday. Knew my rank. Someone got into my file and read it to her. She knew everything about me."

"We already knew she had friends in high places," the colonel said. He didn't seem the least surprised to hear they had a mole in the agency.

Huet grunted. "This Madame woman probably fucked half the cabinet members and has photographs of them hidden in safes all over the country. And your nephew, too."

"Captain?" the colonel said.

"Yes, sir?"

"Shut up."

Kingsley covered his mouth to hide his smile.

"How were you treated while you were there?" the colonel asked Kingsley.

"Like a pet," Kingsley said. "Or a toy."

"A toy?" Huet said. "You're a decorated *legionnaire*."

"To you I am. To them, I was a toy. They played with me. Then they were done playing."

"And you're not angry about that?" Huet asked.

"I was in the house thirty-six hours and I got to be with two beautiful women. For work. And I'm supposed to be angry why?"

"Yes, for work," Huet said. "This is your job, not a game."

"This mission wasn't my idea," Kingsley said, leaning back in his chair again. "You all sent me in. Don't get angry at me for, well, going in. And in. And in . . ."

Kingsley had left out the part where Polly had done most of the "going in." They didn't need all the dirty details. Only some of them. Only the details that didn't involve objects being inserted into his ass.

The colonel sat down hard in his chair behind his boring

brown desk. Huet took over pacing duty. "I suppose you didn't happen to determine the street address while you were there."

Kingsley shook his head. "Blindfolded on the way there," he said. "Unconscious on the way back."

"Leon didn't tell you where you were?" Huet demanded.

"No," Kingsley said. "And I wouldn't have either, if I were him. He doesn't want to leave. If they hadn't sent me packing, I'd still be there. On my mission, of course. Fact-finding and all that."

The colonel raised his eyebrow. "You liked it there."

"Who wouldn't?" Kingsley asked. "I was on vacation." *En vacances.*

"A vacation in a cult?" Huet asked, disgusted.

"If that's a cult, I'm a virgin," Kingsley said. "Now am I free to go?"

"Not yet," Huet said, turning around. "We have to decide what to do."

"Do?" Kingsley repeated. "There's nothing to do. Leon is nineteen years old. If he wants to live in a commune and sweep floors, that's his business."

"You heard the colonel—his mother wants him out," Huet said.

"Well, I want to meet my mother for lunch in an hour, but she's been dead nine years," Kingsley said. "We don't always get what we want, do we?"

"No," the colonel said with a sigh. "We don't."

"We'll just have to go in and extract him," Huet said.

"Extract him? Like a bad tooth?" Kingsley asked. "He doesn't need extracted. He's happy. He's not there under any duress. He was healthy and unharmed. Leave him be."

"Leave him?" Huet asked. "You didn't even try to talk him out of there, did you? You had one job, and you failed."

"They cut me loose before I could—"

"No," Huet said, cutting Kingsley off. "They got to you, just like they got to him. Listen to you, arguing that we should just leave him there with those insane women."

"Just because they wanted to fuck me more than you doesn't make them insane," Kingsley said. "Sounds like proof of a sound mind, if you ask me."

"Lieutenant, no one asked you," Huet said.

"Captain, sit," the colonel said.

Huet flushed with anger and sat on the boring brown chair next to Kingsley's. He moved it four inches away out of pure spite.

"May I speak freely, Colonel?" Kingsley asked.

"When do you not, Lieutenant?"

That was a good point.

Kingsley smiled in apology and leaned forward. "Sir, you know some English phrases, yes? Like 'rough trade'?"

The colonel coughed. "Yes," he said. "I speak English."

"Well, I speak some American. And here's an American phrase for you—*young, dumb, and full of come*. Ever heard it?"

The colonel cocked an eyebrow at him.

"That's your nephew," Kingsley said. "His cock is making all his decisions right now. Trust me, even if he wasn't in that house, his cock would be making all his decisions for him. Mine did at nineteen."

"Still does, I hear," Huet muttered.

Kingsley ignored him. "I understand it's embarrassing and awkward that your nephew has moved into a commune where his one purpose in life is to serve women on his hands and knees. But this isn't our job," Kingsley continued. "We shouldn't be wasting the resources of this office to babysit an adult."

"We determine the allocation of resources, not you," Huet said sharply. He looked at Colonel Masson. "He talks his way back in, gets Leon to give up the location—"

"It won't be that easy," Kingsley tried to say but Huet talked on over him.

"We tail him," Huet said. "We follow. We go in, pull Leon out, and we make sure this never happens again."

That got Kingsley's attention.

"Make sure what never happens again?" Kingsley demanded. "We make sure grown men don't get laid ever again?"

"If we do a little damage to the house," Huet said, "that'll make this Madame person think—"

Kingsley stood.

"Lieutenant?" the colonel said.

"There is an infant in that house," Kingsley said. His voice was unsteady. "Six weeks old. He's the son of one of the women. We do not go guns blazing into a house of women and children."

"They have the colonel's nephew," Huet said.

"And I've already told you that he hasn't been kidnapped. He's there by choice. Even if it's a stupid choice, it's still his choice," Kingsley said. He looked at Huet, back at the colonel. "I'll hunt KGB for you. I'll hunt gun runners and war lords for you. I'll happily hunt arthritic eighty-year-old Nazi prison guards into the deepest circles of hell for you, and I won't come back until I have their black hearts in my back pocket. But this is a witch hunt. I don't hunt witches. The only monsters you ever catch in a witch hunt are the men holding the matches."

The colonel leaned back in his chair and lifted his chin. "I suppose we do have to remind you who you answer to," he said.

"The president," Kingsley said. He pointed to a photograph of the president hanging over the colonel's desk. "I'll go have a little talk with a reporter or two. I'm sure the president will love to read about how his officers are conspiring to hurt women and children on French soil for the sole purpose of saving a man who doesn't need or want saving. That will play well on the front page of *Le Monde*. I'm trying to save your career, Colonel."

The colonel didn't speak. Captain Huet looked too angry to say what he wanted to say.

"Leave them alone," Kingsley continued. "Leon will come back when he's ready."

"They drugged you and dropped you into a hotel room like a sack of dirty laundry," Huet said. "And you defend them?"

"I told her she could do anything she wanted to do to me," Kingsley said. "Considering killing me was one of the options, I got off easy. Now . . . may I go?"

"One more question," the colonel said.

"Yes, sir?"

"This Madame person . . . what's she like?"

Kingsley hadn't expected such a question from the colonel.

"I'll say this," Kingsley said, "I wouldn't fuck with her if I were you."

"I'll fuck with her," Huet said.

Kingsley turned and punched the prick in the face.

"Christ," Huet said, blood spilling down his face. His nose was bleeding like a busted pipe. "What the fuck is wrong with you? This is . . . this is insubordination." He looked at the colonel for back up. The colonel said and did nothing. "He broke my nose!"

Kingsley massaged his knuckles. "You go near that house or those women," he said quietly to Huet, "and I will make sure your own mother won't recognize you. You hurt a hair on their heads, and I'll sell you to the first KGB officer I find. I'll trade you to him for a half-empty bottle of vodka and a pack of cigarettes."

"Are you going to let him threaten me like that?" Huet demanded of the colonel.

"Yes," the colonel said. He turned to Kingsley. "Lieutenant, you're dismissed."

Kingsley left the office and nearly ran straight into Bernie, who'd been eavesdropping outside the door.

"Bernie . . ." Kingsley grabbed the man by his lapels and steered him away from the colonel's office. "You're going to get yourself killed doing that one of these days."

"Did you just hit the captain?"

"I would appear so. Got any ice?" Kingsley shook his hand out. It was throbbing already.

"I'll get you some," Bernie said. "How much trouble are you in?"

"Not enough, considering."

The colonel really had let him off easy. Too easy. Probably because he'd always wanted to punch Huet's perfect nose, too.

"What's wrong?" Bernie asked.

"Nothing," Kingsley said, a lie maybe. He could still feel Jacques's tiny fingernails digging into his chest.

Bernie found Kingsley an icepack. With it wrapped around his hands, they left via the echoing industrial back staircase. Bernie had asked him a thousand questions yesterday after Kingsley had called him from The Opulent, but he'd refused to answer any of them until he'd spoken to the colonel. Kingsley knew any second now Bernie would start up again with the interrogation. He was right.

"Can I ask about the tuxedo?" Bernie said.

"I got married."

Bernie's eyes went wide.

"Not a real wedding," Kingsley said. "It was a party game."

"Who'd you marry?"

"An eighteen-year-old girl."

"Pretty?"

"Stunning, charming, spirited, loved being fucked."

"Does she have a sister?"

"You'll have to ask her, if you can find her."

Bernie pushed the front doors open and they went out onto the cold gray winter streets.

"Was the house nice?" Bernie asked.

"Very big, very elegant," Kingsley said. "But pretty cozy for the headquarters of a sex cult," he said as they reached Bernie's car.

"Did they really make you shave your balls?" Bernie asked.

Kingsley stared hard at him. "Take me home," he said.

"Yes, Lieutenant."

Bernie's little Citroën wove in and out of Paris's Sunday traffic. The world spun by Kingsley's window so fast he felt dizzy. But he'd felt dizzy ever since waking up in that hotel room yesterday morning. It wasn't a drug-induced dizziness, but the dizziness of a child who'd been taken off a carousel he would have been happy to ride for the rest of his days.

"You miss them?" Bernie asked.

Kingsley tore his gaze from the world outside the window. "Who?"

"You know who. The house. The women." Bernie waggled his eyebrows at Kingsley. "Your bride."

Kingsley smiled. *His bride*. He glanced down at his left hand —unharmed—and at the gold band Madame had put on him and had left on him for some reason.

"No," he said, finally.

"Why not? I would be."

"Because they're not done with me yet," Kingsley said.

"How do you know?"

"Madame's a sadist. And she hasn't broken me yet."

"Broken you?"

"I was a toy," Kingsley said again, not that he imagined Bernie would understand what he meant. Few did or could. "Children only stop playing with their toys when they get bored or they break them. Do I look broken to you?"

Bernie glanced at him, smiled with pity. "A little."

It might have been the first astute thing Kingsley had ever heard come from Bernie's lips.

Kingsley sighed. "Ah, maybe they are done with me then."

"This will cheer you up," Bernie said. "New assignment. Good one, too."

He handed Kingsley a red file folder.

"What's this?"

"Six-month stakeout. French national helping rich assholes launder their dirty money."

"How's that good?"

"What's your favorite city full of rich assholes?" Bernie asked.

"New York?" Kingsley asked.

Bernie grinned. "Are you happy now?"

Kingsley smiled. If anything could help him forget Madame and Polly, Colette and Jacques, it was Manhattan.

"God bless America."

II

SUMMER

28

A new dream.

Kingsley has never been in this part of the forest before. In his waking life, yes, but not when he dreams. This is a summer forest, dense with leaves and the sweet damp scent of rot. He walks barefoot across soft emerald moss under a sea green canopy of aspen and oak trees. It's cool in their shade but hot the second he steps free of the shadows. When a breeze blows past him, he smells something in it that doesn't belong.

Winter.

Kingsley hears a twig snap.

It is the only warning he's given before impossibly strong hands grab him and thrust him back and hard against the rough trunk of a tree. The bark bites into his back, but in the dream Kingsley doesn't feel anything except arousal.

"Were you looking for me?"

The question is asked by the blond boy, who is wearing all black in this dream—black trousers, black jacket, black shirt and black tie. So much black he could pass for a priest. But no black shoes. His feet are naked like Kingsley's.

"I'm always looking for you," Kingsley says. "Everywhere I go, I look for you. I never find you."

"You know why that is."

"I do?"

The blond boy nods.

"Because I don't find you," Kingsley says. "You find me."

The boy in black nods again. "Very good."

"But you don't ever find me, do you?" Kingsley asks.

"I'm here," he says, and for one single second, the blond boy looks hurt. It's something that can only happen in a dream. The boy has no heart, no mercy, no sympathy, and no conscience. He gives pain. He does not feel it himself.

"You're not here," Kingsley says. "This isn't real and you're not real."

"In that case . . ." He releases his grip on Kingsley's shirt and turns to leave him.

"Don't go," Kingsley cries out.

The boy stops, turns around. He stands still, hands clasped in front of him and waiting.

"I'm sorry," Kingsley says. "You are here. I was wrong. You are always here inside me."

"I am inside you," he says. "So what would you have of me?"

"Just be with me," Kingsley says. "Stay and be with me."

"I'll stay if we can play."

"Anything," Kingsley says. "Any game you want as long as you don't go away again."

He walks over to Kingsley, bringing with him the scent of snow. The bite of ice.

"Here's a game," the blond boy says. "It's called Blood."

"How do we play?"

"We kiss," he says. "And the first person who bleeds, loses."

"What do they lose?"

The blond boy smiles. "Blood, of course."

Then he kisses Kingsley.

The kiss isn't kind, isn't erotic, isn't sensual, isn't sweet. It's punitive. It hurts. Kingsley loves how much it hurts. His mouth is invaded, taken over, conquered. Violated. A slap would hurt less than the kiss, and in seconds Kingsley tastes salt and copper in his mouth.

"I win," the boy says, stepping back from Kingsley and the kiss. The boy in black lifts his fingers to Kingsley's lips and touches them. When he holds them up in the light there is rust-colored blood on the tips.

"That's where you're wrong," Kingsley says. "You kissed me. I win. I need your kisses more than I need my blood. Kiss me again. Even when I lose, I win if you're kissing me."

The boy raises his eyebrow. "You're starting to learn," he says. "Ready for a new game?"

"Always."

"This game is called Choke."

The boy pushes Kingsley to his knees in the forest and no one has to tell him the rules to this game. Because it is a dream, he doesn't need to fumble with zippers. Because it is a dream, the blond boy's beautiful cock is in his mouth in an instant. The boy's hands are in Kingsley's hair, rooting him to the spot. He cannot move, cannot run, cannot breathe. He doesn't want to move. He doesn't want to run. He doesn't want to breathe. Kingsley sucks deep and lets the full unyielding length into the back of his throat. The boy in black presses in deeper with his hips. Though the core is hard as iron, the surface texture is smooth as satin, heaven on Kingsley's tongue. Kingsley wants to keep sucking it for eternity. If he were to be trapped in a dream for all eternity, he would want it to be this dream, this eternity.

"This is how it could have been," the boy in black says as Kingsley sucks him. "If you hadn't run away from me. What more did you ever want than this?"

Kingsley can't answer in words, but he can shake his head slightly to indicate he doesn't know.

"You do know," the boy says. "If I know, you know. Ask me to tell you and I will."

Kingsley can't ask. He can't speak. The boy in black only laughs and shoves his cock in deeper. Kingsley tries to move away, to free himself but he can't. He starts to choke.

"See?" the boy says. "I win again."

And the forest is filled with two sounds—the sound of one man choking and the sound of one boy laughing.

29

MANHATTAN, NEW YORK. 1989.

With a gasping cough, Kingsley woke up. The sound was loud enough to wake up Maggie, who rolled over in bed and sat up, wide-eyed with concern.

"King?" she asked. "You okay?"

"I think so."

"Bad dream?"

"No," he panted.

She put her hand on his erection and stroked it. "Good dream," she said, chuckling to herself. "I hope she was cute."

"Cute isn't the word I'd use for him," Kingsley said, and Maggie laughed a little louder.

"God, you're even a pervert when you're unconscious," she said. "Marry me."

"Suck me off and then we'll plan the wedding," he said.

"Lay back," Maggie said. "If you please, my sir." She'd told him early on she'd felt silly calling him "*monsieur,*" even if it was French. But since "*monsieur*" meant "my sir," they'd come up with that as a compromise.

Maggie grabbed an elastic hair tie off the bedside table and pulled her thick hair into a ponytail. She did that sort of thing before a blowjob, to keep her own hair out of her mouth. He loved that about her, how practical she was even in bed. She made practical look sexy. She had pert, well-formed breasts, and she was still wearing the leather cuffs on her wrists he'd put on her last night (before he'd secured her spread-eagle to her bed, cropped her, flogged her, and ridden her pussy into the mattress). Memories of last night's encounter flooded his mind as she prepared herself to take him. There were worse things in the world than waking up to a naked woman preparing to give him a blow job.

Oh yes, fucking Maggie was one of life's simple pleasures. Although considerably older than him, she was a natural submissive. He barely ever gave her orders. Didn't have to. She reminded him of the stereotype of the perfect English butler. She knew what he wanted before he had to ask for it. What he wanted was her soft, warm mouth wrapped around his cock . . . and that's exactly what he got.

She licked him and licked him and licked him, wetting every inch of him from the base to the tip and all around the sensitive tingling head. Kingsley kicked the covers off his legs as the temperature in the room shot up to a thousand as Maggie worked her magic on him. Her lovely lithe hands caressed his stomach and sides, and Kingsley gently pumped his hips, fucking her mouth. They were in her luxurious bed in her luxurious Manhattan penthouse apartment overlooking the Hudson River. City lights filled the floor-to-ceiling window opposite the bed, blinking blue and white and red. And a beautiful naked woman had his cock deep in her throat and she was sucking it like she'd been poisoned and this was the only way to get the antidote. In seconds, the dark forest was gone. The blond boy was gone. The dream was gone. Creeping across the sky was the first light of morning, sending the night and all its inhabitants, including dreams, fleeing for cover. By the time the sun showed its face, Kingsley had almost forgotten he'd dreamed at all.

He was close to coming, very close. He stopped Maggie by pulling on her hair. His perfect submissive, she stopped and moved into position on her elbows and knees. He took her by the waist and entered her from behind. Her vagina yielded to his penetration easily, letting him in deep and surrounding him with her warm, soft wetness. She grunted softly as she took his rutting thrusts. Some women tolerated rough deep fucking. Some hated it. Maggie got off on it. She wouldn't come from it, most likely—he'd take care of that later—but she did adore being used. He knew how she felt.

Although Kingsley knew no one could see them fucking unless they had a telescope trained on Maggie's bedroom windows, he still liked to imagine that the entire city was watching them. He'd never quite recovered from that night when Madame had watched him take Colette's virginity, that moment Madame had stroked his side and back and hips and thigh with the flat of her small soft hand. He'd never forgotten that intimate moment when their eyes met, and she saw him, really saw him. He'd craved that sensation and sought it here in New York.

Then he'd found Maggie in a kink club in the Village. An hour after meeting her, he'd fucked her on a table while the entire club—at least twenty people—had gathered round to watch. It wasn't quite the same as that night with Colette, but it was close enough he'd gone home with Maggie that night and hadn't spent more than a night apart from her since. It wasn't love. Just sex and kink and mutual respect. And out of his deep and abiding respect for his lover, Kingsley pulled out of her right before coming so he could ejaculate all over her beautiful bare back.

When he was spent, he collapsed onto his side on her bed. Maggie rolled onto her back next to him. He slipped his hand between her thighs, wetted his fingertips inside her body, and stroked her swollen clitoris until she came for him. It didn't take long. It rarely did with Maggie, especially after he'd fucked her. Her body tensed and her head fell back and her clitoris pulsed and throbbed against his fingers as she came.

She gave him a little drunken sleepy laugh and rolled her head onto his shoulder.

"Good morning," she said happily.

"It is," he said. Kingsley pushed two fingers into her for no reason other than he could. Maggie had given him ownership of her body. Whenever he wanted to put his fingers inside her, he did and she didn't complain.

"You should dream more often, my sir," Maggie said.

"I dream every night," he said.

"This must have been a good one then. Was it?"

He shook his head. "I don't remember anything from it now." This was a lie but he didn't have the energy to tell her the whole truth. He kept too many secrets from her, he knew. It was something she hated, barely tolerated, but there was nothing for it.

"You sure about that?"

He blinked the sleep from his eyes, kissed Maggie's upper arm.

Maggie was about to ask another question when her alarm clock went off. Six a.m. again. She started to reach over to the nightstand to shut it off, but Kingsley's fingers were still buried inside her.

"King," she said.

"Yes?"

"Do you mind?" she asked.

"Very much," he said. "But that noise is horrible."

He extracted his hand from inside her, and she closed her

legs, rolled over and slapped her hand down on her alarm. "Come on, my sir," she said as she crawled out of bed. "Join me in the shower, please?"

"I'm going back to sleep," he said. "I'll fuck you in the shower tonight after we get back from the gym."

"Promise?"

"Swear," he said and rolled over, ready to sleep if only for another chance to return to that dark forest.

Meanwhile he heard Maggie in her kitchen, putting on coffee and calling the night service to get her messages. He'd never fucked a corporate lawyer before. He'd quickly found it had its upsides. Maggie was filthy rich for starters, but that wasn't the best part. As a corporate attorney, she had to be the big bad boss all day long. When she got home at night, all she wanted to do was submit. When they went out on dates, he picked out her clothes. When they dined, he ordered for her. When they played, he was king, and she his willing slave. Last week she'd even made a joke that she found him so attractive she could happily suck his cock for two straight hours without complaint. He'd made her prove it. Longest two hours of his life, but he still smiled when he thought of it. Maggie had no idea, none, that he too had a submissive side. He never showed it with her. Maybe he'd left it in that château.

"King?" Maggie said. "You have mail."

"When the master is sleeping, the servants are silent," Kingsley said, his face still turned to the pillow.

She raised her voice a few decibels and tried again. "I said, KINGSLEY EDGE, YOU HAVE MAIL."

He looked up at her. There was an overnight envelope in her hand. Maggie respected him enough not to press him for any information about the work he did. She was an attorney. She knew better than to ask any incriminating questions. But she wasn't dumb. She knew he did something important and secret.

This wasn't the first overnight envelope for "J. Kingsley Edge" he'd received since he'd started living with her five-and-a-half months ago.

He held out his hand and took the envelope.

"I'll be in the shower if you need me," she said with a wan smile.

She disappeared into the bathroom and left him alone with his envelope. He ripped the strip and opened the flap. A minute later he was opening the door to the bathroom to join Maggie in the shower.

He took her slick, naked body into his arms and kissed her under the steaming water.

"I thought you said you were going to shower with me tonight," Maggie said as she pressed her firm breasts into his chest. He took them in his hands and cupped and massaged them. He didn't say a thing.

"Got it," Maggie said. "There is no 'tonight' anymore, is there?" She wrapped her arms around his shoulders and rested her chin on his neck. "I should have known having my own personal live-in French pervert was too good to be true."

He'd warned her this could happen, that he might have to leave without much notice. It didn't make it easier for either of them. He kissed her without saying a word because the only word he had to say was "*Adieu.*"

By midnight, he was back in Paris.

30

K ingsley was not in a good mood for the next week. True, he had no cause to complain. He'd completed his assignment in Manhattan, therefore it was no real surprise they'd recalled him. He thought, at first, that they'd brought him back because they needed him for another job. Oh, but no. They'd brought him back because they were done paying for him to live in New York. They could keep a closer eye on him in Paris. He'd learned from Bernie that his superiors worried he was a "risk" since he had dual U.S./French citizenship. Better to bring him back to France and remind him who he worked for than to leave him in New York in the bed of a rich, beautiful woman who was happily letting him take advantage of her money, her penthouse, and her body. They did have a point. In Paris, he had to pretend to be an American as part of his cover. In Manhattan, he could be as French as he wanted. He felt more French there than here.

And he fucking loved living in New York. If the feds had come knocking on his door and offered him a job, it would have been "*Au revoir,* Gay Paris" and "*Bonjour,* Big Apple" in a heartbeat.

C'est la vie, this was the job. No one had lied to him about what he was getting into when he'd signed up for it. Once more he was John Kingsley Edge, struggling American writer trying to live out his Hemingway-in-exile dreams. Picking up university students and taking them back to his garret apartment as he waited for his next assignment to come down the pike, as his American grandfather would say. Kingsley had never figured out what "the pike" was, but apparently things to do came down it.

And every night he dreamed of the dark forest where the boy he loved and hated in equal measure met him and hurt him and made him regret his every waking hour. He despised the boy for invading his dreams, but despised himself even more for not despising the boy enough. Finally, on the eighth morning after eight nights of dreaming, Kingsley gave up and called Madame.

He didn't know why he did it, other than he wanted to see what would happen if he went back to that phone booth and dialed that number again.

The phone rang.

And it rang.

And it rang.

And it rang.

After the fifth ring, Kingsley hung up. He stared at the black phone in the cradle and tried to tell himself he was glad no one answered. Perhaps he could let go of that part of him that wanted to submit and to serve, he could finally let go of that part of him that still loved that ice-cold boy who lived in the forest in his dreams. Life had given him so much pain and suffering, it made no sense to him that he craved more of it. Maybe that's why he'd called Madame. Because if anyone knew the answer to why he craved pain when life had given him more than enough of it, it would be her.

But it wasn't meant to be. Perhaps Madame was done with him, after all.

Kingsley left the phone booth and started to walk away. He made it five steps before the phone rang behind him.

He froze. The phone rang again.

He turned.

The phone rang again.

He ran.

On the fourth ring he answered it. "Looking glass."

"You've been missed, my boy," Madame said.

Kingsley sagged with relief at the sound of her voice. "You're the one who kicked me out."

"You were never kicked out, nor were you kicked. Carried. But not kicked."

"Why did you make me go?"

"It's our—"

"Way, yes, you said that."

"We couldn't have Colette getting enamored of you."

"And she was?"

"Far too much and far too quickly. She'd been talking about you nonstop since the moment she spoke to you in the phone booth."

"And that's bad? I like her, too."

"Yes, you like her. She adored you. She pined for you for months after you left. How long did you pine for her?"

Kingsley didn't want to answer that question. He'd had sex with someone else two days after leaving the château.

"Not months," Kingsley finally said, wrinkling his nose as he answered.

"Too much partiality can fracture a community such as ours," she said. "Time apart is best to cool the blood."

"Is Colette's blood cooled now?"

"I can't read her heart, but she has stopped asking me about you every day," Madame said. "But don't think for one moment she's forgotten you. You made quite an impression."

"I haven't forgotten her either," he said, though in truth he'd given her little thought since meeting Maggie. It was Madame who'd haunted his waking hours. She was the puzzle. She was the enigma.

"Is that really why I had to go?" Kingsley asked. "So Colette wouldn't fall in love with me?"

"Or perhaps so that you wouldn't fall in love with Colette. Considering it's taken you months to contact me, it seems to have worked."

"I was gone," he said. "On assignment."

"Welcome home."

"How's Leon?"

There was a pause. "Content."

"No one else has come around asking about him?"

"You threatened to leak highly-classified details of your agency's operation to the press, after all. Not necessary, I assure you, but truly appreciated."

"I don't want to see any women or children getting hurt. I suppose that sounds old-fashioned."

"Polly tied you to her bed and anally penetrated you for her pleasure and yours. I believe we can safely say you are not a man bound by tradition."

"Only bound by lovers," he said.

"Why are you calling, Kingsley? The first time you called me, it was for your work. What is it you want now?"

Kingsley considered the question carefully.

"I don't know," he said.

"What is it you are missing that you think I can help you find?" Madame asked. She didn't sound angry or impatient. Merely curious. She was probing him, looking for chinks in his armor, he imagined. Chinks she could sneak through, slip a finger through. Slip a knife through . . .

"I thought," Kingsley started. "I thought you could tell me something."

"Ask."

"It's human nature to flee from pain, yes?"

"Yes," she said.

"Then why do I miss being hurt?" Kingsley asked.

"We never hurt you here," she said.

"He hurt me. And I miss it. Why? Do you know? I think if anyone might know it's someone like him."

"The boy who hurt you was a sadist. Don't you think it's strange you've come to another sadist for help?"

"Makes perfect sense to me," he said. "Takes a thief to catch a thief? Takes a sadist—"

"To beat a sadist?" she asked.

Kingsley laughed softly. "Something like that."

"If I let you come back, I will hurt you," she said.

"Good."

"I will play games with your mind."

"I'd be disappointed if you didn't," he said.

"You'll be devastated when I do," she said. "You understand this, yes? And you accept the risk?"

Kingsley tensed, swallowed, exhaled.

"Yes," he said finally.

"One more night," she said. "And you'll serve me and only me."

"That's what I want."

"I will cut your heart open, Kingsley. Cut it open like a surgeon. And you might not like what we find inside. What do you have to say to that?"

Kingsley smiled to himself. He was standing in a phone booth in a Paris alleyway, hard as a rock.

"I'd say . . . my scalpel or yours?"

Madame's car fetched him from outside a florist's in the Latin Quarter at four the next day. The driver, Henri, gave him the choice of either wearing a blindfold or spending the next few hours in the trunk of the car. Kingsley chose the blindfold. Although he was curious about the château's location, he wasn't curious enough to jeopardize his night with Madame. For now, it was best he didn't know the location. What he didn't know he couldn't tell anyone, and he had the feeling the case of Leon wasn't quite closed yet.

Kingsley spent the next two hours in the backseat of the sedan, hidden behind the window curtains and half asleep on the leather bench seat. The driver didn't speak to him, and Kingsley didn't mind the lack of conversation. Likely it was one of Madame's orders. The silent treatment was a form of psychological torture, and she'd hinted that mind games were her particular favorite.

Kingsley was sound asleep when they arrived. His watch told him it was nearly eight. The sun rested at the very edge of the horizon, drowsing like a cat on a fence. Its late evening rays bathed the grand old house in golden light. The creeping ivy was a vivid emerald green. The flowering shrubs along the walkway to the front door were a riot of blues and pinks and yellows. Summer was at its ripest and richest and wildest. Winter did not live here.

The front door opened before he reached it. Madame came out wearing navy blue trousers, a crisp white shirt and a red scarf around her neck. She looked jaunty as a sailor, and her smile was one of true pleasure at seeing him again.

"Kingsley," she said, clasping him by his upper arms and kissing each of his cheeks. "Welcome back."

"You look lovely," he said.

"You look wild," she said. "What is this hair?" She ran her fingers through his hair, which now reached almost to his shoulders.

"I grew it out when I was on assignment," he said. "Do you like it? Hate it?"

She gave him an appraising look, her hand tucked in a fist under her chin and her eyes narrowed. He hadn't known how to dress for the occasion. There was nothing in the fashion magazines about appropriate attire for a civilized evening of sexual and psychological torture. He'd opted for his usual off-duty uniform of faded jeans, black boots, and light jacket over a t-shirt. If she didn't like it, she could always undress him.

"Quite dashing, if rather disheveled," she said. "You look like a pirate."

"Better than looking like a soldier."

"You know why soldiers are supposed to have short hair, yes?"

"Why is that?" he asked.

"So the enemy can't do this." She grabbed a wavy lock of his dark hair and tugged it hard enough he had to take a quick step forward or she might have yanked it out.

The pain was bliss.

"You see?" she said. "Short hair for a reason."

"I'm not doing much soldiering these days," he said. "And you're flirting."

"I'm old enough to be your mother," Madame said. "Would you flirt with a twenty-four-year-old at my age?"

"Absolutely," Kingsley said, grinning.

"Wicked boy. Come inside. Your wine is waiting. Very impatiently, I might add."

Madame waved her hand toward the door and they walked side by side into the house.

As soon as they stepped into the marble foyer, he heard a squeal. Polly stood at the top of the stairs in a floral summer dress that clung to her marvelous curves.

"Kingsley," she said, skipping down the stairs, all legs and bouncing cleavage. She caught him in an embrace. He had missed this house.

"Polly, behave," Madame said. "You're making a fuss."

"I like fusses," Kingsley said, kissing Polly on the lips, a friendly peck she returned with pleasure.

"I don't," Madame said. "Say goodnight, Polly."

"Goodnight, Polly," Kingsley said.

"I wasn't talking to you," Madame said.

"Goodnight, Polly," Polly said, squeezing his hand. "If you're still alive tomorrow morning, we'll have breakfast."

"If?" Kingsley said, but Polly had already disappeared.

Madame looked at him without smiling.

"The games have already begun," he said.

"They began six months ago," Madame said. "Come, come. *Tout de suite.*"

The second her back was turned, Kingsley tucked into his pocket the note Polly had secretly passed him when she'd hugged him.

Madame led him to the sitting room they'd talked in his first night at the house back in January. Now July, there was no fire in the grate, only red flowers bursting out of tin milk buckets. The entire sitting room was full of flowers. They sat in glass jars on the tables, glass vases on the window ledges, and in porcelain milk jugs on the fireplace mantel.

"Have a seat," Madame said, shutting the door behind her.

"Chair or floor?" he asked.

"You decide," she said. "You'll be submitting to me all night. It can start now or later. I'm in no rush. Perhaps you are."

"No rush," he said. He chose the chair nearest the fireplace, the one opposite Madame's. She handed him a glass of wine that she'd apparently poured earlier and set out to breathe.

"How are you feeling?" she asked as she took her own glass and sat across from him.

"Better," he said. "A little."

"Already?"

He nodded. "I barely know you. And you barely know me. But I feel at home here. Is that presumptuous?"

"Only natural," she said. "If I were in Mexico or Greece on holiday and found myself sitting at a cafe next to a French family, I'd feel like I'd found old friends, too."

"You're very understanding," he said.

"Empathy is the bedrock of civilization," she said. "Lack of it is the foundation of chaos. This home of mine is a civilized place."

"And yet you're going to beat me tonight."

"At your request and with your permission."

"*Touché*," he said, and lifted his glass in a toast.

The wine was rich and fruity, a vibrant taste that set his palate singing. The sun disappeared and night filled the window. For the first time since being summoned back to France, he was happy.

"Is Colette here?" he asked.

"Ah, your bride. You miss her?"

"I'd like to see her again. Is that rude?"

"When you come to serve one woman, it's perhaps for the best not to inquire about another."

"I apologize," he said. "I was just curious."

"Colette is here," she said. "And well. I'll tell her you asked about her."

"Can I ask another question?" Kingsley said.

"You ask many questions. Enough to be punished for asking so many."

"I'll ask another, then. If I'm going to be punished, I want to earn it."

"Earn it then," she said.

"Why did you let me come back?"

"We have much in common, I think," she said. "I suppose I see a little of myself in you."

"You still love your husband."

"And you still love your monster," she said.

"I wish I didn't," he said.

"And that's why I say we have much in common. And . . . perhaps I let you back because you're so lovely to look at. I like looking at lovely things."

He reached out to stroke the petals of a scarlet red lily. "I can tell."

"And," she continued with a lilt to her voice to match her lilting smile, "perhaps as much as you need a night with a sadist, I need a night with a masochist. The games I play can be a little rough for the men of the house. For the sake of peace and civility, I tend to spare them."

"You don't have to spare me," Kingsley said. "I can take a lot of pain."

"Kingsley, Kingsley," she sighed. "I'm so glad you called me. So very glad."

He warmed at the sensual tone in her voice. She was a very beautiful strange lady and he couldn't help but feel he'd wandered into a dark fairy tale. But what was she, this Madame? The wicked witch? A princess in disguise? Or something else altogether . . .

"I'm glad, too," he said. "Although I'm not sure I can believe someone as little as you can do a lot of damage to me."

"That's a failure of your imagination, then."

"Maybe I just want you to prove me wrong."

Madame stood and set her wine glass on the mantel. She walked to him in his chair and stood in front of it. Gently she stroked a long lock of his hair, and then gently she wrapped her hand around his neck. Gently she pushed her thumb against his Adam's apple.

And then it wasn't so gentle anymore.

Kingsley tensed immediately and fought off the instinctive animal panic that hit him the second she pushed against his throat. She pushed harder and he fought the panic harder. She pushed harder still and then the panic was gone, replaced by dizzying desire.

"You're letting me choke you," she said. "You see, it's not what I *can* do to you. It's what you'll *allow* me to do to you. If your willingness to suffer is infinite, then my capacity to hurt you is bottomless. Do you understand?"

Kingsley nodded, her hand still on his throat. He could have pushed her away easily, without batting an eyelash. He didn't.

"Come with me," she said, staring down into his eyes. "Let's go and find out what else you'll let me do to you . . ."

32

Kingsley followed Madame up the curving stairway to the second floor where she led him down a long hall. There were three doors. One to his left, one at the very end of the hallway, and one to his right.

"My bedroom," she said, pointing at the door on the left. "Bathroom." She pointed at the middle door. "My private room." She pointed at the right door. "I want you to go into the bathroom, take a hot shower, and then come into my private room after. Take your time under the hot water. Ten minutes at least. You can leave your clothes in the bathroom. You won't be needing them the rest of the night."

And with that she slipped into her private room and shut the door behind her before he could see anything inside. He stepped into the bathroom and turned on the light. He'd been waiting for this chance and now he took it. From his jacket pocket he pulled the note Polly had slipped him. He unfolded it and read it, his heart racing.

You need to see Colette, but Madame might not let you. She's in the room you spent your wedding night in.

Ah, a *billet-doux*. How sweet and very like a smitten teenager.

214

His Colette wanted to see him. He wanted to see her, too, though he wouldn't risk antagonizing Madame by slipping off now. After six months what could be that pressing? Surely Madame slept sometimes.

In the meantime, he had a date with a sadist, one that was long overdue. He flushed the note down the toilet to protect Colette and Polly and stepped into the shower. He let the scalding water run over his body until he felt every muscle and every nerve go lax.

When more than ten minutes had passed, he toweled off and went naked into Madame's private room. So stunned he was by the sight that greeted him, he nearly forgot to close the door behind him.

The room was a civilized, genteel version of that dank hell-hole in the basement. It looked one part torture chamber, one part cabinet of curiosities, and two parts gentlemen's smoking room. The hardwood floor was covered with a large silk rug of red and blue and gold. Sitting on it, parallel to the windows, was a low twin bed covered in white sheets. Over the bed hung a polished brass chandelier—a hanging wooden wheel that held two-dozen burning white candles. Kingsley saw one scalding drop of molten wax fall from the chandelier to the narrow bed. By the light of the candles, he glanced around and took in all that he saw hanging on the walls. Ropes and whips and floggers and canes and every other instrument of pain he'd ever seen or heard of. There were antique apothecary cabinets, too, with dozens of little drawers holding secret things he could only imagine. And Madame wandering barefoot around the room in a pale blue nightgown and matching peignoir, peeking into drawers, gathering supplies into a basket like a witch gathering ingredients for her potions.

She glanced his way only once and said, "On the table, please, face down."

He laughed to himself.

"What's funny?" Madame asked.

"Nothing."

"You laughed."

"You said 'please.' That's all. He never said please when he was going to hurt me. I did all the pleasing and the thanking."

"Did he make you beg?"

"God, yes," he said, and laughed. "Tied me to the cot once and touched every part of me but my cock. Kissed and touched me and made me beg to come. In my memory, I was tied to that cot for ten hours. More like . . . forty-five minutes. But it felt like a full day. God, such a bastard. Not nearly as polite as you."

"Polite? *Moi?*" She seemed amused by that.

"You had me shower to relax me before a beating. That bastard once made me strip naked in twenty-degree weather in a fishing hut on a frozen lake. You let me fold my clothes and leave them in the bathroom. He'd throw them on the ground and walk on them."

"Sadly, far too many of our kind have never learned basic manners," Madame said.

"He had manners. He just didn't use them with me. I was beneath him."

"Good manners are beneath no one. Remember that."

Kingsley smiled. He had to wonder if all sadists were this imperious. He hoped so.

He carefully laid on the table, his head turned to the windows and his arms at his side. "Polly did tell me you like things . . . genteel."

"Civilized, that's all," she said. "That's what always appealed to me about this world of ours. The rules. The decorum. The rest of the world can mindlessly copulate if they want. I respect my partners. They deserve to have their bodies treated with dignity and ceremony."

"There's a lot to be said for mindlessly copulating."

"If that satisfied you, you wouldn't be here begging for something more."

"No, you're right. It's fun, but it's never enough."

"For someone like you . . . No, I imagine it never would be."

"Is there something I'm supposed to say if I want you to stop?" he asked.

"Say 'stop,' " she said. "But there's no guarantee I will."

She had a smile in her voice when she said that. Kingsley had missed being threatened.

"You're nicer than he was, but you're just as bad," Kingsley said. A high compliment.

"Worse, I'm sure," she said. "He was a young man. He didn't know any better. But I do. Yet I do it anyway . . ."

She stood at the head of the narrow bed and stroked his hair. Kingsley closed his eyes and allowed himself to enjoy the simple nonsexual touch.

"Thank you, Kingsley," Madame said.

"For what?"

"For entrusting me with your body." Madame moved his right arm to the top of the bed, wrapped a rope around it, and secured it to the bed leg.

"It's what I want," he said as Madame tied his left arm over his head and then to the bed as well.

"The correct answer is, 'You're welcome, Madame.' "

Kingsley nodded. "You're welcome, Madame."

Madame moved to the end of the bed and tied his left ankle down. "See? Etiquette."

"Should I thank you?" he asked as she worked on his right ankle.

"You can thank me now," she said. "You certainly won't thank me during."

With both hands, she caressed him from his ankles up this

thighs and all the way over his back and shoulders. "Don't be afraid to scream," she said. "The walls are soundproofed."

So much for comforting.

A drop of hot wax fell from the chandelier again and landed on the small of his back. It was so hot that at first it felt cold. Small as it was, the molten drop sent a jolt of pain through his whole body. Even his toes curled.

This would be a long night.

Madame stood at his head and placed one hand on his face. She stroked the arch of his cheekbone gently with her thumb. "We're going to try something," she said. "Perhaps it's impossible. Perhaps not."

"What is it?" he asked.

"If I could make you forget him, I would, but I'm too old and therefore too wise to know that's not possible. But perhaps I can make you want something—or someone—more than him if only for a minute or two. What do you think of that?"

"I don't think it'll work, but if it does, I'll be yours forever."

"That's what I'm hoping. I do enjoy a challenge, after all. Especially when the prize is so . . . dear." She bent over and pressed a soft kiss on his lips, a kiss that excited him nearly as much as his night with Colette. "Wish me luck."

"*Bonne chance*, Madame." The sentiment was sincere. This is what he came here for, after all—to be free once and for all of the hold that boy in the forest had on him.

Or die trying.

She smiled one last time at him.

And then she proceeded to break him apart.

She started with a strap. A leather strap, narrow and with a handle. Without preliminaries, she brought it down on his back. It was a quick hard strike that set a strip of his back burning like wildfire. She struck him again, and then again an inch or two lower. All along the right side of his back from his armpit to his hip, she set him on fire. It didn't take long before he was panting hard and twisting away from the source of his suffering.

He didn't count—he couldn't count, under the circumstances —but it was probably a dozen solid hits before she abruptly stopped.

"Let me answer a question you asked me yesterday on the phone," she said, sounding professorial. He almost didn't hear her over his own hard breathing.

"Question?"

"Yes," she said. "You asked me why you miss it. The pain. In Victorian England, a romantic practice arose. Giving gifts of flowers coded with secret meaning. The language of flowers. If a girl passed a male friend a jonquil, she was confessing she wished him to return her affection. A primrose was a promise of eternal love. A red poppy an invitation to an evening of pleasure. White for purity. Pink for affection. Black for death and dark magic."

As she spoke she caressed his scalding flesh where she'd scored it with the strap. Her fingers were cool against his hot skin, and though it hurt where she probed him, he welcomed the pain.

"We, too, have a language of sorts," she continued. "A secret language that only those of us who live this life understand. Your lover, the boy, did he tie you down to the bed?"

"Yes," Kingsley said.

"You know what that means?"

"He wanted to make me feel like a prisoner."

"No," she said. "He didn't want you leaving him."

Kingsley didn't speak, couldn't speak.

"Did your lover bite you?" she asked.

"I told you he did."

"What do we bite every day?"

"Food."

"Correct. Do you eat what you like, what tastes good to you, or what you despise?"

"What I like," he said.

"He bit you because he loved your taste and you nourished him like food. Food for the heart. Food for the soul. Did he strike you?"

"All the time," Kingsley said.

"Why?" Madame asked.

"He's a sadist."

"But why strike you when there are so many other ways to hurt someone?"

"I don't know."

"The same reason I struck you," she said. "Because it leaves marks. What do we mark?"

"What do you mean?"

"What is the last thing you wrote your name on?" she asked.

Kingsley swallowed. "A book."

"What book?"

"*Histoire d'O,*" he said. "It was my parents' copy. If it got lost, I would want it back, that's all."

"Exactly," she said. "He tied you up to tell you he never wanted you to leave him. He bit you because you were the food to his soul. He struck you to mark you as his possession, as a valuable he would want returned to him if lost or stolen. That's why you miss it, Kingsley. That's why you miss the pain. Because every time he hurt you, he was trying to tell you in the only way he could how much he loved you."

"I want to believe that."

"No, you don't. You want to deny it. Because if you believed it, it meant you left him for no good reason."

"I had a good reason for leaving him. It's just . . . I don't know what it is."

"Let's keep playing then. Maybe we'll find that out, too."

33

After the strap came the crop. A flexible black leather crop that she wielded against him with terrifying precision. If a fly had landed on his back, he had no doubt she could have killed it with one quick snap. All along his body from his shoulders to his ankles she struck him over and over again. A light hit would follow a dozen hard hits. A dozen light hits after one hard hit. He had no idea what would come next, and where, and how hard. Then she stopped and caressed his hair again, damp with fresh sweat.

"What does it mean?" Kingsley asked between heavy breaths. "When you hit me, I mean."

"I put bruises and welts on your body for the very same reason I put flowers in vases on my mantel. Because I find them beautiful to look at, and I love to decorate. The question is, Why do you let me hit you? What does it mean to you?"

"I don't know," he said.

"Yes, you do."

"Maybe it means . . . the first time he hurt me, I was covered in bruises. Took me weeks to heal. When I stood naked in front of a mirror and saw what he'd done to me, it was like looking at my real self for the first time."

"That's why you let me hurt you. You want me to see the real you. This . . ." She touched a burning welt. "This is you."

"This is me," he said. He found it harder to admit than he expected. Doing it was so much easier than saying it. Even Maggie, who'd been his lover and girlfriend for nearly six months, hadn't known about this part of him.

"The real you is very beautiful," she said. "Let's make you even more beautiful."

After that there was little talking. The only sounds that could be heard in the room were the slaps of straps and the flicks of whips. And, of course, the cries, the gasps, and the moans of a man being pushed to his breaking point and left there hanging. The pain was so insistent, so merciless, so abundant that he lost track of time. One second Madame was taking a thin cane to the soles of his feet, and the next second the clock struck one in the morning. He only became aware of himself again when Madame ceased her beatings and instead laid her hands gently on his back. For a long time she simply rested her hands on him, letting her body heat scald his raw flesh. He felt flayed open on that table and so when her bare skin touched his, it seemed they melded for a moment into one single person—or, if not one person, one purpose like rain falling on the ocean because all that mattered was water.

"There, there," she said as Kingsley took great gulping breaths, his back shaking and his legs trembling. Her hands roved all over him, scouring his skin again. As the tension left him, she soothed him with the very hands that had scourged him.

He forced himself to open his eyes. He saw her standing at his side, her eyes half-closed and hooded, the slightest smile on her lips. Moonlight surrounded her, and she appeared utterly at peace. Her facial expression was the same he'd seen in religious arts, in icons of saints who'd been given glimpses into the world beyond and whose eyes had never completely returned to earth.

"You're beautiful," Kingsley said to her. Or to himself. Or to the room. Or to the world.

Madame's smile disappeared. He wished he'd said nothing.

"Are you trying to make love to me?" she asked.

"I would love to if you would let me."

"I won't." She leaned over and kissed his shoulder, put her lips to his ear. "But don't think I'm not tempted."

He smiled.

"You've earned another hour's beating for trying, however," she said.

He stopped smiling.

The hour took an eternity to end. She brutalized the back of his thighs with tawse, then a thin metal rod that both stung and left bruises. Shallow pain and deep pain all at once. He didn't scream but he came close a few times. He thought if he could make it through the beating without screaming, he might earn her respect. And also . . . perhaps . . . if he could keep from screaming, she would keep torturing him until he did. He wasn't sure why he loved it so much, why he didn't want it to end. Maybe it was because his little cries and grunts of pain seemed to have an erotic effect on Madame. For every sound of suffering he made, he heard her make an equal and opposite sound of pleasure. A quick intake of air when he flinched. A gasp when he grunted. A sigh when he cried out. Lovely sounds, like a woman being fucked by a man who knew how to fuck her.

Of course, the beating had an erotic effect on him as well. The pain set his nerves and skin singing. He was hard against the table and had been for hours. As the minutes passed and the beating continued, he grew so aroused by his pain and her pleasure that he writhed on the table. Blood pumped through his hips. His cock was an iron bar between the table and his stomach. He'd never been so close to coming but so unable to come in his life. If she just touched it, he would spill everywhere. He was so desperate he started begging, first softly so that she couldn't hear his words but then louder, out of sheer desperation.

"Please," he said, panting. "Please, Madame."

"Please, what?" She stroked his hair, now wet with sweat.

"Let me come. Please. Touch me or let me touch myself or something. Anything."

"If I let you come, then I'll have to stop watching you squirm like a whore."

"I am a whore. I'll pay you to let me come."

"Do you need me to explain to you how whoring works?"

If he hadn't been so out of his mind with need, he might have laughed. Instead all he said was "please" again. Madame untied his wrist.

"Don't touch yourself," she said. "If you do, I will be deeply disappointed in you."

That wasn't much of a threat, but it worked far better than any threat would. He sensed she knew that.

She untied his other wrist, and then both ankles. She ordered him to turn onto his back. Putting his weight onto his ravaged skin was equal parts agony and ecstasy. The greatest test of Kingsley's willpower in a long time was not touching himself the instant he was on his back with his hands free. But he wouldn't do that because that would mean disappointing Madame. And he'd rather cut his hands off than disappoint Madame.

"I will let you come," she said. "But only when I say you may."

He nodded and waited as patiently as a man with a throbbing erection could wait as she secured him to the bed again, both arms over his head, both ankles strapped down. He was at her mercy again and at her mercy was exactly where he wanted to be.

He watched in eager anticipation as she took a bottle of oil from a shelf and poured it into her hands. If it were possible for him to grow more aroused, he did. His breaths came fast and hard and sweat beaded on his forehead. Everything between his left hip and right hip ached. And Madame standing at his side rubbing oil into her hands was not making the wait any easier.

"If you come before I tell you to," she said, "you will be in a car and on your way back to Paris in five minutes. You will never be allowed back here again."

"I won't, I swear," he promised, although he wasn't sure if he could keep such a promise. The second her hand touched him, he would probably lose all control of himself. Did she sense that? Is that why instead of taking hold of him she simply held her hand out, palm down over his straining cock without touching him?

"Fuck . . ." he breathed, in English and with extra syllables —*fu-uuuuck*. She was so close to him he could feel the heat of her hand radiating against his skin. He'd die if she didn't touch him.

She did not touch him.

He died a little.

"Please," he groaned. Tears leaked from the corners of his eyes. This was real pain. This was real torture. The crops and the canes and the straps had been nothing but foreplay compared to the unbearable, unbelievable, incredible misery of her beautiful wet hand hovering a centimeter over his cock.

"You brought this upon yourself," she said. "Every secret you tell me is a weapon in my hand."

"God," he breathed. He'd told her about the time he'd been tied to the bed and wasn't allowed to come until he'd begged and begged and begged. It was happening again. And he was just as desperate to come now as he'd been all those years ago. If he had to beg just as hard, he would.

"Please," he said again, softly this time as he fought the near overwhelming urge to lift his hips off the table and push himself against her hand. Madame must have heard the note of anguish in his voice because she finally met his eyes.

"Please," he said again and swallowed.

"Why should I let you?"

"I want you to see me come."

"Why?"

"To please you," he said. "It will, won't it? You touched me when I was inside Colette. You didn't mean to. I saw it in your eyes—you didn't plan to. You couldn't stop yourself."

"Arrogant boy."

"You call me arrogant but you don't call me a liar. Let me come for you, Madame. I want you to see what you do to me."

She moved in closer, close enough he could feel her breath on his face. She slipped a hand into his hair and pulled it back, forcing his chin up.

"Don't blink," she said. "Don't close your eyes. Don't look away. Not because I've ordered you to, but because you want to see nothing but me when you come."

"What else would I look at?" he asked. "There's no one else in the world."

She touched him.

34

Finally. At last. Thank God, she touched him.

With a slick hand she grasped him and stroked the full length of his erection. The contact hit him like a bolt of lightning, but Kingsley managed—a miracle—to keep his eyes open and locked onto hers. She stroked again, harder, once up and once down. He pulled on his bonds and writhed on the bed, but even as he reached his climax he didn't break eye contact. As she stroked and massaged and caressed and pulled, he fucked her hand with everything he had. And when the climax came, it came from the bottoms of his feet and worked all the way up his legs to his aching testicles and cock. A nerve twitched inside him, one tight little nerve, one quick little twitch and he flinched in pure pleasure. The first spurt of semen shot out of him and onto his stomach. Waves of release washed over him as he came and came in hot spasms. For one insane moment, the only parts of his body touching the table were the back of his head and the heels of his feet. He arched so hard he would have floated to the ceiling if he hadn't been tied down. It was a violent orgasm. It wrenched everything out of him and when it passed, he was left with nothing. He was empty and spent. He had no will, no breath, no energy, no hope, no dreams, no nightmares.

"Thank you, Madame."

"My pleasure."

Limp as a rag, he lay on the table as Madame untied him. His eyelids were so heavy he could have slept there, despite being covered in his own come and suffused with pain from the hours' long beating.

It started to rain. Warm rain. Gentle rain. Kingsley opened his eyes and saw Madame sponging his body off with water from a porcelain bowl. With infinite care she bathed him clean, washing the come off his stomach and chest and then ordering him onto his stomach again to tend to his back, which was still scalding from the beating and bleeding from a few small wounds. Her touch was so very tender it was almost impossible to believe this was the same woman who had just inflicted a beating on him that had lasted half the night.

"I'd forgotten about this part," Kingsley said.

"What part?"

"When it's over," he said. "And you monsters turn back into human beings again."

"Was he kind to you after he hurt you?"

"Sometimes. The second time we were together, after he'd beaten and fucked me, he held my head in his lap and said, 'You did well.' I almost cried. I would have taken ten times the pain, a hundred, just to hear him say those three words."

"You did well," she said.

"Thank you," he said, smiling to himself. Those three words worked their magic again on him. He had pleased her. That's all that mattered. He had pleased her and nothing could have pleased him more.

"Don't fall asleep," she said. "We're not done yet. Up."

With a groan, Kingsley rolled up.

"Come here," she said, motioning with her finger. She walked to the wall where a tasseled blanket hung over something. She pulled it off to reveal an oval mirror, full-length with a silver frame. It wasn't the same mirror that had hidden the passage into the dungeon, but he felt a twinge of guilt just the same.

"There we are," she said, taking his hand and pulling him close so he could see his own reflection in the looking glass. "Who do you see?"

He saw a man covered in welts and bruises, so many of them that they looked like shadows on his back. He saw those same shadows around his wrists and his ankles, marks from where she'd bound him, from where he'd flinched so hard that the cords had cut into his skin. He looked like a man who'd survived.

"I remember him," he said softly.

"He remembers you, too."

He turned to Madame, still looking prim and perfect in her nightgown and peignoir.

"Can I kiss you?" he asked.

"Of course."

He started to bend his head to touch his lips to hers.

"Not there," she said.

He smiled and went down on his knees. He removed her silk slippers and kissed the tops of her feet. He sat up, still on his knees. It had been a long time since he'd kneeled for anyone.

"Please let me serve you," he said.

"You already have."

"I want to make you come," he said.

She smiled and touched his hair. "If I thought I could be with you without thinking of him, I would."

"Your husband?"

"You are not the only one wearing the shackles of an old love

229

around your ankles."

"Maybe if I can take off your shackles, you can take off mine," he said.

"Ah, but you know the truth, don't you? About you and me? You know."

He nodded slowly.

"Say it," she said.

"We don't want to take them off."

She brought her fingers to her lips and kissed them and then pressed those just-kissed tips to his mouth. "Come with me," she said. "I'll let you serve me tonight. You've earned it, and I need it."

She snapped his fingers, and he followed her across the hall to her bedroom.

Her room wasn't what he expected. After seeing where she played, he assumed where she slept would look equally dark and strange. But no, the walls were painted a pale yellow with white wainscoting. A blue-and-silver damask armchair sat by a white fireplace. A Tiffany lamp sat on the bedside table. And the bed itself was neither intimidating nor grand, but simple and elegant, with a plain iron frame and a white quilt on top and a large gray and blue striped rug underneath. It wasn't a bit frilly, yet it was undeniably feminine.

"That room we were in," Kingsley said as Madame switched on the lamp. "Was it your husband's bedroom?"

"It was," she said. The lamplight illuminated her lovely face and her somber eyes. "I burned his bed after I sent him away. Too many memories. It's the only room I ever use when I'm hurting someone. Why do you think that is?"

She seemed to want an answer, a serious answer. King thought about it. "To spite him?"

"That's childish, isn't it," she said. "Even sadists were children once, too."

She reached out and stroked the silken covers on the bed. "I couldn't burn this bed, however. This was always my bedroom. Though he shared it with me some nights when he fell asleep after making love to me. I burned his bed to punish him. I kept mine and all its memories to punish myself." She smiled to herself. "He wouldn't be pleased to learn I let you in here."

"I won't tell if you won't tell," Kingsley said, as if telling her husband were even an option. He wondered who the man was. Did Madame keep photographs? She didn't seem the sentimental type, but then again, neither did he. But he still owned a certain boy's black leather belt that he'd stolen long ago . . .

She sat at her dressing table in the corner of the room. Without her ordering him to do it, Kingsley carefully pulled the pins from her hair and laid them on the table. When he finished he brushed her hair with a silver-plaited hairbrush. He found her pure white hair both thick and soft, and when she closed her eyes he used his fingers to comb out her curls. When she opened her eyes again, she smiled.

"Time to sleep," she said. She rose from the stool and faced him. He reached for the sash of her peignoir and slowly untied it, feeling himself grow warm and aroused as he loosened the knot. He pulled the robe off her shoulders and hung it on a brass hook behind the door.

"You'll sleep on the floor," she said. "Here." She pointed to a patch of rug by the side of her bed.

He laughed.

She raised her eyebrow. "Ah, yes, he made you sleep on the floor, too. Didn't you tell me that?"

"He made me do it a few times. When I deserved it. Usually when I didn't. What does that mean in your language of pain?"

Madame came to him and placed her hands on his face.

"It means we want you close but not too close," she said.

"Why not?" he asked.

She gave him a tight-lipped smile. "Because it's terrifying to be a sadist in love," she said. "You get close enough to someone, they might accidentally see who you really are."

She dropped her hands from his face, walked to the bed, and waited. Kingsley followed her, reached past her and pulled the quilt and sheet down for her, folding them back neatly. She slipped into bed and rolled onto her side as Kingsley pulled the covers over her to her shoulder.

"There's a blanket in the linen chest," she said, nodding at a large steamer trunk at the foot of the bed. "I'll let you have one. But only one."

"You're too kind, Madame."

"I know. You bring out the best in me. It's very embarrassing."

Kingsley took out the blanket and laid on the rug. The rough fibers bit at his brutalized back so he rolled over onto his side. Glancing up he saw Madame's small delicate hand resting over the edge of the bed. He reached up and linked their fingers.

"Close but not too close," she said.

"I thought you were going to break me until I wished I were dead. Instead I wish I could live here forever."

"That's your cock talking."

"Probably," he said. "But sometimes it talks sense."

"Sleep, boy," she said, squeezing his fingers. "I'll break you yet. I've only just begun."

She released his hand and he reluctantly settled down under his blanket. He wanted to sleep, desperately, but he wanted to stay awake even more. Luckily, the bruises on his back screamed at him every time he tried to get comfortable so sleep was unlikely. Eventually it was obvious from her deep steady breathing that Madame had fallen asleep.

Quietly as he could, Kingsley rolled up off the floor. He glanced at Madame in the bed. Her eyes were closed, her face was smooth and slack in sleep. When he touched her hand again, she didn't stir. Though he hated to leave her and risk her disappointment, he had to. He slipped into the bathroom and pulled on his jeans and t-shirt. He snuck out into the hall.

Polly's note said he needed to see Colette. If he didn't do it now, he might not have the chance before Madame sent him back to Paris.

His heart pounded and his blood raced as he crept along the long corridor to the old part of the château, toward the room he'd spent his "wedding night" in. He ran up the stairs and down the hall. He had to remind himself he was a guest in a lovely lady's home and not on a mission. And yet, the low-level fear remained for some reason. Had Madame already broken him to the point that the mere thought of disappointing her was enough to spike his anxiety?

One of these days he would have to figure out why he was always falling for sadists.

At Colette's door he paused and rapped lightly with his knuckles. No answer. He was afraid of that. If he knocked louder, he would wake the house; if he didn't knock louder, she wouldn't hear him. He only hoped the door was unlocked.

It was. With excruciating care, Kingsley turned the knob, wincing as the latch clicked. He stepped into the bedroom and closed the door behind him. It took him a moment for his eyes to adjust to the dark, but there Colette was in the bed, lying on her side with the ornate gold comforter pulled up to her neck and pillows all around her like a harem maiden in a technicolor illustration from *1001 Arabian Nights*. Praying she wouldn't scream when he touched her, he reached out and lightly tapped her shoulder. At once her eyes flew open and she sat up. Kingsley stared at her and realized in an instant why Polly had told him he had to see Colette before he left.

Colette was pregnant.

35

"Kingsley," Colette said, gasping his name in shock and wonder.

He couldn't speak. He'd lost all his words. He could only stare at her. She had on the same gown she'd worn the night he'd taken her virginity, but she wore it very differently now. That night it had been loose and flowing. Now it hugged her softly-protruding stomach. Five months along? Six months? Six months . . . He'd come inside of her six months ago. Six months ago he'd come inside of her.

You should see Colette . . .

Madame might not let you . . .

"Kingsley?" Colette said again, covering herself with the sheets to hide the evidence. Too late for that. Her voice broke with nervousness and finally he found his voice.

"Is it mine?" he asked.

"Kingsley, I—"

"Is it mine?" he asked again, his voice growing colder, harder. Not because he was angry, but because if he didn't get control of himself immediately he might lose all control entirely.

The door opened behind him. He turned to see Madame standing there. She hadn't been sleeping so deeply after all.

"Kingsley, come with me," Madame said.

"Is it mine?" he demanded.

"Leave Colette alone and come with me," she said very slowly. "We'll discuss this like civilized adults in another room so Colette can sleep. She needs her rest."

"If I go with you, you'll tell me?" he asked.

"Yes," Madame said. "If that's what you want."

Of course that was what he wanted. More than anything on earth, he wanted to know if Colette was pregnant with his child. He would have cut off his arm to know, gouged out his eyes to know, killed an innocent man in cold blood to know.

"This way," Madame said. Leaving Colette in that room was torture, but he knew he had no choice but to follow Madame. He looked back at Colette from the doorway, at her scared lovely face and her swollen stomach barely hidden under the blanket. It was his. He already knew it was his. Why else would Polly have told him to see Colette if it wasn't his? Why else would Colette have asked Madame about him for months after he'd been sent away?

All the way down the hall he thought of what to do. He'd have to live here, wouldn't he? Unless Colette wanted to live with him? He'd have to resign his commission. He couldn't keep risking his life for his work once he had a child. No more drinking either. No more smoking. No more picking up university students at bars and bringing them back to the garret apartment. Already that life seemed a thousand miles away and a thousand years ago. Already he didn't miss it.

He followed Madame down the stairs and into her sitting room. She turned on a lamp but didn't sit. Neither did he.

They stood facing each other in front of the cold fireplace. "Is it mine?" he asked.

"You really wish to know?" she said. "I'm impressed. Most men your age when learning they might have fathered a child would rather be left in blissful ignorance."

"I am not most men. And you have no right to keep the truth from me."

"No right?" she asked. "Can you get pregnant? Can you carry a child? Can you give birth? Nadine almost died having Jacques. She's still not back to her full strength."

"Are you going to make me beg?" Kingsley asked. "I will. I'll beg all night and all day and all night again. I have no shame. I will do anything to know. Please, I beg of you right now, tell me. Is it mine?"

His voice broke. He was on the verge of tears, nearly hyperventilating. Madame, however, looked calmer and crueler than he'd ever seen her. He would have taken a month of beatings over this torture. A year of beatings. A lifetime.

"Nothing," Madame said, "comes free in this house. You want something, you have to pay for it."

"No games," he said. "Just tell me if it's mine."

"No games?" she repeated, her tone mocking, almost sneering. "Did you think I brought you here for coffee and conversation? Did you think I brought you here for charity? You are here for me to play with. You can only win if you play."

"I can only lose if I play, too."

"True," she said. "But that's the risk we take."

"I won't make my child into a game for your entertainment," he said.

"Then go," she said, tossing off a gesture with her hand that said he could go and be damned for all she cared. He was tempted to call her bluff, but he knew he would die before he crossed the threshold of the château without finding out if the baby was his.

"Why are you doing this to me?" he said, closing his eyes as if in prayer.

"You know why," she said.

"It's your way," he said, meeting her eyes. She waited. He waited. One of them would have to blink first. And it would be him. It had to be him, because for her this was a game and for him ... for him this was his entire life.

"I'll play," he said.

"Light a fire," she said.

"What? It's July."

Madame said nothing, merely raised her chin. Some dark, feral animal part of him briefly entertained the thought of wrapping his hand around her neck and squeezing until she answered his question. He didn't, but it scared him how much he was tempted to do it.

He lit the fire. It didn't take long, but even those four minutes of putting down paper and dry kindling felt like a tortured eternity. Meanwhile Madame went to her writing desk on the other side of the room and took out pen and paper. What she was doing, he didn't know ... but he had a feeling he wouldn't like it.

When the fire started going strong, he stood up and faced Madame again. "Your fire. There. Now ... Is it mine?"

Madame stood with her back to the fire. In her hand she held two sealed envelopes. She held one envelope up in front of her.

"This envelope marked with a *C* on the front contains the answer to your question about Colette. The other contains something else equally valuable to you. A letter."

"A letter from who?" he asked.

"Marcus Sterns."

Kingsley's heart plummeted to his feet.

"No," he said, shaking his head.

Madame ignored him. "You may open only one envelope. The other I will burn in the fire."

"You're insane," he said.

"This is the envelope that contains the letter. As you see, it's marked with an S."

"S for Stearns?" he asked, already knowing the answer but asking the question anyway.

"No," she said. "S for Søren."

F or the second time in half an hour, Kingsley was rendered speechless.

By the expression on her face, Madame was in seventh heaven. Or one of the circles of hell. "He told me his real name because he knew you would need proof I was telling you the truth," she said.

"How?" he asked.

"I called your old school," she said simply, like it was the easiest, most obvious thing in the world to do. "I left a message for him. A priest at the school passed it onto him. He called me two months ago. We had a lovely talk."

"I don't believe you."

"He's quite an arrogant bastard," she said.

Kingsley swallowed a hard lump in his throat. "All right. Maybe I do believe you. What's in the letter?"

"Things he wants you to know. And that's all I'll tell you. Now . . . what is your choice? If you don't answer in . . ." She glanced over her shoulder at the mantel clock. ". . . thirty seconds, I'll burn them both."

"I could kill you and take them from you."

"What if the envelopes contain nothing?" she asked. "What if the letter from your Søren is hidden in my house? You kill me, you kill the answer."

"Colette will tell me if it's mine."

"If you harm me, she won't tell you anything except to go to hell. And she certainly won't tell you where Søren's lovely long letter to you is hidden."

"Don't say his name. You don't deserve to say his name."

"The clock is counting. Twenty-three seconds, Kingsley. Decide."

"What did I do to deserve this?" he asked, half-sick with rage.

"You were warned."

"It's a child, not a game."

"Everything is a game," she said crisply, briskly, coldly.

"This isn't sadism," he said. "This is sick."

"Then why are you playing along?"

"What choice do I have?"

"You have two choices—his letter to you or the answer to your question about Colette's pregnancy. It's very interesting that you haven't decided yet."

"I've already decided. I'm just not telling you yet."

"Or you're stalling because you don't know who you love more—your possible unborn child or him."

"I would always choose a child over him. Always."

"You were very quick to tell Colette you were already planning a future with children for you and her. Is that why you left him all those years ago?"

As soon as she said it, a locked door in his heart popped open. That was it. Of course that was it.

"Ten seconds left. By the way, your Søren gave me a message to give to you."

"What is it?"

"He says he still plays Ravel for you," she said, and shook the envelope marked with the *S*.

"You bitch," he said shaking his head.

"Three . . . two . . ."

Kingsley reached out and snatched from Madame's hand the envelope marked with the *C*.

In a flash, Madame turned and threw the other envelope into the fire. In seconds it had been consumed, consumed before Kingsley could even rip the envelope in his shaking hands open.

He did, at last, finally tear it open. He pulled the folded sheet of paper out and looked at the page. There were no words on it. Only a small white feather stuck inside the fold.

He stared at it, then at Madame.

"A feather?" he asked, looking at her. "What the fuck does that mean?"

Madame smiled slowly. "All the pillows in this house are feather pillows, Kingsley."

He understood at once, and the shock was strong enough to send him falling to his knees. Disappointment? Relief? Grief?

"She's not pregnant," Madame said. "It was only a pillow under her gown."

Kingsley fell further, collapsing onto his elbows. He was bereft, utterly bereft.

"Why?" he said, his voice barely more than a low moan. "Do you hate me?" he asked.

She shook her head. "Not at all," she said. "Quite the opposite."

He looked up and saw the last of the envelope, the last of Søren's letter, turn to ashes and die.

"Was the letter in there?" he asked. "Really?"

"What letter?" she asked.

"The one from Søren."

"There was no letter, you fool. We've never even spoken."

"You know his name. You know he's arrogant . . ."

"I know he's arrogant because you told me so yourself. And I know his name and that he played Ravel on the piano the day you met because you talked about him when I'd drugged you. Oh, you told me so much about him I feel like I know the boy. We'd have a lot to talk about if we ever talked. Too bad we haven't."

She took a step forward so that he could have kissed the top of her foot again. Or he could have reached out and grabbed her ankle, yanked her to the floor and strangled the life out of her. He did neither.

He breathed through his nausea, his head on the floor, his stomach lurching.

At first it started as a low chuckle. Then a soft laugh. Then a loud laugh. On his hands and knees, he laughed until his back hurt from laughing. He bruised his bruises. He looked up and saw Madame staring at him with wide eyes. Clearly of all the things she thought he might do, laughing like a maniac was not even in the top ten.

"Kingsley?"

"You did warn me," he said.

Slowly, a smile spread across her face. She curtsied.

"I warn everyone. Everyone," she said, waving her hand to indicate the whole wide world. "No one ever believes me. I say, 'I'm going to destroy you if you let me.' They say, 'Ha, do you worst, Madame, you daft old lady.' Then a few days later, they're vomiting on my rug and seeing a psychologist for the next decade. I'm impressed with you, Kingsley. The last time I played with a man so viciously, he pulled a gun on me. He didn't laugh. Not once. I made him think his daughter had killed herself, so maybe I deserved it. But I did warn him. As I warned you."

"It crossed my mind to snap your neck," he said, sitting up and back on his knees. He wiped sweat off his forehead with his shirt. Sweat and tears.

"But you didn't."

He rubbed his forehead. "I will call you a piss cold whore."

"Ah, that goes without saying," she said with a careless toss of her head as if his insults were nothing more than a buzzing fly.

She stepped closer to him, and he collapsed against her thigh.

Now that he'd stopped laughing he was nearly on the verge of tears again. Why? Catharsis? Disappointment? Relief?

"I'm not sorry," she said.

"I'm going to throw up," he said.

"Not the rug, please. On the hardwood only." She stroked his hair like he was a puppy. He didn't throw up, but it was close. His stomach cramped again, and his mouthed tasted like copper. Yet he managed to breathe through it. Although he almost wanted to vomit if only to stain Madame's rug.

"I fucking hate you," he said. He felt like he'd just run a marathon, he was so spent and rung out.

"Would it help if I told you I had a reason?"

"I don't know if there's a good enough reason in the world for you to do that to someone. Other than demonic possession."

A fresh wave of fury washed over him at the thought of being played so brutally. He closed his eyes tight and let loose with a flurry of insults. *Putain. Salope.* When he ran out of French insults, he switched to English. Madame kept petting his hair and saying over and over, "That's fine. Let it all out. It doesn't hurt me. Nothing hurts me." When he finished verbally excoriating her, he lay on his stomach on the floor in utter defeat, exhaustion, and misery.

"You know now," she said, putting her foot on the small of his back. "Yes?"

"Maybe," he said. The floor was cold on his face. It soothed him.

"You picked your unborn child over him," she said, toeing his hip to turn him onto his back. She gazed down at him, pointed. "You said it was impossible to want someone more than you wanted him. Not impossible at all, you see."

"Someone who doesn't exist."

"But someday," she said. "If you stay."

Kingsley rolled up to a seated position but stayed on the floor. Seemed safer.

"If I stay?" he asked.

"If you stay," she said again. "I want you to stay."

Kingsley was shocked into silence.

"Do you think I would play my best games with someone I cared nothing for?" she asked. "I beat you. I let you in my bedroom. I let you kiss me. Do you think I do that with simply any man? I haven't let a man kiss me on the lips since . . ."

"Your husband?"

She nodded.

Kingsley couldn't believe it. "You really want me to stay?"

"Not only me," Madame said. "Polly, too. And Colette. And Jacques, he told me so."

God, Jacques. Kingsley had missed the little boy almost as much as he'd missed Madame . . .

"Look at me, child," she said. Kingsley met her eyes. "I'm asking you to stay with us. Inviting you. I don't extend this invitation often, but I am now, to you. If you stay, you can sleep in Polly's bed with her any night she asks for you, and I promise that will be many, many nights. If you stay, you can sleep on my floor. I'll give you two blankets and a pillow. And I will beat you often—for my pleasure and yours. And if you stay, you can have a child with Colette. In a year from now you could be a father. And . . ." Madame did something he never expected her to do. She knelt on the floor right in front of him so that they faced each other eye to eye.

"Madame?"

"Listen to me. Kingsley . . . if you fall asleep anywhere in this house, anywhere at all, wherever you wake, you'll know you're home," she said as she took his face into her hands. "You'll have a home and a family. You won't be lost again. You won't be cold again. You won't be alone again. You'll be mine, you beautiful lovely wonderful horrible wicked little boy . . ."

She kissed him on the mouth. He kissed her in return, passionately. She pulled away from the kiss quickly and touched her lips as if he'd burned her. Slowly she smiled.

Home.

Family.

Children.

Everything he ever wanted. Everything. Every last thing. Except for one thing.

There had to be a catch.

There was always a catch.

"But what about—"

"No," she said, her tone sharp as a razor. "If you choose to stay with us, you must choose us and us alone. It's us or him."

"What do you mean, you or him? I haven't seen him in years."

"If he calls this house asking for you, I will not let you talk to him. Nor will you be allowed to call him if you find out where he is. If he writes you a letter, you'll burn it unread. If he comes here and knocks on that door looking for you, I'll send him away without you ever knowing." She shook her head. "I can't let you be a part of this family if you're only going to run off the moment he crooks his little finger at you."

"I wouldn't abandon my child for him."

"But you don't have a child yet. What if he comes tomorrow? Would you leave us for him tomorrow? A week from now? If he came and asked you to leave with him, would you take Colette and the child with you? Would you tear up my family for him? I can't allow that. I'm offering you everything you want. But there is a price. Is it really too much to ask? When a man out there in the old world gets married, he promises to forsake all others. That's the vow. Can you make that vow to us?"

A terrible question, but a fair one. More than fair. He wasn't being asked to commit to one woman, but to an entire house of them. Madame wasn't asking for monogamy. He could have ten women, a beautiful sumptuous château to call his home. He could have safety, security, and children of his own.

All for the seemingly low price of turning his back on a boy he hadn't even laid eyes on in over seven years.

Kingsley leaned forward and rested his head against Madame's shoulder. She wrapped her arms around him, held him close, and lightly caressed the back of his neck.

"My mother used to do that," he said, "when I was sick or had trouble sleeping."

"Rub your neck?"

"Yes."

"You like it?"

"Love it."

She kissed his forehead.

"Madame . . ." he said.

"Yes?"

"You never told me your real name."

She laughed softly.

"Will you ever tell me your name?" he asked.

"Never, no," she said. "Why do you ask?"

"He told me his real name," Kingsley said. "The first time we were together."

She stopped laughing.

It hurt worse than the beating she'd given him, but Kingsley pulled away from Madame's arms and her tender motherly caresses.

"I'm sorry," he said.

She exhaled heavily and nodded. "Don't be."

"I should be. I am."

"You know he may never find you," she said.

"I know," Kingsley said.

"You're making the wrong choice."

"Ah, I've done it before and survived."

"This is it, you know," she said. "No second chances. Next time you call me, I won't call back."

"I understand."

"Colette will be heartbroken," Madame said.

"Tell her . . . tell her something that won't hurt her," Kingsley said. "Tell her I can't leave my job or they'll storm the house."

Madame nodded. "Of course. You're kind to want to protect her feelings."

"I shouldn't after the trick she pulled on me."

"It was all my doing," Madame said. "They take orders from me. Everyone in this house obeys me. Even you."

"Order me to do something then," Kingsley said.

Madame rose to her feet with indescribable grace, rolling back onto her toes and standing straight up. For a split second he saw the young girl who'd once served a powerful man who thought he'd put a puppy on a leash only to find later it was a wolf. Kingsley had always loved wolves.

She placed her fingers under his chin and lifted his face to meet her gaze.

"Leave," she ordered.

Kingsley reached into the pocket of his jeans and pulled out the gold band, his "wedding band," and placed it on Madame's ring finger, next to her own wedding band.

Then he kissed the back of her hand.

"*Adieu*," he said. "You unbelievable bitch."

By the time Colonel Masson arrived in his office at eight a.m. the next morning, Kingsley had already been waiting a full hour.

Kingsley sat behind the colonel's desk, his feet on top of some very important papers.

The colonel paused in the doorway. "Lieutenant? Your feet are on my desk and you are in my chair," he said. He didn't look happy. "Why is that?"

"Because it would please your wife to know I put my feet on your desk, wouldn't it?"

The colonel did not ask him again to remove his feet from the desk. He shut the door behind him and locked it. "My wife," the colonel said at last.

"Your wife," Kingsley repeated.

"You went back to the château."

"I did."

"Without permission."

"I had her permission. Hers is all I need."

"It's my house," the colonel said. "She stole it from me."

"You don't actually have a nephew, do you?"

"No," the colonel said. He slowly sunk down into the chair across from his desk. "But I do have a son."

Kingsley wasn't surprised. He hadn't been expecting that, but he wasn't shocked either.

"Leon's your son," Kingsley said. "But not hers?"

The colonel nodded.

"You were still together with her when you had him," Kingsley said.

"I can do arithmetic, too, Lieutenant."

Kingsley stared at the colonel, this tall, handsome, strapping aristocratic man with his iron gray hair and obsidian eyes. A stubborn old fool dying of loneliness and male pride.

"She wanted children of her own," the colonel said. "I told her 'no.' "

"No? Why?" Kingsley asked, his brow furrowed. What man would deny his own wife a child? "She loves children."

"Plutarch tells a story," the colonel said, "of the Athenian general Themistocles who is famous for saying his son was the most powerful person in all of Greece. As he said to his son, 'The Athenians command the rest of Greece, I command the Athenians, your mother commands me, and you command your mother...' "

Colonel Masson glanced up at the ceiling as if he was too ashamed to meet Kingsley's eyes.

"You couldn't stand to share her with a child?" Kingsley asked. "Your own child?"

"Her family lost everything in the war. Everything. The Nazis killed her brother, burned the house, the fields. When I say everything, I mean everything. But my family, we were lucky. Her father and mine served side by side as spies. Her father saved my father's life. I knew I'd marry her before I even saw her. Both families expected it. And then I met her. I'd never seen a more beautiful girl. So innocent, too. I was besotted. Before we even married I paid off all the debts her mother owed and bought her a house, sent her sisters to school. I thought she'd worship me as a god, a savior at least. I thought she did." The colonel paused, tapped the arm of the chair. "She's a good actress. Too good. I thought I was enough for her. Couldn't bear to think of her loving someone more than me, of sharing her body with someone other than me, being commanded by someone other than me."

"But you have a son," Kingsley reminded him.

"I had an affair. Meaningless. Lasted two weeks," he said, "and Leon was the result. I visited him here in Paris, sent money. When my wife found out I had a child . . . I think she'd been waiting for her moment and that was it. For years . . . since our marriage probably, she'd secretly kept notes and photographs and files on every man who ever dropped his trousers at that house or picked up a whip. Princes and Generals played under my roof. And they weren't going to be happy to see their names in print. With what she had, what she knew, what she was willing to tell or sell . . . she could have destabilized whole regions, started wars. And I would have been a dead man. But that wasn't enough for her."

Kingsley had to admire the woman for her cunning—to keep secret files, blackmail material, to use it to control rich and powerful men . . . God, what a woman.

"I saw what you did to her," Kingsley said. "The bloody bed. Did you keep her a prisoner in the dungeon?"

The colonel laughed. He laughed and laughed.

"What?" Kingsley demanded, ready to kill the man. He had his Beretta under his jacket. Would serve the bastard right.

"Why am I not surprised she never cleaned up that mess? She probably goes in that room and pleasures herself thinking of what she did to me there."

"What did she do to you?"

"She drugged me, tied me to the bed, and kept me there a week until I agreed to her terms. Everywhere I looked, I saw her words to me from our wedding night. She'd scrawled them all over the walls. I'd given her a phrase to use if I went too far. Thought we'd need it. I wanted her so much, I didn't even trust myself. I beat her and she never used the words I gave her—just kept saying, 'I don't like this. I want to go home.' I gave her the phrase to protect her and now she mocks me with it."

"Looking glass," Kingsley said.

The colonel nodded. "I thought she was playing along, playing scared, playing innocent. I told her a hundred times before that when she wanted me to stop to say 'looking glass' and I would stop. But it had to be that word. It couldn't be any other word. She never said it."

"Looking glass," Kingsley said. "What's the joke?"

"You don't know?" the colonel asked. "Thought it would be obvious."

Finally, Kingsley got the joke.

"Her name is Alice," Kingsley said.

"I told her I was taking her to a kind of looking-glass world where everything was a little different, a little mad. But anytime she wanted to go back to the real world, the safe world, she only had to say 'looking glass' and I would take her back," the colonel said. "But she didn't want to go back. She just wanted it all for herself."

"I saw blood on the bed in the dungeon. Yours?" Kingsley could imagine Madame castrating the colonel on that bed. He liked to imagine it, in fact.

"Hers," he said. "From our wedding night. Same rule. If I'm hurting her, she was supposed to say the phrase. She didn't. The room was dark. I thought she was . . ."

"Wet?" Kingsley said.

"She wasn't," the colonel said.

Kingsley cringed and muttered "Christ" under his breath.

"She lay there in the dark," the colonel continued, "dead silent, playing the martyr, while I fucked her to shreds. I was furious at her for not telling me I was tearing her. I would have stopped, if she'd only . . . Ah." He shook his head. "She looked so innocent after when she'd said, 'I only wanted to please you.' Cold-blooded and calculating even then."

"Or a scared eighteen-year-old girl forced into marriage with an older man who her mother told to obey completely, because his family had saved them from starvation?"

"Tell yourself that," the colonel said with a defiant lift of his chin. "But I know better. She kept the bloody sheet for a reason and it wasn't sentimental. Kept it, saved it, and used it to torture me. She's mocked me for years. Mocked me with love letters, then refused to see me. Played mind games with my agents. Turned my best agent against me. Kept the fucking house?" The colonel laughed, not a happy sound. "That house has been in my family for two hundred years. But if I so much as step foot on the property, she'll send her files to *Le Monde*. That's why she went after Leon, you know. I tried to go see her. She sent a note to the front gate, carried by one of her pets, the one with the scar. You know what the note said?"

Kingsley shook his head.

"It said, 'You come here again, and I will slit your son Leon's throat and send you the sheet he bled out on as a Christmas gift.' "

Kingsley's eyes widened.

"As if threatening him wasn't enough," the colonel said, "she found him. I'd done everything I could to keep him hidden but she worked her magic, her connections. She found Leon, played with his mind, and seduced him into moving in with her. God only knows what she's told him about me."

"If it makes you feel any better," Kingsley said, "he's very happy there. And she hasn't slit his throat. Yet."

"That doesn't make me feel better."

Kingsley stood up, looked down at Colonel Masson. He thought about saying something, then decided it wasn't worth it. He turned for the door, but stopped when the colonel said, "Did you sleep with her?"

"How is that any of your business?"

"So you did?"

"I don't kiss feet and tell," Kingsley said. "I will say this: If you go near her or send anyone else to her . . . ah, no reason for threats. You know what I can do to you."

They both knew. The colonel had overseen Kingsley's training, after all. And Kingsley was thirty-five years his junior.

"She must have been very good to you to inspire this kind of loyalty," the colonel said. "What did she do to you? Play your sweet *maman*? And you were her little lost boy? It's all an act. No matter how kind she was to you, it's nothing but a con. I was her first victim. She played the role of the perfect wife for fifteen years."

"No, she wasn't kind to me. She did the cruelest thing a woman can do to a man, and I will still burn you if you go near her and her house again."

The colonel laughed a sad little defeated laugh.

"I had a feeling you two would get along."

Kingsley started to tell him just how well he and Madame had gotten along, but the colonel dropped his guard for a split second and Kingsley saw such longing on his face, such loneliness . . . He recognized that look. God knew, he'd seen it in the mirror enough times.

"Did she tell you she was my wife?"

"She didn't have to. I guessed when you didn't punish me for breaking Huet's nose."

"I still love her," the colonel said. "After all that . . . I still love her. And she still loves me. Almost as much as she hates me."

"Can't you make peace with her? Apologize? Grovel?"

And to that the colonel said simply, "No."

"Your loss," Kingsley said.

"You don't understand. This is the game. As long as I keep playing with her, she's still in my life. The second I forfeit, the game ends."

"It's a stupid game," Kingsley said. "You shouldn't have dragged me into it."

"You're right. But it's all I have. What do you have?"

Kingsley wanted to give him a smart answer.

He didn't have one.

The colonel's shoulders slumped, the fight gone out of him. "I retire in two months. I think we can pretend this never happened, yes?"

Kingsley shrugged. "What happened?"

Without another word, Kingsley walked down the hall of HQ and wasn't surprised to see Bernie sitting on a chair right outside the door to Captain Huet's office.

Kingsley paused and narrowed his eyes at Bernie. "How old are you?"

"Twenty-five," Bernie said. "Why?"

Jacques's our first boy in twenty-five years . . . Our last boy—I call him my nephew . . . he moved away years ago, but he's still drawn back to us. He visits me often, brings me all the gossip. The children of this house are all very loyal even if their parents are not . . .

She has someone on the inside. I never told her my last name. She knew it anyway . . .

"No reason," Kingsley said. He'd left the château, and he was never going back. Some things were better left a mystery.

Kingsley left Bernie without another question, without another word and walked out onto the Paris streets sweating in the full heat of a city morning. Exhausted and sore as he was, he walked back to his apartment rather than take a taxi. Paris was bright and thriving that day, buzzing with voices, with beautiful women in trim high heels with silk scarfs of every color dancing behind them as they strode the sidewalks. Tourists thronged the parks and nannies pushed carriages and men sat at café tables drinking coffee and solving the world's problems. He bore the marks of Madame's château on his body, but only on his body. By trying to break his spirit, Madame had helped heal an old wound. Maybe now that he knew why he'd run away from Søren, he could find a way back. He thought of this when he turned the corner and saw the very same phone booth he'd used to call Madame that first day. He stepped inside and closed the door. He put in all his coins and dialed a phone number he shouldn't have known by heart but did.

After three rings, someone answered.

"St. Ignatius Catholic School for Boys?" A woman's voice. They must have hired a receptionist. "How may I help you?"

"Is Marcus Stearns there?" Kingsley asked, in an American accent.

"No, he no longer teaches here. I could relay a message to him, if you like."

A message. He'd leave a message and in an hour or a day or a week, he'd get a phone call. Is that what he wanted? A call back? A long chat?

Or nothing.

He could leave a message and wait and wait and wait and his phone might never ring.

And that would break him in a way Madame could only dream about...

"No message," Kingsley said. "Thank you."

He hung up.

If Søren wanted him, he would find him. In the meantime...

Kingsley returned to his apartment, stripped out of his clothes, and crawled under his sheets. They embraced him like an old friend. He closed his eyes and felt sleep creeping along the floor toward him, ready to join him in bed. At last sleep came to him.

He did not dream.

III

WINTER

3 8

K ingsley stood in the clearing of the snow-filled forest. He saw the stone. He saw the chess board laid out upon it. He saw the boy with the January eyes and the ice in his veins.

But this was not a dream and the boy was not a boy anymore. He was a man, a beautiful man with blond hair going silver, gray eyes vital as struck flint, his face and jaw granite though his heart was red and warm and alive. If there had ever really been ice in the boy's veins, it had melted decades ago.

Kingsley walked toward the chess board, leaving a trail of footprints in the snow. His breath steamed in front of him and rose to the tops of the trees like incense in a cathedral.

"What the hell are you doing?" Kingsley asked.

"Are you going to sit and play chess with me?" Søren asked. "Or stand there laughing all night."

"It's fucking freezing out here," Kingsley said, shivering. "I never should have told you about that dream."

"But you did, and now we're going to sit out in the cold and the snow and play chess until one of us wins. Never let it be said that I haven't made all your dreams come true."

"I have better dreams than this," Kingsley said.

"But it's this dream you told me about. Sit."

Last night Søren had bestowed a rather cathartic beating onto him. During the aftermath, Søren had ordered Kingsley to tell him a secret, something he'd never confessed before to anyone. Maybe it was the wine Kingsley had drunk or the happiness of getting to be alone in a cabin in Maine with his lover, but Kingsley had told him a story he'd kept secret for over twenty-five years. The story of the château.

"Well?" Søren said, moving his white pawn forward. "I'm waiting. And I'm not letting you back in the cabin until you play with me."

Kingsley sighed so heavily, his breath turned into a cloud around his head before dissipating.

He sat across from Søren and moved his pawn.

Søren sacrificed a pawn almost immediately.

"The Danish Gambit," Kingsley said. "I should have guessed."

"Yes, you should have. I'm going to beat you."

"I hope so."

"Whore," Søren said.

"Always."

"I beat you last night. And today."

"And tonight?"

"Win the game and I'll consider it," Søren said.

"I already won," Kingsley said.

"Did you?"

"I'm playing with you," he said. "Therefore, according to you, I win."

Søren looked at him with utter disgust. Kingsley grinned maniacally in response.

"I didn't actually say that," Søren said. "A twisted, absurd dream version of me said it."

"It sounded like something you would say."

"Did it?"

"It was obnoxious and arrogant," Kingsley said. "And pompous. Smug, too."

"Yes, point taken."

"Self-important. Self-righteous."

"Kingsley."

"Yes?"

"Checkmate."

Kingsley looked down at the board. "Thank fuck," he said. "I'm freezing my balls off out here."

"This was your stupid dream," Søren said as he packed the chess pieces away. "Not my fault your subconscious is as much of a whore as you are in your waking hours."

"What's that supposed to mean?"

"You dreamt I was a wolf that sexually assaulted you."

"It wasn't assault. It was consensual," Kingsley said with a shrug.

"My God, Freud would have a field day with you."

"He'd have an entire field year with you. Field decade. Field century..."

"I have perfectly normal dreams, thank you," Søren said as they walked back to their cabin, the snow up to their ankles now.

"Such as?"

"For starters, I've never dreamt about having anal intercourse with apex predators."

Søren held the door of the cabin open for him and Kingsley walked through without a retort. The man had a point.

A fire smoldered in their fireplace and Søren nodded toward it. With a put-upon sigh, Kingsley squatted by the hearth like some caveman of old and built up the dying fire with shredded newspaper and other kindling. Søren stood by the steadily building fire holding out his hands to warm them.

"I still can't believe you never told me about Madame and her cult," Søren said. "What other cults have you nearly joined and not told me about?"

"It was just the one cult. And I was only there about three days total," Kingsley said. "After a week it felt like it had all been a dream. After a year it felt like something that had happened to someone else. After this long, I'd almost forgotten it ever happened at all."

That all was true. He had nearly forgotten it. Until Søren had prodded him, and it had all come back to him like the words to an old song when he'd heard a stray bar or two.

"I have so many questions," Søren said. "I don't know where to begin."

The fire caught at last, and Kingsley stood with his back against the mantel. "I probably don't have the answers," he said. "I still can't figure out what Madame meant when she said she'd lied to me only once, but it was a big one."

"I may know that one," Søren said. "Her big lie was telling you how innocent she was when she married her husband. I was eighteen once. Was I innocent?"

"You think she really planned to overthrow him for fifteen years?"

"She did say he gave her a copy of *Histoire d'O* a week before the wedding. If I remember correctly, at the end of the book, O is discarded by her lover, and she asks for permission to commit suicide. Maybe your Madame read that and decided to write a better ending for herself. What do you think?"

"Your guess is as good as mine," Kingsley said.

"What happened to your colonel?" Søren asked.

"He retired, like he said he would. Never saw him again. I

want to think he finally humbled himself enough to beg her forgiveness, but I doubt it. Funny thing though . . . as soon as the colonel retired, Bernie quit our agency. Never saw him again either. I hope he went to Madame to serve."

"You think he wasn't as stupid as he pretended to be?"

"Maybe. Still don't know if Bernie was working for Madame or the colonel. Or both. Or neither," Kingsley said. "I don't want to know. I like to imagine he was secretly the best spy in the agency."

"And Captain Huet?"

"We made up eventually," Kingsley said, a little smile playing at the corner of his lips. "He forgave me for breaking his nose."

"You slept with him, didn't you?"

"No comment," Kingsley said. A better answer than the truth. Yes, he had slept with the good captain—gentle kisser, rough blow jobs. They were lovers for almost a month before Huet was sent to Argentina to arrest an escaped Nazi war criminal. He'd died on that mission, but at least he took the Nazi down with him. They'd sent Kingsley to retrieve Huet's remains. *There but for the grace of God go I,* Kingsley remembered thinking as he looked at his lover's destroyed body.

One week after that, Kingsley became Captain Boissonneault.

"I really shouldn't be telling you any of this," Kingsley said. "Supposedly all my work was classified."

"But this assignment at the château was unofficial, yes?"

"Everything I did for them was unofficial."

Søren went very silent and his brow furrowed.

"What?" Kingsley asked.

"Colette," he said. "Did you see her with your own eyes *after* your Madame said she wasn't actually pregnant?"

"No. Madame ordered me to leave. I left right away."

"So she could have been pregnant?"

Kingsley glared at him.

"Will you ever stop fucking with my mind?" Kingsley asked.

"It wouldn't be this easy to fuck with you if you'd used condoms a little more often," Søren reminded him.

"True. But if I had, there'd be no Nico."

"And no Colette Junior out there somewhere weeping in her pillow at night, pining for her lost *papa*."

"If you must know, I got a postcard a week later," Kingsley said. "It said, *Sorry we tricked you.*"

"From Colette?"

"No," Kingsley said. "From Georges, the tick."

Søren laughed. His laughter died, and Søren looked deeply into Kingsley's eyes. "I want to ask you something, and I'm almost afraid of the answer."

"You don't have to be," Kingsley said. "Ask."

"Do you ever regret the choice you made?"

"Madame's choice?" Kingsley asked.

Søren nodded.

"No," Kingsley said without hesitation.

"She offered you a home and a family, children, comfort, safety, lust, pain, and love. And you chose to wait for me to find you instead."

"I wasn't wrong. You did find me. Eventually. And I have two beautiful children. I have a home. I have a family. I have comfort, safety, love *and* lust. And you for pain."

It pleased Kingsley to count his blessings. His Juliette—his lover, his better half, the mother of his daughter and the joy of his days. His Céleste—his daughter, his angel and his princess. His Nico—his son, whom Kingsley not only loved, but admired and respected. His home in New Orleans. His friends. His work. His life.

And Søren. The boy in white who now wore all black.

"I do wonder sometimes what would have happened if I'd

left you a message that day I called our school," Kingsley said. "Would you have found me sooner?"

"Yes," Søren said. "And I would have come to you that very same day. And I would have taken you home."

"Ah," Kingsley said. "One more regret for the butcher's bill."

"But I would never have let you hear the end of it," Søren said.

"Maybe I don't regret it then." Kingsley leaned forward, wanting to kiss Søren, and it seemed—for once—Søren would let him. At the last second, however, Søren brought his hand up and clapped it over Kingsley's mouth.

"If you ever try to kiss me again without permission," Søren said calmly, "I'll eat your heart like an apple and throw the core on the ground and let the worms have the rest."

Ah. Still a wolf. No matter how much he denied it, Søren still had the teeth, still had the claws, still had the bite.

Kingsley smiled. "You tried that trick last night," he said. "I have the bite marks on my chest to prove it."

Søren raised an eyebrow at him. "Are you complaining?"

Kingsley shook his head. "Never."

"Good," Søren said and though his tone was stern, his eyes were alight with amusement.

"But," Kingsley said, "I do have a question."

Again, the eyebrow went up.

"Did you . . . when we were young, I mean, back in school . . . did you pick me up when I was sleeping and put me into bed with you? Or did I just dream that?"

"You want to know?" Søren said.

"I've wanted to know all my life," Kingsley confessed.

"The answer is . . . ." Søren leaned in and put his mouth to Kingsley's ear. Kingsley caught his breath and held it tight. He had truly wondered about that night for thirty-three years.

"Yes?" Kingsley said.

"The answer is . . ." Søren said again, and grabbed Kingsley by the back of the neck and pulled his mouth to his for a long, hard, passionate kiss.

Ah. Well. So be it.

Between the kiss and the answer, he would always pick the kiss.

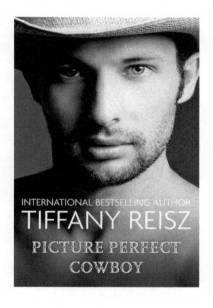

Jason "Still" Waters' life looks perfect from the outside—money, fame, and the words "World Champion Bull-Rider" after his name. But Jason has a secret, one he never planned on telling anybody...until he meets Simone. She's the kinky girl of his dreams...and his conservative family's worst nightmare.

Picture Perfect Cowboy **is a standalone erotic romance from** *USA Today* **bestseller Tiffany Reisz, set in her award-winning Original Sinners series.**

8th Circle Press • eBook and Paperback

ABOUT THE AUTHOR

Tiffany Reisz is the *USA Today* bestselling author of the Romance Writers of America RITA®-winning Original Sinners series from Harlequin's Mira Books.

Born in Owensboro, Kentucky, Tiffany graduated from Centre College with a B.A. in English. She began her writing career while a student at Wilmore, Kentucky's Asbury Theological Seminary. After leaving seminary to focus on her fiction, she wrote *The Siren*, which has sold more than half a million copies worldwide.

Tiffany also writes mainstream women's suspense fiction, including *The Bourbon Thief* (winner of the *RT Book Reviews* Seal of Excellence Award) and the RITA-nominated *The Night Mark*.

Her erotic fantasy *The Red*—self-published under the banner 8th Circle Press—was named an NPR Best Book of the Year and a Goodreads Best Romance of the Month. It also received a coveted starred review from *Library Journal*.

Tiffany lives in Lexington, Kentucky with her husband, author Andrew Shaffer, and two cats. The cats are not writers.

facebook.com/littleredridingcrop

twitter.com/8thcirclepress

instagram.com/tiffany_reisz

ALSO BY TIFFANY REISZ

Standalone Novels

THE BOURBON THIEF

THE LUCKY ONES

THE NIGHT MARK

THE RED

THE ROSE (April 2019)

The Original Sinners Novels

THE SIREN (Book #1)

THE ANGEL (Book #2)

THE PRINCE (Book #3)

THE MISTRESS (Book #4)

THE SAINT (Book #5)

THE KING (Book #6)

THE VIRGIN (Book #7)

THE QUEEN (Book #8)

PICTURE PERFECT COWBOY (standalone — November 2018)

The Original Sinners Novellas

THE CHRISTMAS TRUCE

THE GIFT (previously published as SEVEN DAY LOAN)

IMMERSED IN PLEASURE

THE LAST GOOD KNIGHT (PARTS I—V)

LITTLE RED RIDING CROP

MISCHIEF

THE MISTRESS FILES

THE SCENT OF WINTER

SOMETHING NICE

SUBMIT TO DESIRE

The Original Sinners Collections

ABSOLUTION (Australia only)

THE CONFESSIONS

MICHAEL'S WINGS

Harlequin Category Romances

THE HEADMASTER (e-Shivers)

HER HALLOWEEN TREAT (Blaze)

HER NAUGHTY HOLIDAY (Blaze)

MISBEHAVING (Red-Hot Reads)

ONE HOT DECEMBER (Blaze)

SEIZE THE NIGHT (Red-Hot Reads)

CPSIA information can be obtained
at www.ICGtesting.com
Printed in the USA
LVHW050458020519
616374LV00001B/15/P

9 781548 681951